The Last Best Hope

A Civil War Era Alternate History

The Last Best Hope
A Civil War Era Alternate History

By David L. Parrott

STORYTELLER
A Publisher of Quality Fiction

ISBN-13: 978-0-9847254-9-6

Book Website
http://www.parrottpen.com

Give feedback to:
parrottpen1@hotmail.com

THE LAST BEST HOPE: A CIVIL WAR ERA ALTERNATE HISTORY is a work of fiction. Apart from the well-known actual people, events and locales that figure in the narrative, all names, characters, places and incidents are the product of the author's imagination or are used fictitiously. Any resemblance to current events or locales, or to living persons, is entirely coincidental.

Cover art by Kathey Amaral
kattnboys.deviantart.com

Storyteller Publishing
www.storytellerpublishing.com
Email: info@storytellerpublishing.com

Printed in U.S.A

ACKNOWLEDGEMENT

Many thanks to my sisters and family for serving as "first readers;" to friends Gary Gilmore and Dennis Shaffner, historians, civil war re-enactors, and insightful critics; to Susan Beates, curator of the Drake Well Museum for allowing me access to their archives and to local historian Steve Karns for "walking the grounds" of Pithole with me and imparting his wisdom and enthusiasm for the ghost town of Pithole, PA; to Lorin Oberweger, Jayne Magee, and Goldie Browning for editorial advice; and finally, to my late father, Lawrence Parrott, who took me on a train ride through the Oil Creek valley and started this whole enterprise.

DEDICATION

This book is dedicated to my wife, Leslie and children, Travis and Lauren, whose support and patience with my writing obsession is much appreciated.

Historians have often asked, "What if the South had won at the Battle of Gettysburg?"—what if, indeed?

PART ONE

There is a fountain, filled with blood
Drawn from Emmanuel's veins
And Sinners plunged beneath that flood
Lose all their guilty stains.

William Cowper, hymns, 1779

Chapter One

Day One of the Battle of Gettysburg
July 1, 1863

Ezekiel Edwards

The last Rebel soldier I had killed stared down at me, his arm draped across my chest like the embrace of a lover. As daylight turned to dusk, his vacant eyes took on a fiery orange hue and then a deepening purple while tendrils of mist crept over us both, finally separating me from that unblinking stare.

In pain and despair, I gazed up at the fog. It reminded me of nights at my home in Salem, Massachusetts; but unlike the sea mist, this purple haze was heavy with the smell of gunpowder and the stench of the dead and dying. Once more I tried to lift my head, to raise an arm and free myself, but a stab of pain shot through my shoulder. The weight of the pile of Confederates on top of me was slowly crushing me to death. A line of scripture came to my mind: *Romans 6:23—the wages of sin is death.*

My vanity had brought us all to this. All my fault. I saw an image of myself, saber raised above my head shouting, "Come on, you Bucktails!" I could still feel the hot wind in our faces, the thrill of the charge, the boom of the cannon close at hand, the deadly shards of canister mowing us down—and we fell, like ripe hay before a keen scythe. All of us doomed...all my fault.

But now, from deep within the pile of fallen men, I heard singing. I thought at first that it was one of the dying men.

"Help me. Oh, dear mother, help me!" a different voice cried out from nearby.

I felt an odd sensation on my free hand, something curled around my forefinger. I craned my neck and saw that a butterfly had landed on my finger, its wings as black as the approaching night—a glimmer of hope in the darkness.

And then the singing again—a chorus of men's voices? Or were they angels?

"*Swing low, sweet chariot,*" one deep voice began, and then the others sang in reply, "*Comin' for to carry me home . . .*"

The men who had been moaning all around me grew still, listening. This is my last chance, I thought. If only I can let them know I'm buried here.

I tried to call out to them, but with so little air in my damaged lungs my voice made the sound of a croaking toad. I choked on dust and blood. I thrashed with my legs trying one last time to free them, but another jolt of pain swept through my body, and I thought in despair: *even the angels shall forsake me.*

The voice of the lead singer rang out again, his voice rich, deep, beautiful. He was closer to me now, just steps away. I spat out a clot of blood and tried to shout, but only a gasping "Help me" came from my lips.

And then, the light of a lantern and the voice of the lead singer said, "Wait, I heard somethin'."

The singing stopped. The light grew brighter.

Fighting against the pain, I waved my free hand and croaked my plea again, "Help me."

The light parted the mist, and I saw a company of slaves. They were gathering the injured Confederates. The leader stepped close, so close that I blinked from the brightness of the lantern. Then I saw his face, a kind and gentle face, with scars from some unknown accident or heathenish ritual. At first his eyes expressed shock and fear, and he stood there staring.

"Help me," I mouthed the words a third and final time, feeling as if no breath was left in my chest. Please God, don't let him turn away.

In the same rich voice I had heard singing, he cried out, "Here's one!" He began to pull the bodies of the men on top of me aside and he said, "This man's alive."

The face of that great, gentle Negro came just inches from mine, his arms encircled me, and he lifted me from the pile of men. I saw the faces of the other slaves now, gazing in wonder. Both joy and a sharp pain filled me as breath reentered my crushed lungs. He hoisted me up and stepped away from the pile of dead men. He carried me on his shoulders toward a wagon of injured men, stepping with strong legs over the rutted and blasted field.

Once again, he began to sing that song about the flight to freedom.

The chorus of voices joined together in response. As I slipped into unconsciousness I thought, perhaps they were angels after all.

Chapter Two

Two Years Later
Oil City, Pennsylvania
March 1865

"Captain Edwards! Captain Edwards!" the boy shouted, "we're coming into the station, sir!

I had been dozing, but his shrill voice woke me, as always to that dull pinch of pain. My eyes opened fully, and I saw the grinning face and elfin eyes of the boy. Wincing, I smiled.

"We're coming into Oil City, Captain!" the boy repeated, his eyes lit with excitement.

"Jesse, get back here," the boy's mother said from the seat behind him. I had been secretly admiring her throughout the trip; an auburn-haired beauty with clear blue eyes, dressed in a deep green woolen coat that set off the rich hue of her hair. Some fine gentleman's wife, I mused—polite, but not interested in a scalawag like me.

"He's fine, ma'am," I said to the woman. "It's time for me to be up and about my business."

"I'm sure you are a man of many talents," she said as the train lurched and threw her close to me. Did I see a twinkle of mischief in those bright eyes, or was it only wishful thinking?

I stood and went into the small lavatory, leaning toward the hazy metal mirror as the train jerked to a final, screeching stop. I patted my pockets for the one that held the spoon. Again, I felt the padding of the greenbacks sewn into my vest, a reassuring weight against my ribs. Things were going well for me on this trip. A short jaunt up to Pithole, and I could have a nice dinner and a good, long rest.

I uncorked the bottle of medicine and poured a spoonful of laudanum, taking care not to spill a drop. I lifted it to my lips and took it down, feeling if only in my imagination, the warm glow spread from my belly up to soothe the pain in my shoulder.

"Just one tablespoon until we get to Pithole," I said, pointing my spoon at the fuzzy image of a gaunt, sandy-haired man in the mirror. The words of Saint Paul came to mind: *for now we see through a glass darkly, but then we shall see face to face . . .*

"So keep that in mind," I admonished him. I lifted up the bottle to the light and saw that it was more than half full. Good. I was keeping to my dosage quite well. I looked at myself in the mirror again and said, "Now, get to work. They're waiting for you."

I stepped from the compartment, gathered up my haversack in my good hand and headed for the door. As I stepped into the queue of departing travelers, I smiled. The narcotic's effect had boosted my sense of well-being, and I was ready to start my new venture in life.

"Jesse told me you were heading to Pithole to work a lease," the boy's mother said, brushing an auburn wave of curls from her brow with a gloved hand.

"Yes, ma'am. Some mates from my unit came from Titusville. They've already begun working on the hillside of the Holmden Farm. I expect to join them in a couple of hours."

"The last stage to Oleopolis leaves right now," she said, glancing out the window where the sun hung low in the late-winter sky. "You might make it before nightfall."

"Oh, I'm confident I will," I said, reaching into my pocket and pulling out a tattered stagecoach schedule. "My associate mailed this to me in Salem just last week. According to this, I should have plenty of time."

She looked at it as the line inched forward. She bit her lower lip, a fetching gesture, and said, "I'm afraid this is a schedule from last November. I think it might be a bit out of date, what with the rail line about to open and—"

"My uncle is the richest man in Pithole!" Jesse interrupted. "His name is Soloman Stottish, and he's got *millions of dollars!*"

The woman laughed. "Jesse exaggerates, Captain Edwards. But he does have an uncle who is in the oil business now. If you happen to meet him, tell him Lydia sends her greetings." She paused to steady herself as she stepped down onto the platform, and I caught a glimpse of a well-turned ankle. "And you may even meet my fiancé, as well. His name is John Wilkes-Booth. He's an actor. Perhaps you've heard of him?"

"I'm afraid not," I answered, thinking she must be a pretty war widow and not yet remarried. Our eyes met for just an instant as I stepped down close to her, and I thought she blushed slightly.

"Oh, look! There he is," she said, pointing to a well-dressed man standing up in an open carriage beside his Negro driver. The clouds parted, and a shaft of sunlight shone on him for an instant—John Wilkes-Booth. Not only Lydia, but several other women on the train turned to gaze at him. I should have felt envy, but I didn't. I saw the fine clothes and carriage, his fine hat and admirable countenance—they all spoke of one thing— success. That's just what I had traveled so far to gain.

"Stage to Oleopolis! Stage to Oleopolis! Fifty cents!" cried a man standing on a muddy lane just off the platform.

As Jesse and his mother headed down the platform toward Booth, she turned and said, "Hope you make it to Pithole before dark, Captain Edwards."

"Thank you, ma'am. I'm sure I will!" I replied, tipping my hat to her.

Her son turned back toward me, "Captain Edwards, be careful! There's a murder a day in Pithole City!"

His mother jerked his arm, shaking her head in exasperation. I headed for the open door of the stagecoach and pressed the fare into the hand of the driver. He tossed my haversack above to the cargo hold. For the first time, I noticed a pungent odor in the air. As the driver latched the door to the coach I asked, "Pardon me sir, but what's that smell?"

"Why, that's the smell of the grease, sir. That's the smell of *oil!*"

As I settled back to endure the bumpy stagecoach ride, I looked out the window at the river. Two riders sat across from my seat pointing at the railway line being built. "I thought they were much further along," one of the men said.

"Pitiful," his associate answered.

The only other passenger was a lumberjack with his long axe and a bag of tools. He wore tall leather boots, which looked expensive. I saw him glance at my footwear and sneer.

We had only traveled a few rods farther when one of the railway men shouted out the open window, "Say, driver, stop the coach for a moment. We need to talk to the bridge crew." I recognized the accent—a Tidewater drawl.

They stepped down from the coach into the miry mud along the road. Across from me in the coach the lumberjack pulled out his timepiece, looked at it and scowled. "We'll miss the stage to Pithole for sure, now. Railroad men!" He spat a stream of tobacco out the open door into the muck.

The railwaymen clambered up to the gang of men sawing beams for a small bridge. In the fading sunlight, I at first took them for former Union men in their dark woolen uniforms. But in the silence of the evening, I heard them singing softly—and then I spotted the overseer with his whip. The workers were slaves. If only…I thought. But I pushed that idea away as useless. We had lost the war, and this was the result.

The singing stopped as the railroad bosses conferred with the slave master. It grew uncommonly quiet. I noticed the lumberjack also watching the slaves and railwaymen, and it brought back to mind the slaves who had rescued me at Gettysburg. I mentioned this to the lumberjack, saying, "Slaves like to sing of trains and chariots and such."

He lifted an eyebrow. In a quiet voice he responded, "They're singing about a different kind of railroad."

"Like, *this train is bound for glory*—that speaks of heaven."

"No."

"*I looked over Jordan.*"

"The Ohio River."

Comin' for to carry me home, I thought to myself with growing awareness. It was a message sung in code. I was just about to ask him another question when he raised an eyebrow, put a finger to his lips and glanced upward at the driver. I knew what he meant. We were in enemy territory. We might be overheard.

The stagecoach driver let the horses forage for grass that poked through snow along the berm of the road, and they pulled us closer to where the railwaymen now spoke in heated tones to the slave driver. Something to do with how many boards they were sawing in a day.

"But sir, we can't." I heard one of the slaves say.

And then came the crack of the whip, a muffled cry and then another. I reacted without thinking, leaning forward to launch myself out the door and at the slaver with the whip. But before I cleared the door I was yanked rudely back into the coach. The lumberjack had horse-collared me, his dark eyes meeting mine in the fading light.

"Push it back," he said. And in the impotence of my rage, I knew what he meant.

We missed the stage from Oleopolis to Pithole by just a few minutes. We could see it clattering along the ridge-top on the long roundabout road that the stagecoach drivers used. It would take several hours to follow it on foot, but the lumberjack said he knew a shortcut.

"But I wouldn't recommend it," he said and shook his head. "You gotta follow the unfinished rail line and ford the Pithole Creek several times."

"Looks more like a river than a creek, to me," I said to him.

"That's why I'm wearing these tall boots."

"I forded many streams below the Rapidan during the war. I was often below enemy lines."

"I got two good eyes, Captain. I can see you still bear scars of that war, but these are not the gentle streams of Virginia. This water had ice across it just this morning, and the bottom is caked with oil from the wells of Pithole. It's rocky, slippery, and as cold as December. Take my advice: go back to town. There'll be another coach in the morning." He put his axe on his shoulder and stepped out into the stream. The water came almost to the tops of his fine, tall boots. He crossed the rushing torrent, more than once putting his axe in the water to steady himself against the current. When he got to the other side he stopped and shouted something, but it was lost in the roar of the water.

In just a few moments he vanished from sight. I pondered what to do. Perhaps with a walking stick I too could ford the stream. My feet would get wet, but they would dry out. I'd had wet feet before and survived.

Finding a fallen beech branch with its snake-like silver skin still attached, I snapped an end off and made a passable walking stick. I launched myself out into the stream, but the slimy bottom was a surprise. Still at the edge, I fell to one knee and almost went under completely as I floundered, trying to hang on to the stick. It snapped in half and floated away in the icy torrent, and for a moment I imagined myself being carried along like the stick, crashing head first into rocks and over waterfalls. I would have to either go back or hike the cliffs. Perhaps, if I climbed over a couple of them I could reach the roadbed of the unfinished rail line and the walking would be easier. Surely it couldn't be that far? I stepped back out of the water and began ascending the first steep hillside.

Each cliff seemed to sap my energy. My hands became bruised and my palms bled as I struggled to find handholds in the rock face. On the fourth one I stopped at a small opening to catch my breath, my shoulder throbbing. The moon had begun to slip beneath the trees on the far side of the ravine. I tried to gauge how much time had passed. Surely it was time for another dose of laudanum? I pulled the warm bottle from my vest and fumbled for the spoon. My aching fingers lost their grip, and the spoon clattered away below me, catching the light at it bounced from rock to rock and then disappeared in the icy torrent below. I cursed. One false step and that would be me.

I lifted the bottle to my lips and was about to take a swallow when I heard an angry growl. In an instant I leapt away from the opening in the rock, expecting the teeth of a black bear to sink into my flesh from behind. I clambered up the rock face and flung myself over the cliff top and onto the damp ground above. Another low growl came from below, but the bear, or whatever it had been, was not pursuing me. I rolled to my feet and stepped cautiously back into the woods. Then, I realized I'd lost my medicine. For the second time in as many minutes, I cursed out loud. Words from the Book of James came to mind: *the tongue is a raging fire, who can contain it?"*

A sense of resignation came over me. I had no pack or gear for sleeping outdoors, only clean clothes for living in the town of Pithole. Wonderful. I looked around for a low pine tree where I might at least find refuge until dawn, which would be many cold hours away.

"After hubris, comes nemesis," my old Latin teacher once told me.

"Pride goeth before a fall," I had responded.

But he had shaken his head and replied, "Hubris is arrogance. There's a difference."

"Pride is good; arrogance bad?" I had then asked.

"No," he had said, smiling with those crooked teeth of his," they are just different sins."

An owl hooted. I turned toward the sound and spotted the light of a cabin through the trees, a ways deeper in the woods. Perhaps Providence guided me still.

I surveyed the scene carefully as I approached, a habit developed while behind enemy lines. Several horses stood tethered out back and to my surprise, a small covered carriage had been rolled out of sight in the trees. The cabin must have been the work of some earlier lumberman or maybe a pioneer because it looked surprisingly well-built and inviting. A wisp of smoke rose from the chimney, and the smell of roasting meat made my mouth water. Perchance I could find not only shelter, but a meal?

Shadows in a back window moved about in the light. Old habits die hard, so instead of approaching the front door I circled quietly around back, closer to the window. As I approached, what I had at first thought were two figures now appeared to be only one. Maybe one of them had left the room? But as I got closer I could see that the two had not separated, but had become as one. They stood in a lovers' embrace, the man in shadow, the woman near the light.

The first thing I noticed was her hair—a shimmering cascade of auburn curls highlighted with golden hues from the reflected candlelight. My breath slowed. *Turn away*, an inner voice told me, but my limbs disobeyed, and I stepped closer still. After all, I reasoned, they wore their outer cloaks, so this was not some married couple in bed. But as I watched, it became evident that he was slowly undressing her, and I became more entranced.

I remembered my own wedding night before the war. My hand at the top button of my bride's dress. Her hand reaching to mine.

"No," she had said.

"It's all right. I'll be gentle."

"Please, stop."

Had that been the moment we began to part? Because I had not stopped, had I?

There was movement in the room in front of me, pulling me back to the present. The man took her overcoat from off her shoulders, and my eyes were drawn to the fine texture of the freckled skin of her throat. For a moment I thought of the pretty widow at the train station. This could well be her younger sister, now in the first bloom of her maidenhood.

From the shadow behind her, the man's gloved hand now reached to the top button of her dress and was enclosed in the milky white hand of the woman, freezing that motion in time. I leaned closer still, and I saw her mouth part slightly—was this passion, or was she going to protest to the man to go no further? I took one more step, knowing I shouldn't. Yet it had been so long since I had been with a woman, and this woman was so stunningly beautiful. *Turn away*, part of me said again—but I couldn't.

My lust betrayed me when a dry twig snapped as I leaned forward. Through the hazy glass the woman's eyes met mine, and she screamed.

I staggered backwards, dead foliage making even more noise, and I turned to run away feeling both fear and shame at being discovered. I circled back toward the front of the house following a moonlit path that would lead me back to the cover of the woods. But as I stepped past the porch, something moved in the shadows. Before I could raise an arm to fend off the blow, the cudgel struck the back of my head and drove me forward toward the frozen ground. The pain was so intense I felt as if I'd been shot with a minie ball. Time slowed as I fell and in that instant of time, one clear thought came to my mind: *this will change everything.* Then, I smashed face first onto the stone steps and lost consciousness.

Chapter Three

I found myself on the cabin porch in the morning. An old quilt that smelled of horses had been thrown over me. My head ached on two accounts: because I had been bludgeoned and fallen, and because I was overdue for my morning dose of laudanum.

I patted the pockets of my vest, and then I remembered losing the spoon and later the bottle and finally coming to this cabin. Then, I realized something much worse had happened. My attackers had stolen the money hidden in my vest. A cold, sinking feeling went from my chest to my belly as I frantically searched the vest once again, but I found only one loose thread. Someone had searched the vest and found the money and now, the last of my inheritance was gone.

"Oh, Lord," I said and sat up, my back against the rough siding of the cabin. "Now what am I going to tell Tinker and Daniel?" The smell of the woods and the newly sawn pine boards of the cabin filled my nostrils, but brought me no comfort. Where was I going to find the money to keep our venture going? I shook my head and felt a sharp pain from where I'd been bludgeoned the night before. None of this would have happened if I hadn't looked into that window. But I couldn't tell that to my mates. I couldn't tell them I'd been peeping into the window at a pair of young lovers and so, lost our chance at making a fortune. Once again, rash action on my part had ruined everything. Now, what could I do?

Reaching a tentative hand to the back of my head, I found a crusty scab. Finding something wet there, I wiped blood from my fingertips onto the blanket. I would look a sight when I finally got to town. Hardly the grand, confident entrance I had envisioned when I set out for Pithole the day before.

Upon standing, I was greeted by more pounding pain in my forehead. I would need to obtain some more laudanum—soon. I looked around for my hat and for evidence of where my attackers might have gone. Hoofprints dented the soft grass around the porch along with fresh ruts from the departure of a carriage. Robbers with a carriage? That didn't make any sense.

I started to follow the ruts that were clearly visible in the soft earth of the woods. A wagonload of thieves? But it sounded more like a small cavalry detachment to me, which would mean they would move more slowly, so I picked up my pace from a steady march to double-quick. Perhaps my money was not lost after all.

Chapter Four

Chastity Stottish
Less Than a Mile Away

Farther ahead on the same road the carriage bearing the former president clattered along slowly through the woods. Two Bucktail guards, Tom Mortenson and Elisha Stiles, rode on horses out in front, their sidearms always near at hand. Miss Chastity Stottish sat beside Lincoln in the carriage, holding his hand as they clattered over the rough road. Commerce on this stretch was heavy with teamsters and oil wagons, seeping dark greenish crude oil into the road and adding to the gooey mire. The horses labored to pull the carriage with just two riders, and when they hit a tree root concealed in the mud the carriage jerked. He squeezed her hand, in pain even though she'd given him a draught of sedative, as she always did when they moved him.

She sighed, wondering if it were her fault that they had to seek a new lodging. She thought of the events of the night before which had forced them to abandon the comfort and safety of their hidden cabin and move the former president to another location.

She shouldn't have let Marcus into the room, she thought. She must be resolute in her dealings with him, for where could her attraction to him lead?

"We can go north," he had said. "I've been assured of a situation in Montreal. The arrangements for my departure are almost complete."

"But what sort of life would there be for me there?" She asked, noticing that he had stepped closer, that his soft dark hand caressed hers. In the other room the guards dozed by the fire, and the President snored loudly from the other small bedroom.

"Do you miss the life of a young society girl in Pittsburg?" Marcus asked softly. "Is that what you want?" His lips brushed her cheek and neck for she had turned her head away.

"I do not miss Pittsburg. But I also do not wish to live the life of a poor nurse forever."

"I lived quite well before the war was lost," Marcus said. "In a free country I would find a good position again. I am quite sure of it. Montreal is a fine town. Or, perhaps you would prefer Paris?" he added with the curve of a smile. Then, he played his trump card, "You will be free of your father. Come away with me..."

He had kissed her again, this time without her face averted, and he had raised his hand to her cloak—to the top button. She had caught his hand in hers and said, "Marcus, the other men..." But her protests were weak, her desire for him strong. Then, she just stood there while his fingers had undone the top button of her dress, and she felt his warm hand slip inside—this time, she did not stop him.

But then, she heard a sound from outside and saw a face clearly through the glass. A face she knew from somewhere. He looked at her intently, lustfully. She screamed, and the man disappeared. She jerked away from Marcus. Her hand flew to her open dress, pulling it closed, her fingers fumbling for the button. In the front room she heard the President's guards fly out to confront the intruder.

Marcus snorted in disgust, and then he slipped out into the main room as she rebuttoned her dress and joined him.

"The stranger who looked in your window is unconscious. I hit him soundly on the back of the head," Mortenson said when he came back inside, lifting up a walking stick he'd used as a weapon. A few light hairs were stuck in the hickory grain at the end. The sight of it was enough to make her feel ill. "Marcus, could you watch over him for us? I'm not sure how long it will be until he awakens."

Marcus, playing the toady once again, dutifully headed toward the open door as Mortenson added, "Check the pockets of his coat and vest for a weapon. He may have been sent by our enemies. Elisha and I will gather the President's belongings and prepare to move him."

Gently, tentatively, Chastity had prodded the President awake. He was angry at being rousted from his bed to travel once again, and he grumbled until his draught of narcotics kicked in.

"My letters. Don't forget my letters!" he groused at her as she helped him out of bed.

"Yes, sir. I'll put them in the carriage directly," she answered, trying to be patient. She wanted to think that he was improving. She wanted to think that now that she was caring for him his bitterness and melancholia was lifting, but it seemed his precious letters from out West meant more to him than her ministrations.

As the sun rose higher the small company continued on to their next hideout. Chastity flicked the reins of the matched set of bays that led the carriage deeper into the forest, following the lead of the ever-capable Tom Mortenson. She thought once again of Marcus and his offer of a new life in the cosmopolitan city of Montreal where they might be accepted as equals. Was this her life's destiny? Could she accept the sour looks and condemnation that some would give her as the wife of a free black man? Could she really trust Marcus, or was he a bit too much like his flamboyant owner, John Wilkes-Booth?

Too many questions. She sighed and glanced across at her companion in the carriage. He was covered with a cloak to the chin to protect him against the cold, the top of his head covered with a floppy old campaign hat, sleeping soundly—until the wheel on the carriage fell off.

Chapter Five

Ezekiel Edwards

I had been on solo missions behind enemy lines before, usually to scout the approach to an enemy encampment or locomotive facility. Once, near Chattanooga, I had found a heavily wooded path through what others said was an impenetrable forest. It led us to a railroad bridge that the ever-resourceful Tinker was able to blow up with black powder. So, following a trail like this through an unknown forest was nothing new. What was new, however, was this pain in my shoulder coupled with an even sharper pain in my head from last night's altercation. Both conspired to slow me down.

As I struggled along I reflected on what had happened last night. Could someone have known I was carrying a large sum of money in my vest? Could they have followed me from the train station seeking an opportune time to rob me? And did I give them that opportunity when my lust got the better of me as I lingered at the cabin window? My aching head made it hard to come to a clear conclusion on any of these questions.

At the crest of the hill, at most a mile from the cabin, something about the wagon tracks changed. I stopped and bent over to examine them. They had ended here at this spot. Something unusual must have happened. Muddy footprints. A discarded tree branch with handprints marring the frosty bark. A piss-hole in the snow at the base of a nearby tree where someone had relieved himself. Whatever had happened would have slowed them down. I moved forward looking for more evidence in the snow and mud.

The first shot thudded into a tree next to my head. I dove into the underbrush of a mountain laurel and listened to the report of another rifle shot. Two shots now, both very close. Time seemed to slow down, the way it does when you're in a fight. The report of the gun echoed through the rocky hillsides. Sharps carbine, I guessed. Whoever was shooting at me was not some muzzle-loading squirrel hunter.

I rolled to my right, trying to see my attacker. Another bullet whizzed by, just over my head. I ducked lower into the bush, flattening myself against the earth as I lay on my back. An odd calm settled over me—I would either die or not die—it was in God's hands. Or the shooter's. Three small black and gray birds landed in a bush nearby and began pecking at little red berries, oblivious to me and my plight.

If I had come another step into the open I would probably be dead right now, for these men were professionals. What were they doing out here? Who did I know with those kinds of skills and weapons? Confederate cavalrymen, mostly—Mosby's Rangers or J.E.B. Stuart's or Fitzhugh Lee's men? I turned on my side to get a better look at them, the side of my face pressed to the earth. Someone mounted a horse wearing a dark blue woolen coat. That didn't mean anything—half the Confederate army had stolen Union coats. Not that their former owners often complained; most of them were carcasses long since picked clean by carrion birds.

There was silence now. A slight wind in the trees, a murmur of voices up ahead. Deciding whether to attack down the hill or finish me off, most likely. None of this would have happened if I hadn't looked in that cabin window at the lovers. *The wages of sin is death.*

Or go back one step further—the pride and stubbornness that made me think I could hike to Pithole alone at night.

Or, earlier still, the hubris of carrying a large sum of money on my person—as if I were impervious to attack.

Should I go back even further and curse the day of my birth the way Job did? For now, the wetness of the frozen, damp earth was seeping through my garments. Why had I made this journey? Why was I here? Why was I cowering under a bush? I would rather be dead than a coward…so I rolled over and stood up.

But they missed my gallantry for by then they'd already gone; the sound of horses galloping up the hill, the cavalrymen's rear guard action finished. They had my money. They had good weapons. I was not going to stop them with a rock or a pocket knife. I would have to march to Pithole and face my mates—if no one else ambushed me along the way.

At the top of the hill I found where the carriage and horses had rejoined the main road that was heavily trafficked. A myriad of wagon ruts in the thick, oily mud obscured their tracks making it impossible to tell which way they had gone. No matter, my goal was to reach town, not follow them. To my right I heard the sharp clang of a steel hammer, and

I turned that way. A work crew was busy just over the crest of the hill—slaves again. Were all the work crews of the North now slaves? I tried to repress my anger for even at this distance I could see their overseer had a Kentucky long rifle across his lap. I adjusted my hat to cover my injured head and approached.

"Does this track lead to Pithole?" I asked, pausing to catch my breath.

One of the slaves, a slight man wearing a tattered brown coat and a new workman's cap that bore the railway's logo, looked up to me and answered, "Yes sir, couple miles on that way." He pointed down the hill to the east. From his speech I could tell he was from the North, perhaps New York. Once a freedman—now a slave.

"What rail line is this?"

"It's the Garnett and Amistead Railway," a voice from behind me said. I recognized an accent I had heard before in North Carolina. "Who wants to know?"

I turned and saw the slave driver. He wore a long black duster to ward off the weather and under that, a butternut shirt. On his head was a gray slouch hat with a bit of tattered braiding. An officer for t'other side.

"Just an oil man," I said, answering his question. "We'll want to be shipping our product out by rail as soon as possible."

"Then quit pestering my crew and get on your way."

"Good day to you, then," I said and pulled my boots free of the iridescent goo. They made a smacking sound of lips kissing. Leaning heavily on my walking stick I began to make my way past the line of slaves shackled with leg irons who shoveled gravel against the virgin steel of the new rails.

As I passed, the slaves began to sing a working song. One voice sounded strikingly familiar, a rich baritone. That singer was near me, and I paused beside him. Sensing my interest, he lowered his eyes and looked away. They started another verse of the song about John Henry, and I could hear his voice again, though softer now. Was it the same slave who had rescued me? I looked at the back of his legs. Through tattered trousers I could see his strong muscles, as if they'd been chiseled out of black walnut. Could it really be him?

The snort of a horse came from behind me. The overseer was turning my way. I must go. But I wished that I could stop and talk to the slave. His eyes caught mine, and I could see they were white and rimmed with fear. Reluctantly, I moved on toward the town.

I smelled Pithole before I saw it. The stench wafted through the trees and over the ridges. A familiar smell, the smell of open latrines at an army camp—but with a twist—for intermingled was the smell of raw crude oil. The odor made my belly ache. It brought back the memory of dysentery and stomach ailments that killed more in our company than minie balls.

When I broke through the trees to see the town itself I felt a new sense of hope. This was the place I had chosen to start my new life. A mad jumble of oil derricks, shouting teamsters, blasting steam whistles, shouted oaths and imprecations.

Pithole, I thought: *thou art well-named "Pithole."* I stood transfixed watching the men who raced about all over the town, like crabs scuttling for cover under a pier.

And so I hurried down the hill to join them.

Chapter Six

I descended to the flats where the drillers labored. My belly was tight, and my head still hurt—as much from the lack of laudanum as from what I knew I must do now— explain to Tinker and Daniel how I had lost the funds needed to keep our venture going. I followed Pithole Creek until it intersected with Holmden Run. That much I remembered from the map of our lease. To my surprise, I spotted the tattered Bucktail flag on the derrick almost immediately. These two men and a tattered flag were all that were left of our Company.

I steeled myself for what lay ahead as I heard Daniel shouting from overhead, "Captain Edwards! Hey Tinker, Captain Edwards is here!"

The two of them climbed down the rickety scaffolding and rushed to greet me.

"'Bout time you showed up. We're almost ready to start drillin'," Tinker bellowed.

He looked even taller and thinner than I remembered him. Had he been getting enough to eat? It didn't look like it. His belt was cinched tight with glossy marks where it had been drawn tighter, the ragged end hanging free, a sure sign of illness or short rations that had reduced him to a wiry minimum.

"How'd you get here before the morning stage?" Tinker asked.

"Walked," I said, reluctant to divulge all that had happened within hearing range of other drillers.

"All the way from Beantown?" Tinker shouted up to Daniel, still descending, "Look, Daniel, the Cap'n hiked here from Beantown, all by his lonesome."

Daniel came down and stood beside him. He wore a floppy, wide-brimmed felt hat to protect him from the cold March weather.

"Barely recognized you with that hat," I said.

"This here's a driller's hat," Daniel said in his soft Virginia hill-country drawl. "I'm gettin' it worn in proper before drillin' commences. All the fellars wear 'em, 'cept Tinker, of course. He still wears his Union cap. He's a believer in lost causes."

I glanced at Tinker. He was still wearing his well-seasoned Kepi. It was taller than most with a skinny, dark brim. He could have been in Napoleon's infantry with that hat. But at six feet tall and with the ropy muscled arms of a former lumberman, no one was going to knock his cap off.

"Speaking of lost causes, how's it going here?" I asked him.

"Good, Captain. We're making some real progress. Yesterday I hired a smithy to help with the tools. His name is Enos Yoder. He's from a family of salt drillers down by Tarentum. He really knows his tools."

"That's good news," I said and then, knowing I had to tell them, swallowed hard. "But I have some bad news. I was robbed last night. They took almost all the cash I had with me—roughly three thousand dollars."

Their faces fell, but Daniel said softly, "Captain, we're no worse off than most of these men here." And with that, he swung his dark hand wide to indicate the surrounding wells. "They have to sell shares in their wells. We'll just have to do the same."

Tinker frowned and cursed, "Dammit Captain. That ruins *everything*."

"I know. I should have taken greater precautions. But trusting it to a bank can be risky too. Banks fail. Banks get robbed."

Tinker strode away kicking clods of frozen dirt. "Dammit, dammit, dammit," he said, turning back toward me. "I should have warned you that these woods are full of thieves." He stomped the ground one more time. "We should go after 'em!"

I thought of the sound of the carbine, the whiz and thunk of the bullet beside my head. "I saw these men. They were not just hoodlums from the city. They were well-armed and mounted. We can't afford casualties in an ill-planned attack."

"So we just give up?"

It was just like Tinker to see everything in black, but that wouldn't help us much now. "Let's not panic. Like Daniel said, these other men are keeping their wells going, and probably with less money than we started with. We'll just have to sell some shares."

"We'll lose control of the operation," Tinker protested. "We had a chance to be independent drillers. That's a rare thing."

"But a profit is a profit," I countered. "We'll not make our fortune on just one well. We have to start over somewhere. In fact, I already have one person I can try."

"Who?"

"There's a man named Solomon Stottish, whose niece I met on the train." I began to feel this might be the way out of our dilemma, but Tinker objected.

"He's tightfisted with his money," said Tinker. "All those Pittsburg iron men are." He paused, looking with frustration at the partially finished derrick. "I had hoped we could start drilling in a few days . . . and I have to pay Enos for his first week's wages when he gets back from McClachey's hardware."

Daniel whistled a few notes and looked away. This was not the joyous reunion I had envisioned when I set out from Massachusetts, but I strove to make the best of it—someone had to lead. "I'll head up the hill and see if I can find Mr. Stottish. And I do have some funds still available in my account at Prather Bank." I spoke with increased confidence. "Those investing in wells might have knowledge and expertise that we can use. Things will work out. You'll see."

"Captain, with all due respect, I've heard those words from you before." He turned to Daniel, and I knew what he was thinking. They were the only ones left after the charge— the ill-omened charge I had led that wiped out their friends and brothers-in-arms. All dead, except Tinker and Daniel and me.

I met his gaze. Back when I was in command I might have struck him for the insolence of that stare. But those days were past, so I averted my eyes and turned away. I headed from the flats up the hill toward the ramshackle town. I had to weave my way through the jumble of derricks and up the slimy, boulder-strewn trail to town. It was enough to make me wish myself back on the icy cliffs over Pithole Creek. Lots of the wellheads flew the Stars and Bars or other Confederate rags. Some had picturesque names, like the Allemagoozelum Well. Some stood silent. Dry holes? Broken tools? Out of money? Would that be us if I failed to find new investors?

Lots of signs warned against smoking, with varying degrees of threats scrawled below them—*SMOKE AND GET SHOT!* was one. I climbed on past, but my throbbing forehead would not be stilled until I got some laudanum. Cresting the hill, the town of Pithole stretched out before me looking even more ramshackle and disreputable up close than it had from a distance. I stepped onto the rough-board sidewalk of the main thoroughfare named Holmden Street and began to look for a drugstore. Just one block south, where the sun slanted low in the sky, was Second Street. And on that corner was Christy's Drug Store.

"Jim Christy, at your service," the proprietor greeted me as I came inside. A wood stove roared away in the corner fighting to dispel the late winter chill.

"Good morning, Mr. Christy. My name is Edwards. I'm new to town and I was hoping to fulfill my scrip for laudanum from my home physician."

I opened my billfold and handed him a tattered missive with my name and a description of my infirmity. As he looked at it, I reflected on the bizarre fact that the person or persons who had robbed me had not taken my billfold. The thief must have been in a hurry. At least he hadn't taken the money I'd hidden in my boots.

Mr. Christy continued to read the prescription, frowning and tilting his spectacles down to inspect it more closely. "This has been filled numerous times, Captain Edwards. Perhaps you should begin to consider an alternative."

"You have a more efficacious medicine?"

"No, sir" he said, handing back the scrip. "But we have a couple of excellent surgeons in these parts. Dr. Miller, out of Franklin, who served with Burnside. And then there's Dr. Samuel Mudd, from Maryland. He might also help you gain some relief."

Burnside could have kept a whole platoon of surgeons busy, I thought. But I didn't want to raise his ire, so I responded instead, "I am not contemplating any further surgeries at the moment." I thought of the operating tables I had seen set up like the workroom of a slaughterhouse at Gettysburg—and the mountains of human limbs piled outside in the hot summer sun. I shuddered. How much better was laudanum than a surgeon's knife!

Christy shrugged, "If you happen to change your mind, feel free to stop in, and I'll give you directions to their office."

Thankfully, I saw that he had gotten me a bottle of laudanum from a locked cabinet. He wrote my name on the label, and I paid him for it.

"That reminds me of my other errand today," I said, happy to change the subject. "I have some business with a Mr. Solomon Stottish. Do you know where his office is?"

"I believe he's at the Danforth Hotel," he said, motioning out the front window. "Let me show you." He stepped out the door and pointed down the street to a corner several hundred yards away. "You can see the sign right across from where they're building the new jail."

Following his outstretched hand I spotted part of the sign that bore the name of the hotel. While he was turned away, I uncorked the laudanum and took a hearty swig. Patience was never my cardinal virtue. He didn't notice, however, due to a commotion at the end of the street by the hotel. Through the mire at that end of the town, there appeared a cavalcade of well-dressed women on horseback. "Is that a funeral procession?" I asked, wiping my mouth with the back of my hand.

Christy laughed. "This must be your first day in Pithole."

"Yes, well."

"That's what some call *The Parade of The Soiled Doves.*"

"Hookers?" I asked, using the army slang for the camp followers of the intemperate General Joe Hooker.

He nodded.

"What do the respectable ladies in town think of this *parade*?"

"There ain't any. You'd have to travel to Plumer or Oil City to find some of those. I take it you're not married?"

"Lost my wife in the war, so to speak."

Christy raised an eyebrow at that, but simply said, "Once the jail is finished and the new sheriff arrives it might be a more suitable place for young women. And, of course, when the railroad's done you'll be able to travel to the established towns more easily. That should be quite soon."

The women approached, and we both accorded them the deference of our attention. They smiled and waved to an admiring audience of men lining the road. All wore high-buttoned dresses and cloaks, their ankles covered demurely. Some had placards on their saddles proclaiming the establishments they worked for, such as "The New Idea" and "French Kate's." In my mind's eye I compared them to the woman I had seen in the cabin last night. Like the fabled *Snow White*, she was fairest of them all.

But they were available, for a price, for whatever pleasure I might wish to take from them. I had not made it my practice to frequent camp followers during the war as some did. But back then I thought I had a home to return to—and a Company of young soldiers looking up to me for guidance. Not now. And it had been a long time since I'd been with a woman. I should be about my business, I thought. I should not be standing here like a buyer at a cattle auction, but still I lingered.

The parade filed past, and one dark-haired beauty waved at me. She reminded me of the Scottish girls of Cape Anne, with pale white skin, dark eyes and tresses of raven black hair. Her posture was erect and tall, her waist slim. On her saddle a placard bore the legend "McTeague's Saloon." Then, I heard some shouting from the end of the parade.

"The lust of the flesh! The pride of life! This is the work of the Devil!"

"That's the crazy preacher," said Jim Christy.

The man was dressed quite strangely in a long, white robe caked with filth that looked like it might be a curtain he'd cadged from a hotel window. Under that he appeared to be wearing a tattered blue army uniform with the ubiquitous tall boots to slog through the mud. His brownish-gray, shoulder-length hair was a mass of mats and tangles. He shouted again at the men admiring the prostitutes from the wooden sidewalks lining the street. "It is better to *marry* than to *burn*! saith the Lord. If thy right hand offends thee, *cut it off!* It would be better to enter into heaven with *one* hand than…"

A man across the street tossed a well-aimed clod of mud, striking the preacher squarely in the chest. "Shut your mouth, you overripe tomato!"

Stunned for just a moment, the wild-haired preacher nevertheless pointed a finger at the rabble on the saloon porch and yelled back, "It is better to *pluck out your eye* than to *look upon a woman with lust!* It is better to enter into heaven with one eye than to be *cast into the lake of fire* where the fire is not quenched and the *torments never cease!*"

The rabble leaned back to let him pass as he continued to rant at the top of his voice and follow the "doves" on down the street. But even as that odd parade continued out of sight I had to wonder if, perhaps, the crazy preacher wasn't right. I recognized that first Bible quotation he used: *the lust of the flesh, the pride of life.* Was that what had drawn me here? Is that what I wanted? A fat billfold and a prostitute to share it with? I shook my head and heard a voice from behind me. I had forgotten I was not there alone.

"Welcome to Pithole, Captain Edwards," said Jim Christy with a laugh before turning and going back into his store.

Chapter Seven

I found Stottish's office on the corner by the Danforth Hotel. By the time I arrived the dose of laudanum had kicked in, and my aching head and shoulder felt much better. There was even a bit of a spring in my step, no doubt caused by the narcotic effect of the drug. Nothing like a little opium to make the day go better! I pushed the door open, buoyed by a newfound sense of optimism.

In the outer office several men sat at desks with oil lamps burning. They wore green eyeshades and seemed to have been pressed from the same mold. All were dark haired, lean and young. All wore dark gray pinstripe suits with vests and had bowler hats sitting on the corners of their neat oak desks. None of them looked up when I walked in. Apparently, they did not expect visitors.

"I am here to make inquiry of Solomon Stottish concerning an oil well investment."

"Mr. Stottish does not trouble himself with wells," one of the men said, his eyes still downcast as he continued with his bookwork. "Only leases and land. Good day."

"I have been referred to him directly by his niece, Lydia to discuss investments," I said, stretching the truth. "I am Captain Ezekiel Edwards, formerly of the Bucktail Regiment, and lately of Salem, Massachusetts."

This prompted a glance from him, but not an approving response. He sighed, slid out his chair and looked up. "I promise you nothing, but I will consult Mr. Stottish. I hope this is not some sort of ruse to pester him. He is a very busy man."

"I will only require a few moments of his time," I said, trying to be as diplomatic as possible with this front-room dandy. Three years of armed conflict had lessened my patience with what my former colleague, Professor Emerson called "city dolls."

I followed Stottish's factotum to a thick oak door in the back. He knocked lightly, and I heard a growl from within. He opened the door to a richly paneled office almost as large as the front room. A table strewn with maps dominated the room: maps of oil leases and land for sale.

Stottish looked up from his papers and gazed at me sternly. I had once happened upon an eagle devouring its prey that had fixed me with a similar stare.

"This man says your niece, Lydia referred him to you concerning investments. His name is Edwards," the assistant sneered, twirled on one polished shoe and stepped out.

"Captain Ezekiel Edwards, sir," I said, repeating my soliloquy from the front office. "formerly of the Bucktail Regiment and Salem, Massachusetts."

"Not sure I'd mention military service for the defeated Army of the Potomac as one of my credentials," he said, still fixing me with that hawk-like stare. "Now what investments are you here to discuss?"

"My associates from the military and I have procured lease No. 143A on Holmden Farm," I said with a nod toward the plat of leases spread open on the table before him. "We have begun drilling for oil," I said, stretching the truth a bit. "We seek investors to purchase shares."

"How much per share?" Stottish asked, giving me hope that he might be interested.

"We are offering 1/8th shares for one thousand dollars each—and we have four of them available immediately."

I saw him clench and unclench a gnarled fist. "You have only half the money you need to complete drilling? Good Lord, man, you're selling half your well!" He shook his head and looked at the ceiling. "Let me tell you something, Mr…ah, Edwards, was it?"

I nodded and swallowed a lump in my throat.

"If you hadn't mentioned Lydia you would not have even gained entry to my office. Look down in that valley," he said, waving a claw-like hand toward the window. "There are thousands of men drilling side by side down there. All of them think they are going to make a fortune. Almost none of them will. Soon, this field will be played out. A few will learn from their mistakes here and move on to the next field. Most will go back to whatever it was they did before. If they're lucky…" He turned back to me, "What did you do before the war?"

"I taught theology," I said in a voice that sounded plaintive even to my ears.

"Well, then," Stottish said, his tone warmer. "You're an educated man. You probably write well. That's a good skill." He nodded, pressed his lips together and crooked a finger at me. "Take my advice. Go back to Vermont, or wherever, and find a position in teaching. You'll have a much better life. Gambling on oil wells is just that, a gambler's life. You strike me as too much of a gentleman for that. Good day, sir."

"Thank you, Mr. Stottish, sir," I said. I couldn't afford to let my frustration show in my voice. "But if you yourself do not invest in drilling ventures, perhaps you know someone who does? I ask not only for myself, but also for my associates in this venture. We would like to complete the work we started."

"Finishing what you started is always good, I say," Stottish said, turning back to his maps and reaching for his spectacles as he leaned closer to examine them. "You did mention my niece, Lydia. Her, ah, fiancé, Mr. Booth, does invest in drilling ventures. He is also the manager of the Metropolitan Theatre on First Street. You might inquire of him there." He slipped on his spectacles and said as an aside, "Now, good day sir, and best wishes."

I stepped out of the office and closed the door gently, catching a look of triumphant disdain from the office manager who had let me in to Stottish's office. It would have been most gratifying to strike that smile from his smirking lips, but I restrained myself. Instead, I tipped my hat to him sternly and stepped out onto the rough-plank decking of the sidewalk.

The air was cooler now, the sun descending already on this typical March afternoon. Yet I had not accomplished my goal of finding funds to keep our new enterprise going. I thought of how I must have appeared to Mr. Stottish and of his quick rejection of my proposal. Was it the laudanum I had taken? Did it make me appear drugged and disreputable to those hawk-like eyes? Perhaps this was divine retribution for not having broken my addiction to the medicine. Perhaps it made me feel confident internally but made my countenance appear contemptible, like some gin-swilling lackey. Whether this was true or not I couldn't say, but I knew one thing. My options, like the late winter sunlight, were fast slipping away.

I had only one other possible lead to explore: John Wilkes-Booth.

* * *

A Negro servant ushered me into his office. "Good afternoon. My name is Marcus, sir," he said, taking my coat and hat. A row of even, white teeth greeted me when he smiled. His jacket and pants were of fine broadcloth, his shirt a spotless lavender—no plantation darkie, this.

"Mr. Ezekiel Edwards is here to see you, sir," Marcus said, opening the door to his master's office.

"Ah, Edwards. That's a fine New England name," said Booth, coming out from behind his desk to greet me with an outstretched hand, giving me the once-over with those riveting, dark eyes

"No relation to the famous New England revivalist, I'm afraid," I said, "though I did teach theology in Boston before the war."

"I have a girl, ah, that is—many friends in Boston," Booth said, smiling and fixing me with that stare. It gave him a wolfish aspect. I noticed a thin scar under his chin. "What brings a New England gentleman to this god-forsaken wilderness, I must ask?"

"I have several close business associates here," I said, remembering Stottish's remark about not mentioning my war service. "We have begun drilling a well, and I think we have an excellent team."

"And you're running short of funds?" Booth asked, hiking up a knee to sit casually on the corner of his desk. His movements bore the grace of a natural athlete. He reached out and patted my arm. "Don't apologize for that, Ezekiel. There's hardly a well that's been drilled down in the flats that didn't have the same problem." His friendly demeanor and his quick use of my Christian named disarmed me.

"We did experience the loss of some funds which we had expected to have available. But let me stress that my crew is quite competent. Tinker Evans is one of the most knowledgeable steam boiler men in these parts, and we've obtained an experienced smithy to handle the tools. And to round out the crew, I have a hard-working young African as my driller." I added this last, in case Mr. Booth was kindly disposed to the Southern cause—a fact I had guessed from his employment of a house slave.

"It sounds as if you lack nothing but capital," he said, laughing and hopping up to circle the desk. His youthful vigor was surprising. An investor in wells and manager of a large theatre—few in New England had achieved so much, so soon.

"Now, Ezekiel," he said when he paused to examine me, standing closer than before. "You've not been totally forthcoming with me, have you?"

His eyes were mesmerizing, like the turning of a pinwheel. I felt the hackles of my neck rising. What was this about?

And then, just as quickly, he bounded away saying over his shoulder, "I've read about you in the Franklin paper. When I was living there a few years ago the exploits of the daring Ezekiel Edwards and his Bucktail Raiders were all the rage. Don't be coy."

Again, he surprised me. He appeared to be an enthusiastic supporter of our cause, yet wasn't Marcus a house slave? "I've been told that it doesn't serve to mention my war experience."

"Well, I think it shows gumption. And a man *needs* that here in the oil region if he is to succeed. I think you're too modest, by far. Why, I've heard you Bucktails were even on familiar terms with President Lincoln. Is that not correct?"

"Well, he did often visit our camp out at the summer residence," I said. Over Booth's shoulder I saw a framed photograph of our new president, Robert E. Lee, smiling benignly down on me. All was well, he seemed to say.

"But Lincoln did visit you? You would know him if you saw him again?"

"Yes, I was acquainted with him. But unless we should reunite in heaven, I doubt I'll ever see him again."

"Some people think him still alive."

"Yes, I've heard those stories. He's been seen eating chowder in Boston, spotted in a train coach passing through Illinois, he's hiding with the Seneca deep in the Alleghenies. People will believe almost anything."

"Ah, now that's the skeptical professor talking!" Booth said and then laughed gaily. "But seriously, Ezekiel, there are some people who think the former president survived his wounds, and that he still lives. We've heard rumors he might be in these parts."

"Nonsense."

"That indeed may be so," Booth said, moving around the desk again, waving a hand. The man simply could not sit still. "But if I loan you this money, I might call upon you to disprove what you think is only bunk and nonsense. Would you be willing?"

"Seems farfetched, but yes," I said. Was he serious? It seemed too good to be true.

"Well, it's settled then. Of course—I *must* consult with a couple of my associates—but if I had my way, I'd write you a check right now."

That caught my attention. Perhaps our venture might succeed after all, in spite of my slips and starts of the last day. Perhaps Benevolence smiled on our cause after all. Perhaps.

"Thank you for your kind consideration of my offer, Mr. Booth," I said. "You won't be disappointed."

He walked me to the door, still talking. Seeing me hesitate to reach out with my injured arm he motioned for his servant, Marcus to open it for me. Marcus had put on his coat and hat to go out for some errand, and he held the door as I passed through. Something about the Negro in his cloak and gloves seemed familiar, as did his cologne when he leaned close to me to open the door. I had seen him somewhere before, I thought. My eyes lifted to meet his, and he looked quickly away as if ashamed of something. Odd.

But I gave it no more thought as I stepped off the porch into the gooey mud and headed toward McTeague's Saloon. Booth's last words, "I look forward to doing business with you!" rang in my ears as I entered the saloon. A chill had come in the evening air, and a warm bowl of soup would be just the thing about now—and perhaps a little celebratory whiskey!

Chapter Eight

I stepped into McTeague's Saloon just across the street from Booth's Metropolitan Theater. A crowd of boisterous and noisy Irish teamsters sat at a row of tables hoisting mugs of beer. A small chalkboard behind the bar bore today's menu: beef stew and biscuits. I found an open barstool and had just settled myself when I looked up at the imposing figure of the proprietor who was standing there looking down at me.

"Ezekiel Edwards," I said, extending a hand which was swallowed up in the much bigger paw of McTeague.

"Call me Josiah," he said. "Now, would that be *the* Captain Edwards of the Bucktails?"

"In the flesh, or what's left of it. I'm surprised you made the connection."

Without prompting, he put a glass on the counter and pulled out a bottle. He poured a very healthy dollop of amber liquid in, handed it to me and said, "This one's on the house, in honor of your service. Cheers."

"Why, thank you, sir. Do all veterans receive this honor?" I asked, sipping the finely aged whiskey.

"Only those what fought on the proper side," Josiah said and then winked. Once again, from under the counter, came the bottle of the good stuff. He lifted it to my cup.

I put out a hand to stop him, "I'd best have a bowl of your stew first."

"SUSANNA!" Josiah hollered to the serving girl in the back of the room. "A bowl for Captain Edwards of the Bucktails, if you please!"

I wished he would not announce my presence so loudly. The events of the morning made me concerned that I had enemies here already.

"So, I hear tell that you are thinking of trying your hand at *the oil business,*" Josiah said with a sly smile.

"I've started to drill a well down in the flats." I leaned forward so that I was sure only Josiah could hear me, and I added, "with some of my mates from my—um—regiment."

"Those would be the famed Bucktail Raiders?" Josiah asked. "Our friend, Crocus often wrote of you lads in the local rag. Stealing locomotives behind enemy lines, blowing up bridges and tearing up important railway lines and always escaping just before the Rebel Cavalry arrived. Daring! Exciting! as Crocus would say."

I grimaced in response and said, "Much of what we did was not known widely back then. What was known was exaggerated." I said this quietly, but Josiah still did not get the point. Of course, he didn't know I'd been accosted by armed men in the woods this morning, and that there might be Rebels who didn't look on me kindly in this room, even now.

"We all thought your exploits should have been more widely known," he said in his loud Scottish brogue. Now, heads were turning; some of them belonged to men dressed in Confederate gray.

"A toast to Captain Edwards of the Great Bucktail Regiment," Josiah added, raising a glass of whiskey in salute.

Some dressed in blue lifted their glasses—but some did not. I tried to keep my emotions from showing in my face, but the truth was I felt uncomfortable here. This had once been Union country—now I guessed most of those in the room were firmly in the enemy camp. In Massachusetts, I could at least feel safe from former enemies; not so, here.

Josiah must have sensed some of my fears for he said, "I'm told a peace treaty was signed over a year ago. But you wouldn't know it in Pithole. Feelings run high here. There've been shootings, for a time."

I thought of mentioning that I had dodged bullets just to get here this morning but I still did not know this man. My service behind enemy lines had taught me not to trust strangers too quickly, especially those who offered flattery.

Just then, the serving girl approached and set a bowl of steaming hot stew in front of me. It was my first decent meal of the day, and the whiskey had piqued my appetite.

"Lift up your eyes, lass and say hello to the famous Captain Edwards," Josiah said to the waitress.

She glanced up at me and blushed—she was one of the doves I had seen parading through town this morning, the dark haired, pale beauty who had met my glance. She curtsied and turned away.

Josiah thumped the bar and let out a laugh. "Well, now. I've known Susanna for some time, and I've not seen her act like that before! I daresay she fancies you, Captain."

Josiah stepped away to fetch a pitcher of beer for a pair of greasy-looking men at the end of the bar. They seemed in high spirits, and one of them yelled out to a friend across the bar, "Struck oil at one hundred feet! Three hundred barrels since this morning!"

"What's the going rate?" an equally greasy fellow shouted back above the din.

"Nine dollars and change."

"Tremendous! Now you can buy us a round," the man yelled back, bringing a laugh from the crowd of men at the tables. Josiah handed the driller another pitcher brimming with beer to carry across to his friends. I thought of Stottish's sour comments about dry holes and the futility of drilling for oil. You wouldn't know it from this crowd. Perhaps there was still hope for our venture. There seemed to be nothing special about these men yet they had struck oil and begun reaping a fortune. How hard could it be?

Josiah returned to me with the local paper tucked under his arm. "Someone hitting oil is almost a daily occurrence here," he said. "and the price has stayed steady since summer."

"So that driller made three thousand dollars today," I said to Josiah. "That's about what I lost."

He raised his thick Scottish eyebrows in surprise, "Did an investment go sour?"

"No, I was robbed while I slept. I was exhausted from hiking in along Pithole Creek and fell asleep at a logger's cabin. When I woke, my money was gone." I carefully neglected to tell him about my window peeping and laudanum swilling—and the gunfight. Had they known I was coming? Who would have tipped them off?

"These woods are thick with thieves. That's for sure. Most of the teamsters pack rifles and sidearms for that reason. Three thousand, though! That's more than this place cost," he said with a wave of his hand at the rough-sawn interior of his saloon. "Did you see any sign of the one what robbed you?"

"Earlier in the evening I saw a party of travelers in the woods. They had a young woman with them and someone riding in a carriage that I didn't see." I sipped my whiskey and watched the effect of my words on Josiah. Not just words, lies…I had seen a girl getting her clothes removed. I had seen a carriage, but no rider.

Josiah narrowed an eye and said, "A logger and his wife, do y'suppose?"

"The girl was very pretty and well-dressed. Looked out of place in the forest," I said, thinking back to the image I had of her: milky skin and a cascade of auburn ringlets catching the lamplight. The dark hand on her top button, opening, revealing.

Josiah stroked his beard and looked away, musing, "Could be Miss Chastity Stottish."

"Chastity Stottish?"

"She's a high-spirited one, that. Headstrong, willful. Her father's a wealthy mill owner from Pittsburg who's come here to invest. She's been giving him fits for years. Volunteered to be a nurse in Pittsburg at the end of the war. Unheard of!"

I thought back to my convalescence. I didn't remember any red-haired beauties at my bedside. I remembered delirium and pain. But then again, she *had* looked familiar.

"Her father's office manager came in here a few days ago. The old man sent him out to snoop around for her. Of course, he couldn't leave his precious bank ledgers to go look for himself, so he sent that shriveled up prune out to look."

"And they didn't find her?"

"Ah, nah. She's 'gone off again' is all he'd say. We guessed with some man who's taken a fancy to those curls and dimples of hers," Josiah laughed and slapped his knee. "She's not well-named, Miss Chastity!"

I laughed with him. But the idea that she was a woman free with her affections had again roused feelings in me that had lain dormant for a long time. Is that what I had come here to find? A woman who would let me have my way with her? I had known only resistance from my former wife. Were the women here different?

Across the room a man with a red shirt whooped loudly. His friends knocked their beer mugs together, soaking themselves, but too drunk to notice or to care. One of them fell off his chair, and his mug shattered on the floor. The man behind him brushed off splatters of beer and angrily shoved the drunk away from him. Josiah stepped away from the bar and went to intervene.

As he stepped away I noticed a copy of the local paper that a customer had left behind. I spotted the name Crocus on a byline and began reading:

BABE IN THE WOODS—"Word has come to our ears that a rustic woodsman has passed through these parts. Some say he is a traveling preacher—preaching a familiar message of hope and freedom for those in chains. 'Tis no doubt a rumor with only the substance of a wished for dream.

From this strange paragraph he went on to a discussion of how long the current "oil bubble" might last, quoting some who said the price of a barrel of oil would come to just one dollar soon. He then mentioned a meeting of *The Knights of The Golden Circle* to be held at The Metropolitan Theatre. It did not escape my notice that this was the property of my new associate, Mr. John Wilkes-Booth. I was about to read further when I felt a hand on my arm. Startled, I looked up to find Susanna, the waitress standing close to me.

"Josiah wanted me to tell you that we have a complimentary room for you this evening, Captain Edwards," she whispered. Apparently, she did not want the fact that I was being given a room to be public knowledge. Why?

"That is very kind of Josiah," I said and even though I felt a great weariness from all the events of this day I added, "I do still need to speak with my men down at the well before I retire for the evening."

There was more noise from the crowd, and to make herself heard she leaned closer still, so close I could feel her breath against my cheek. I noticed her flawless white skin, raven dark eyebrows and hair and shocking red lipstick that accentuated her sensual mouth.

"If you stop back after your errand I will escort you to your room," she said.

Our eyes met. Her lips parted slightly. The rest of the room slipped out of focus. I saw only those deep brown eyes of hers, with tiny golden flecks. An emotion passed between us—something hard to define, but tangible, as if she had opened and surrendered to me. I folded the newspaper to take with me down the hill and said, "I shall not delay my errand to the flats. I don't want to keep you waiting."

Her eyes crinkled with pleasure, and the smallest of smiles creased her lips, "I'll look forward to your return."

Chapter Nine

John Wilkes-Booth

The placard on the door of the main banquet room of the Danforth Hotel read KNIGHTS OF THE GOLDEN CIRCLE: PITHOLE SWORDSMEN CLUB. John Wilkes-Booth pushed through the ornate oak entry door and went inside. The room was so new that the tang of linseed oil from fresh paint still hung in the air—but not for long. Soon, the air would be rife with tobacco smoke. This was only fitting, for the motto of the club was RCT—Rum, Cards, Tobacco.

Booth took his accustomed chair and surveyed the room like an actor assessing the house audience. A good showing of the members. Excellent. They understood the danger before them. The men sat at card tables spread throughout the room with one lead table reserved for Leonidas Duncan, the president of this branch of the organization. As a waitress set a plate of succulent fried oysters at Booth's elbow alongside his glass of whiskey, Duncan rose from his seat.

"Gentlemen, we have a problem," Duncan said, his brow furrowing. "We have reason to think Abraham Lincoln is still alive."

Booth heard a gasp from one of the young Prather boys seated at his table. Some, apparently, didn't know that this was why they had called the meeting.

There were catcalls and mutters of disbelief, but Duncan lifted up a newspaper from his table and waved it. "You've seen the rumors in the paper. It's not mere poppycock. We think he's been moved close by and is being guarded by former soldiers still loyal to the defeated Union."

Booth listened to Duncan's reasoned remarks and felt a growing sense of frustration.

Leonidas continued, "You know those damned Abolitionists had a highly organized system for hiding men's property, both before and during the war."

Property, meaning slaves, Booth observed.

"Perhaps they mean to take him to Canada," said Duncan, presenting his case in his sober, lawyerly fashion. "We know there is mounting resistance to the policies of President Lee there."

"They can have him!" Prather shouted out, getting a slap on the back from one of his friends. Booth had seen Prather gulp down two cups of hot-buttered rum already this evening. Good, he thought—it helps to inflame the passions.

"Robert?" Duncan said, recognizing a tall woodsman who stood at one of the back tables wreathed in smoke.

"Begging your pardon, Leonidas, but I hear he was spotted in Plumer just this mornin'."

This brought forth a babble of conflicting voices and some shouts of "Kill him! Kill the traitor!" from the back rows.

"Order, order!" Duncan exclaimed, thumping an empty whiskey glass on the table—but the room still buzzed with conflicting voices.

Now was the time, Booth decided. He stood and said, "Leonidas, if I might have the floor for a moment?"

"The stage is yours, Mr. Booth," Duncan said eliciting laughter at his jest.

"Now is not the time for jokes and laughter," Booth said, his blood rising. "We are talking of the very Devil himself, I say! That demagogue! That beast from the pit! *Two hundred thousand men lay in their graves because of him!*" He paused, took in the rapt looks of the men throughout the room and then continued, "If he is still alive, he must be immediately captured and brought to justice, or the vile poison of his pen will infect the whole country again with the wretched plague of his loathsome ideas!" Booth looked around at the stunned faces of the men of the Swordsmen Club.

Freddy Prather thumped his table and cried "Here, here!" in a slightly slurred voice.

"The forest here is an immense jungle of trackless wilds, John," Duncan said in his measured tones. "You could hide an elephant in there. How will we find one man?"

"It has been said he was shot in the spine—can he walk?" Booth answered. "Can he ride?"

"I think not," answered Duncan.

"And those who guard him? Are they many in number or just a few?" asked Booth.

Duncan raised his eyebrows, and Booth was encouraged. He turned about, beseeching the assembled men, "We have an historic opportunity here. He is the symbol of that hated regime we fought with bloody tooth and nail in years past. He is the one man who could rally, again, the forces of Northern oppression to impose their Puritan will upon us. He must be stopped!"

A tense silence filled the room, and then from the back William Holmden stood and spoke out, "I pledge five hundred dollars to the capture of Lincoln!"

"I match that, and raise him five hundred!" said Fred Prather.

"Young Frederick, we are not playing cards now," Duncan said, and everyone laughed. Then, he added, "I believe Mr. Booth is right. This is a new challenge to the very heart of our country. We may have newfound wealth from the oil boom, but we must not neglect that calling that brought us together as Knights of The Golden Circle!"

Fred Prather jumped up and said, "I make a motion we deputize and authorize Mr. John Wilkes-Booth to hunt down and capture Abraham Lincoln—and to bring him back to jail here in Pithole, Pennsylvania!"

"Are you making a motion, Frederick?" Duncan asked.

"Yes, sir!"

"I second the motion," came the strong voice of the elder Holmden from the back. That would sway most men, Booth knew.

"All in favor?" Duncan asked.

A rousing shout of "Yeas!" rose from the assembly.

"Any opposed?"

Booth looked around intently to see if there were any Judases in the young group of Golden Circle men. No one met his eyes.

Chapter Ten

Ezekiel Edwards

Tinker Evans hoisted a tin cup brimming with golden liquid into the air and cried, "Here's to Cap'n Edwards and strikin' it rich on this here well!"

I took a sip and then responded, "Amen to that!"

Then, when Tinker brought out a wide-mouth glass jar with more of his brew I noticed something dark that floated in it, hard to discern by lamplight. "What sort of swill is this?" I asked, wrinkling my nose in disgust.

"Swill!? I'll have you know this here's a shor'nuff delicacy—homemade apple-jack from local apples, no doubt planted by our hometown hero hisself—Johnny Appleseed."

"Yassir, this is the fruit of the vine from ol' Johnny Seedapple," Daniel echoed. "We brewed it up yest'dy evenin'."

"Looks like you've got a dead bat in the jar," I said to Tinker, grabbing it before he could refill my glass.

"Dead bat! Captain, it pains me to hear you say that. This here's a piece of fine white-oak charcoal to give the brew some extra flavoring and filter out impurities."

We hoisted our glasses again, but an uneasy feeling settled into the pit of my stomach. What if the deal with Booth didn't go through? What would we do then? What if Booth rejected our proposal—or his mysterious partners did. One of the lessons I had learned as an officer was that at times a leader had to project confidence even when he didn't feel it himself. So, I smiled and toasted the success of our venture, and I hoped all would turn out well. But a deeper layer of worry shrouded my gay appearance.

After a couple more toasts I staggered up the steep hillside to Josiah's. The promise of a comfortable room after the rough night I had spent in the woods enticed me, as did the prospect of being with Susanna. Had I misread her intentions in the crowded tavern? Did she intend to do more than just show me to my room? It was worth a hike up the long hill to find out.

When I arrived back at Josiah's the crowd had thinned for the night. A small group in the corner celebrated their newfound wealth, but they were near passing out from overmuch jubilation.

"Susanna, would you be so kind as to show Captain Edwards to his room?" Josiah declared when he saw me. The drillers, who had been chatting with her in the corner, appeared a little put out that she was being taken away. One of them opened his mouth to protest, but only mumbled discontent when the big Scotsman said, "Do you have a problem with that, *mate?*"

Susanna led me around the back of the saloon to a set of stairs, and I followed her up to the second floor. The gaslights from the street illuminated the fabric of her dress. It highlighted the shapeliness of her figure as she climbed before me, the black patent leather of her tall laced boots glittering like polished obsidian. For a moment it took me back in time to a church outing, tobogganing on Folly Hill, near Salem. The girl whom I would later marry was there. For the sake of decency, all the girls were wearing trousers while sledding. I remember following Elizabeth up the hill—and that's when I noticed her walk! There was something powerfully alluring in that motion. I wanted her from that moment on— *the lust of the flesh*—is that all that had ever driven me?

We reached the landing and the small, unroofed platform was slippery with ice. Susanna fumbled with the key in the lock, cursing softly. Was she as anxious as I was? Without comment I reached out to help, enclosing her hand in mine. I heard her breath catch, and she turned to face me in the dim light. I could feel her breath, see her pursed lips. I leaned in and kissed her. The scent of whiskey and tobacco lingered on her, but it was not unpleasant or strong. Her mouth was warm and soft against mine, but she pulled away. She seemed surprised.

She leaned back and stared at me oddly, "Most men don't kiss me."

"You don't like that?"

She tilted her chin down, her hand still clasping mine as she turned the key. A furtive smile, the door swung open behind her. "I didn't say I didn't like it…" She looked up and then kissed me more passionately. Too passionately, for she lost her footing on the ice, and I had to catch her lest she fall completely off the shoddy platform.

I lifted her up in my arms and stepped through the doorway. The symbolism of carrying her across the threshold brought a twinge of regret. I should stop. But I could not stop; stronger passions ruled me. I set her down on the bed and trimmed the table lamp that had flared up with the cold air. She must have prepared this room—lit the lamp and tended the iron stove.

Her eyes met mine, her lips parted slightly. She lifted her hands behind her neck, and a brass button caught the lamplight as she began to unclasp her dress. Her breasts rose against the fabric—desire filled me—I pulled her open dress downwards, revealing her creamy white skin. Her hands were at my collar, opening my shirt, deliciously cool against the skin of my chest. Our lips met again, but this time in hunger, like animals devouring each other while our hands removed the last impediments of clothing.

"Ezekiel," she said using my Christian name, drawing me closer.

* * *

When the first rush of our passion was spent, she began laughing. For just a moment I was angry, confused. Did she mock me? But then I saw her leaning forward to unlace her boots.

"I guess we were in a bit of a hurry," she said with a look over her shoulder.

Her raven black hair fell across one shoulder, and the architecture of her bones was revealed in the warm lamplight. I should have felt shame or disappointment being in bed with her. But I did not. If anything, I felt gratitude—she had given herself to me as a gift. I traced the outline of her shoulder blades and the sweep of her spine downwards, feeling the warmth and moistness of her skin from our exertions. We were not cold now, not yet.

"I'll never get these boots off if you keep doing that," she said with a grin over her shoulder.

And she didn't.

* * *

At dawn I got up, measured out a dose of laudanum to ease my headache and sore muscles and washed up at the small lavatory. Susanna lay sleeping as harsh winter sunlight flooded the room from the east window. One slightly muddy lace-up boot lay on the floor at the foot of the bed. The thick quilt comforter was drawn up to her neck, and she was smiling. She was a prostitute. What right did she have to smile?

And what about me? I should feel guilt, for I had done what I always cautioned my men not to do; I had given in to lust and slept with a whore. Had I lost more than blood in the war? Had I lost my faith and personal morality? Or were they lost when the cause itself went down in defeat?

But overruling a sense of remorse was a sense of elation. What was it Caesar had said? *Vini, vidi, vici!*—*We came, we saw, we conquered.* I had not merely purchased her services, I had brought her pleasure—she had laughed then—and she smiled now.

This taught me a lesson. Something had been wrong with my marriage. There had been passion at the start, but only at the very start. Something overpowering—was it guilt? At times I had a strong sense that I had forced my wife into marriage against her better judgment. Against God's will, even. My lust had triumphed in capturing her so that I could have my way with her—something only possible inside of marriage in our New England Puritan society. But once that was accomplished... then the truth was out. I had only wanted her as a conquest, not a wife... and our love had grown cold.

I shook my head, as if to dispel those thoughts. They were too unpleasant to dwell on. *"Forgetting that which lies in the past,"* Saint Paul had said, *"I press on..."* That's what I must do. Leave the past behind—press on to the future.

I left the room quietly so as not to disturb her and went down to Josiah's saloon, drawn by the smell of fresh coffee and bacon. There, I spotted Mr. Booth poring over the latest issue of *The Pithole Daily Record*. He smiled and waved me over to his table. To my surprise his Negro servant, Marcus rose from a chair and said, "Coffee, Mr. Edwards?' and when I nodded he went to the kitchen to get it. My stomach tensed slightly. Should I immediately broach the subject of my oil-well investment or let Booth take the lead? I sipped some of Josiah's strong coffee and waited.

"I had an interesting discussion with some of my investment group last night concerning your proposal," Booth said, setting the paper aside. He flashed his charming smile, and again I noticed a long facial scar partially hidden by his moustache that extended downwards to his chin. He looked at me intently, "We approved most of the funds you requested."

He reached into a pocket of his vest and pulled out an envelope. He placed it on the table and slid it over to me. I had not failed to catch his phrase *most of the funds*. I opened the envelope slightly and saw the stack of Confederate dollars. It looked painfully small. I tried to bite back my feelings of disappointment.

"Now, don't look so glum, Captain. This is two thousand dollars—a small fortune to most men."

"But not enough to fully fund our drilling venture."

"Think of it as a down payment. It is the amount of funds which I personally had available at short notice. My partners have other plans."

"Such as?"

Booth leaned forward and spoke in a lower tone, so as not to be heard by the rough men at tables nearby. "We have one problem here in the North," he said, with a glance to those surrounding us. "Expensive labor cost is crippling the enterprise of our economy. Like these greedy immigrants, the teamsters. Their cost of hauling the oil to the railhead in Corry is often more than the cost of the damn oil itself!"

"You are thinking of replacing them with slaves?" I said, my stomach tightening again.

"No," Booth said, still leaning close. "We are building a pipeline to move the oil to the new railhead at Miller Farm. It will open next week."

"The teamsters aren't going to like that!" I exclaimed more loudly than I had intended.

Booth looked around to see if anyone had heard. He motioned to Marcus to approach and said, "Marcus, some eggs and a rasher of bacon for Captain Edwards, please." When his slave departed he continued speaking *sotto voce*, "We have a solution for unruly wage earners: Allen Pinkerton's men. We have a large contingent of them in Pithole already. And if they are not enough, Vice President McClellan has pledged federal troops to assist us, though I don't think that will be necessary. The Pinkertons have been doing a smashing good job of keeping the lid on things down in Pittsburg. I am sure they will manage here." He grinned with his mouth, but his eyes did not smile.

Marcus appeared with my breakfast and set the plate down beside me. He seemed oddly tense around me. Was it because I was a Union man from an Abolitionist state? Abolitionists often stirred up trouble—perhaps he feared I had come to do the same.

As I began to eat, Booth said, "As I mentioned, my investment group, The Golden Circle Petroleum Company, has big plans for our investments in the oil region. We will need competent staff to move this process forward. Competent and *loyal* staff."

"Are you talking about drilling operations or overseeing your pipeline project?"

"Both," he said. "We would like to expand our drilling operations to new fields and connect our new wells to our own transportation system—even build our own refineries."

"Sounds like a large operation," I said. For just a moment, I saw myself a wealthy operations manager with a fancy carriage and fine clothes. Was this what Booth was hinting might await me? I asked, "What role do you see me playing?"

"Ah, now Mr. Edwards—I'm the actor here, not you!" he said reaching out to grasp my sleeve and laughing, his dark eyes twinkling. "But I do, indeed have a role for you to play. We would like to start with this drilling venture and see how that progresses."

"But what if my well is a dry hole?"

"Most wells *are* dry holes. That's why we need a larger overall operation. Leases, wells, pipelines—all the way to refineries in Cleveland. But it all starts here," he said with a theatrical flourish of his hand toward the window at the battalion of derricks standing in the flats below. "We need a man who can be a bridge between what happens in the field and what happens in our offices here in town, someone who can work well with the drillers and the smithys and the boilermen. Not a general, but a good captain. A man in the field, as my associate, Mr. Duncan put it."

I should have been tickled by his flattery, but it was still the old game of granting titles with one hand and removing money from your pocket with the other. I still would have to explain to Tinker why I had not procured the three thousand dollars I had been promised yesterday. I took a bite of my eggs, trying not to let my disappointment show on my face. But Booth was perceptive; he reached a hand out to me again and tapped the table beside me where the newspaper lay.

"Ezekiel, we have other problems, as well. Look here in the paper," said Booth folding the newspaper so I could see an article on the back page. "This local wit, Crocus has another column about this so-called 'Babe in the Woods'."

He slid the paper over to me with a slim, delicate finger and indicated the offending paragraph. Marcus appeared at my elbow to refill my coffee cup, which was odd because my cup was still full.

"My associates and I think this is some sort of agitator who wants nothing better than to stir up trouble in the oil fields."

I read the paragraph. It declared, "SLAVES IN THE OIL FIELD! WAGE EARNERS IMPERILED!"

It continued, "Hardworking men of the North Woods, your jobs may soon be made *redundant!* The Pittsburg cabal has plans to bring slaves to work the oil fields, just as they brought slaves to work the cotton fields. A small bird has whispered this news into the ear of the Babe in the Woods, and it will surely come to pass. Act Now! Stop this."

I looked up from my reading to see Booth's lips pressed in fury. "We think they have a spy among us. And we have an inkling who this 'Babe in the Woods' might be."

I noticed that Marcus still stood nearby. Why did he linger?

"Some believe Lincoln's funeral was a sham. Perhaps it's him, or some other deposed general of the former Northern army."

"Maybe it's Hooker," I responded. "He'd fit in well here in Pithole."

Booth smiled, raised his coffee cup to drink and said, "That, he would. I wish it *were* him. But," he said, and now the dark eyes stared at me intently over the rim, "we have reason to believe it might be Lincoln himself."

I snorted in disbelief. "You mentioned this before. I'm not convinced."

Booth held his hands up. "Consider this. When Beauregard's troops sacked the White House he was shot in the spine and near death. Loyal bodyguards spirited him North from Washington on the old National Road into Pennsylvania—and those bodyguards were of the Bucktail Regiment."

"Not of my company. Those Bucktails were the President's guards. They never saw combat."

"You're quibbling. They were Bucktails. From the North Woods." Tinker would know. I was about to mention that when I saw Booth's stare and Marcus still standing inanely by with the coffee pot in his hand. Better not…

"And do you know who preached his so-called funeral?"

"Reverend Steadman. The Methodist," I answered.

"Guess where he has relocated since the war?"

"Illinois?" I ventured.

"Pithole! And he's making a damned nuisance of himself, too, I might add," said Booth, his face still red with anger. He turned on Marcus, "What are you doing here! Put that coffeepot back where it belongs and go attend to the chores I told you of this morning."

Marcus's face clouded and with an obsequious "Yassir," he nodded and turned on his heel.

Booth's outburst gave me a moment for reflection.

Then, Booth continued. "I think Lincoln still lives. He has recovered enough to sit in a wheeled chair and spew his detestable doctrines."

As he continued with his diatribe about Lincoln the thought took shape in my mind.

"And we've located his wife. What did they used to call her, 'The Hellcat'?" His glance took in Marcus, who in spite of his words, still lingered near the door to the saloon. With Booth looking on, he ducked outside. "She is in an insane asylum in Pittsburg. Perhaps he makes clandestine visits to her now and then."

My lack of credulity must have shown in my face, for he added, "I know this sounds far-fetched, but we have credible witnesses."

"You need more than that," I said, floating the idea that had occurred to me. "You need an experienced person who would be accepted by former Unionists. And if some of the Bucktail regiment is involved—"

"You would be willing?" Booth asked.

"It could be dangerous."

"How does one hundred dollars sound as a fee, then?" Booth said with one of his winning smiles.

"I was thinking one thousand dollars."

The smile fled his face. I saw his Adam's apple bob up and down, "I don't have that available at the moment, and I would hate to have to approach my investors again."

I tried another tack, "Josiah told me that Stottish thinks his daughter might be nursing that invalid—the gentleman you believe to be Lincoln." I thought of the wagon ruts in the snow. I thought of the young woman with her hand at the top button of her dress. "Perhaps I could kill two birds with one stone, as the old saying goes."

Booth's eyebrows rose. It was clear that this had not occurred to him before. He nodded slightly and said, "You have a point there. She might indeed be tending Lincoln. And who better to find out such information than a Bucktail Raider from an Abolitionist state?"

I could see my offer of service had surprised him. It gave him new leverage with Stottish, whose purse was closed tighter than the shell of a Little Neck clam.

But was this a compact with the devil? I lifted my coffee cup to my lips to finish it off. It was cold and there were grains of coffee in the bottom of the cup. My last sip remained bitter on my tongue.

Chapter Eleven

It was already mid-morning by the time I arrived at the well. Tinker and Daniel were just starting to nail boards onto the side of the derrick.

"Grab a hammer and some nails and come up!" Tinker yelled when he spotted me navigating the ooze as I approached our well.

"Hey, Enos," Daniel said to the stocky blacksmith who stood beside him smoking a pipe, "give the Captain your tool belt."

"Well, I suppose I could do that. Would we be having two men saw boards down here, then?" Enos asked.

"Yeah, give him your belt and a boost up onto the scaffolding. This nice weather ain't likely to last much longer. The snow could return at any time," Tinker added.

"You'll have to cinch it up some, Mr. Edwards. I'm a tad heavier than you…" Enos added. "In fact, rather portly. Or fat, some might say…" he continued under his breath, mostly to himself. This earned another yell from Tinker to hurry up.

I donned the belt and started to climb. Lifting my arm higher than my shoulder gave me a jab of pain, and I gritted my teeth. I was tempted to pause half-way and take a shot of laudanum. But as I was perched on a thin plank high in the air, it seemed unwise.

"You gonna be able to pound nails?" Tinker asked. "I can tell that arm still pains you."

"I can out-nail you with my sore arm tied behind my back. Just call me 'Lefty'."

"Pffft! You couldn't have out-nailed me even before you got blowed up. Now that you're a cripple, I'll win for sure."

I steadied myself on the plank, one hand resting on the tall posts of the derrick above us. Looking down did give me a fright and my expression conveyed as much to Tinker, who exclaimed, "Don't worry, Cap'n. I nailed this scaffold off myself. It's as solid as can be. Watch." He jumped up and down causing the whole thing to shudder and sway violently. I made silent entreaties to the Lord.

"See, like bein' in your mama's arms," Tinker said and then yelled down to the sawyers, "Got the next one cut yet?"

Daniel sawed away at the board while Enos held it steady. He had been owned by a family from the mountains of western Virginia and had excellent carpentry skills. Being fair skinned he could pass for a white man. With his hill country drawl and backwoods skills, he had been a strong asset behind enemy lines. If gentry were around, we pretended he was my slave. With trusted men from the North we sometimes let it slip that he was a Contraband: a black man taken North in the confusion of the war.

"Coming right up," Daniel yelled and handed the board to Enos, who then handed it up to Tinker.

We tacked the board in place, Daniel tossed up our only ruler in a smooth arc to Tinker, and we measured the next board. Then, we nailed the board in front of us off while Daniel and Enos sawed the next one. But as we did so a cloud obscured the sun for a moment, and a shower of snow flurries erupted. I saw Tinker glance down at the plank beneath our feet; in an instant it was covered with melting flakes. I could read his thoughts: *it was bad enough being on a rickety plank forty feet in the air—far worse if it froze.*

"If this well hits we'll be starting another one before spring. Right?" Tinker said to me and then climbed down to reach for the next plank.

I shrugged, "Depends on Mr. Booth, I guess. He has leases all ready to drill—we've got just the one."

"Still seems like makin' a deal with the devil, hookin' up with that character."

"If we can strike oil on a well or two we can go out on our own," I waited for a response, but Tinker still frowned. He held one nail in his mouth and with a couple of swift strikes pounded home another one held in his fist. I heard a clatter behind us and saw a black carriage wending its way around the derricks and outcroppings of rock. "Well, speak of the devil," I said.

The carriage pulled to a stop, and the spry Mr. Booth hopped out, sinking almost to his boot tops in the muck. "Ezekiel, come down!" he shouted in a clear, ringing voice I assumed he must use when on stage.

"Better hop to it, Zaccheus," Tinker said, laughing—until he heard his name shouted also.

"If you're Tinker Evans, climb down." Booth yelled. "Mr. Stottish is here."

As we clambered down the scaffolding another two men gingerly stepped out of the carriage and tried to find a spot to stand on—Solomon Stottish and his prim assistant. Booth darted around shaking hands with Enos and looking quizzically at Daniel. The others stood quietly gazing at the derrick with the rough boards nailed almost to the top and the boiler sitting sideways, not yet hooked up.

"Looks like you *are* making some progress," Stottish said after introductions were made, his hawk-like eyes studying the works. His assistant managed to look both bored and out of sorts. He gazed up at a banner slung from a well just a few yards away that said: *SMOKE AND BE LYNCHED!* I saw him flinch at that admonition, and I smiled to myself.

"It was not easy convincing Mr. Stottish that we should invest in this drilling operation," Booth said rubbing his hands together, his breath forming vapor clouds in the cool afternoon air.

"Risky, risky," the obsequious assistant said looking to the sky and shaking his head.

"It's true," Stottish said. "But I can see the logic of having a crew in the field. It might give us a better understanding of what sort of land is worth developing. What sort of land is likely to bear rock oil?" he asked, "No one seems to know for sure."

"Oil has been thought to lie only underneath streams," Booth said, "but now, a well near Franklin is flowing two hundred barrels a day on a hilltop!"

"Well, sir. We're happy to try drilling anywhere you please," Tinker said from under the brim of his kepi, responding to Booth's infectious enthusiasm.

Stottish, I noticed, did not join in the jovial banter. Instead, he tromped around examining the work we had completed. He reminded me of a bank inspector in Salem, aptly named Peter Coffin, who had visited a home I was building. He had spotted each and every bit of slipshod or hurried work and commented on them all in his rejection of my loan. Stottish's gruff stare now focused on the unfinished plumbing to the steam engine. I tried to repress a growing sense of anxiety. Was our funding about to be revoked?

I followed Stottish around the derrick while the others talked out by the sawhorses. The topic had shifted from oil drilling to some upcoming shows at Mr. Booth's theatre, including one featuring the amply endowed Swedish singing sensation, Hedvig Carlsson.

"We've been rushing to get things done before the weather turns," I said apologetically to Stottish.

"I can see that."

I expected him to chastise me for the shoddy workmanship. Instead, he leaned close to me, so close I could see the gray stubble on his chin and the age spots on his haggard face. "There's something else I want to talk to you about: my daughter."

"Yes, sir," I said, relieved to shift the topic.

"She's...she's run off," Stoddard said. "I believe she has taken up with a man that I don't approve of." He glanced off to the side where Booth was telling a story and waving his arms. "Booth said you might be able to help."

"I offered to go look for her and her employer. For a fee."

"One thousand dollars is a lot of money for a simple errand," said Stottish, bristling.

"Sending some amateur out could be worse. What if there's resistance?"

He screwed up his face like someone who had bitten something nasty. Small wonder he was rich. "Just find her, then."

"And drag her back by her hair?"

He looked down at the snow, his eyes had lost their steely hue—they merely looked tired now. "Tell her that her father misses her. That he loves her still."

And with that, he turned his back on me and strode forcefully back to the carriage. Perhaps his heart was not made of stone, after all.

Over his shoulder he yelled, "Booth, stop your jabbering and get in the carriage. These men have *work* to do!"

I turned to see Booth just finishing his story, imitating a singer at his theatre who always bowed deeply to the audience while men threw money in appreciation. He slapped his thigh in conclusion and grabbed Stottish's assistant by the elbow to steer him back to the carriage.

Tinker watched them climb in, and the carriage struggled to pull free of the muck, the muscles in the horses' necks standing forth in protest. Booth yelled something out the window but it was lost in the noise of Daniel starting to saw a board again. Tinker smiled and returned his wave, "Charming man, that Booth. Not unlike Lucifer."

"Stottish is different," I said.

"What did he want?"

"Wanted me to go look for his missing daughter, Chastity."

"In your spare time?

"No. For Money."

"She good looking?"

"Very," I answered, as we started climbing back up the scaffolding.

"Then I'll go, too. Make sure you don't get in any mischief."

Chapter Twelve

We rode at dawn the next morning, having obtained horses at the Metropolitan Hotel livery stable near Booth's theatre. There, a dark-skinned lad tended the horses. Tinker, as usual, took care of procuring our mounts. He chose a strong bay and knowing how I felt about horses got a dappled mare for me. Her coat reminded me of Gloucester granite, with flecks of gray and black.

"She's gentle and easily led," the youth said as I paid him a coin as surety for the horses.

We stepped into the lantern light at a small stand up-desk where he noted our names in his ledger and gave me a chit noting the time we had taken the horses out, "When you come back this afternoon, you'll need this."

I noted how well-spoken he was and that in the lantern light he looked like an Indian. "Did you go to the Carlisle Indian School?"

"Yes, sir. I did, sir."

"And you are of Cornplanter's tribe?"

"Yes, sir. All this was once our land," he said with a wave out the open stable door to the woods beyond.

"Spoils of war, I suppose," I said as much to myself as to him.

"Indeed, sir."

As we cantered slowly up the hill into the woods I thought of how it had been roughly forty years since the French and Indian War, and now there was hardly a trace of the Seneca nation here. Now, men made great fortunes with mineral wealth from that land right here in Cornplanter's fields.

"You awake yet, Captain?" Tinker asked, noting my silence.

"Barely. Too much of your apple squeezin's yesterday evening."

"I'd a thought you'd be red hot to go find that girl and collect your extra thousand Confederate," said Tinker, following me off the plank road and along the new railway line up the hill.

"Don't want to miss the turn," I said as if that explained my caution—or my lethargy. What was wrong with me? I had always taken the lead and pushed my men hard during the war. So what was I afraid of? I slowed my horse as we reached the section of woods where the trail to the cabin met the railway line.

"Buggy passed this way," Tinker said leaning low in the saddle to inspect the leaf-strewn ground.

"Yes, I passed through here a couple of days ago."

"No, since then. Perhaps as early as this morning. The frost is disturbed."

"Coming or going?" I asked, thinking I should have seen this. I should be taking the lead.

"Hmmm. Looks like going—fresh hoof prints in the mud heading up the hill toward Plumer."

"Are you absolutely certain?"

"No."

"Let's check the cabin first. We can follow their trail to Plumer later."

I pulled my horse around and headed quickly down the hill. When I came near the place I had been shot at the first day I could see the roof of the cabin in the distance. A wisp of smoke rose from the chimney. I held up a hand, and Tinker halted behind me. We dismounted.

I pointed to a sign nailed to a tree: *PRIVAT PROP. STAY OUT!*

Tinker snorted at it.

We tied our horses there and headed to the cabin in silence. I made a motion to Tinker, and he unbuttoned his duster revealing his Colt navy revolver at the ready. We stepped up onto the porch gingerly and darted to the sides of the one front window. Tinker drew his sidearm and quickly leaned in for a look.

He shook his head to indicate the front room was empty. Still moving quietly we circled around to the other windows. I came to the bedroom window I had looked in before. There were footprints in the soft ground, but no sign of my earlier visit—no blood on the grass, no stray dollars of my inheritance blowing around. And as I peered through the glass, no beautiful girl with a dark hand at her breast, undoing buttons.

A dark hand at her breast? A gloved hand?

"Hey, Zeke. This ain't no muse-ee-um," Tinker yelled from the porch. "Give me a hand with this lock."

I shook my head. The memory of that moment still wasn't clear. I climbed to the porch carefully for the stairs were slick with damp, frosty leaves. Tinker stood by the door waiting for me. I took from my pocket a small pry bar and a thin blade I had brought from our supply of tools at the well.

"Lift the door on its hinges a bit," I said.

Tinker lifted the door up by the knob, and I slipped the jimmying device in by the mortise lock and popped the catch. The door swung free.

"Cheap locks," Tinker remarked. "I love 'em."

I nodded once, and he followed me into the room. Tinker approached the small potbelly stove in the corner. He lowered a hand to it carefully and said, "Still warm. Pro'bly an hour or so since they left."

I opened the drapes at the front window more fully letting in more sunlight. It shone on a small desk in the corner beside me. "Looks like an old school desk," I said placing my hand on the worn, wooden top.

Tinker frowned. "Not many school kids here in these woods."

"Someone writes here," I said lifting a freshly trimmed quill up to the light for him to see. I thought of Josiah and letters from the "Babe in the Woods".

"Brilliant deduction. You should be a detective," said Tinker nodding his head and rooting around in the stove with a stick. He pulled out a piece of partially burnt cloth. "Looks like a bandage."

From across the room it didn't look like that at all. It reminded me of a scripture passage that in English read: *Though our sins be as scarlet, he will make them whiter than snow.* But in Hebrew it was a more earthy metaphor about soiled menstrual cloths. I made a face.

Tinker knew me well and he responded, "It's not from the girl. I can see where it was pinned like a bandage. You should know."

I shuddered. I had seen enough of that at the hospital at Pittsburg—the pails and hampers of bloody linens. Not many of the soldiers carried into that place ever walked out again—but I did.

Tinker continued rooting around with a poker in the wood stove. I went to the back room, still thinking of the hospital, the moans of the men at night, some calling out for their mothers or to God. And one demented man who would suddenly yell, "Uncle Herbert! Come here! Uncle Herbert!"

In the back room I came to the place where I had seen the girl. She had left some of her clothing and cosmetic items strewn about the room. A hairbrush lay on the dresser with several auburn hairs caught in the boar bristles. A small vial of perfume sat beside it. I pulled the cork and dabbed a small amount on my wrist. The smell triggered an odd memory.

I was back in the hospital face down on my bed, and a nurse was rubbing my back to prevent bedsores. Her hands were cool, soothing.

She leaned very close as she worked her way up to my sore shoulder, and I yelped in pain. I felt her breath on my neck, "Oh, I'm sorry," she said in a girlish voice. And I had smelled her perfume, the same perfume as now. Her hands on my back had moved lower. Then lower still. Even in my foggy mental state I knew that she had crossed the line from healing to caressing. And she continued caressing and whispering to me, pausing now and then to apply lotion to her hands. It was early evening, and we were separated from the other patients by a curtain.

I became aroused by the touching of her hands, and for one brief moment I completely forgot the pain in my shoulder. I moaned softly—and that's when I heard the screech of the head nurse, "You hussy! What are you doing! Get away from him!"

"Ezekiel, what are you doing in there?" Tinker's voice interrupted my reminiscence. He leaned in the door and saw that I stood in front of the dresser with my hand on a half-opened drawer that held Chastity's clothes—her undergarments, to be specific.

"Shame on you, you horny toad. No wonder you were being so quiet. I thought you'd nodded off from laudanum or something."

"I am conducting a serious investigation, Mr. Evans. One never knows what one will find unless a thorough search is done." I held up a shapely corset and added, "For example, there might be small weapons concealed in this item."

Tinker grinned, shook his head and turned away. As he left I looked down and saw the edge of an envelope in the bottom of the drawer. I lifted it out, pulled out the letter inside and began to read:

Deerest Chastity,

They are treating me quite well here, though I must say the food is still bestly. I think I am doing well, and hope to be re-nited with you and father, that dear man, as soon as possible. That Doll Mary is here now with me I call her Molly as she is such an friend in time of distress. She misses you and says you were the best nurse ever and anon. Much love to your and that dear man, you're beloved father and to father Abraham. I am pleased to know you are still following the path the Lord has lay out for your, and such, and ever and anon are with the angels in my prayers as always.

Much Love and Kisses,
You're Mother,
Constance Mellon Stottish

"Schenley Sanitarium," Tinker said reading from the envelope flap. "That's just over the hill from where I was taken for my injuries. It's an asylum."

"Her mother's maiden name was Mellon. They're bankers. They finance iron mills, railroads, oil drillers," said Tinker twisting his fingers together to indicate cash.

"Maybe you should find her. Improve your situation."

"I'm spoken for," Tinker said. He had recently become engaged to marry, and he hoped our venture was a success so he could finalize his wedding plans.

I held the envelope, wondering what to do with it. I decided to return it to its hiding place and so went to the desk out front to find something to write on. I pulled open the drawer at the small desk and found a nub of a pencil and some writing paper. I was startled to see that the letterhead said *The Executive Mansion*. With the pencil I wrote the words "Constance Mellon" and "Mary/Molly?" and "Schenley Sanitarium" on one page of the lined paper of the pad, then placed it in my pocket.

I looked down beside the desk and saw a crumpled piece of the same paper in a coffee tin that served as a wastebasket. I pulled it out and smoothed the paper out to read it in the dim winter light of the window. It appeared to be a rough draft of a letter with many scratched out lines. I spotted the word *Gettysburg*, and it piqued my interest.

Tinker stood beside the window with the curtain partly drawn. "Someone's comin'," he said.

I stuffed it in my pocket and buttoned my coat as we heard the sound of horses being pulled up, men dismounting. Tinker pulled out his revolver and held it up as he went to the door.

"What're you doin' in there?" came a voice from the trees. I saw a Black Hat rise a bit higher in the bushes—it looked like one of the Iron Brigade men.

"We're visiting homes to announce the opening of the new Methodist church," I yelled from inside. "Reverend Steadman sent us."

Tinker had stepped out onto the porch, his hands held up. He was clearly in danger, so I stepped beside him. "Reverend Steadman wanted us to invite all the un-churched in these parts out to the opening. We saw the buggy tracks and thought a young family might be home."

The Black Hat stepped from behind a laurel bush. "Methodists, eh?" he said and then spat. "You Methodists always break in to houses? Put that gun away."

Tinker pushed the gun down into his coat pocket.

"The door was unlocked," I said. That line usually worked. Tinker nodded in affirmation of this fact.

"What outfit were you with?" the Black Hat asked, motioning to Tinker's kepi.

Tinker turned the cap around so the man could see the worn nub of deer hide attached to it.

The man laughed, "I locked that door myself. And you ain't no Methodists. What were you really doin' here?"

"Stottish sent us to look for his daughter," I said. I noticed that he still held his gun on us. Old habits die hard.

"She was here," he said. "Now she's gone."

"Her father's worried about her. He would like her to come to town and let him know she's all right."

"She's fine. She's doin' what she wants to do. And she's not a girl, she's a woman, fully growed."

Amen to that, I thought. But instead, I said, "Can I speak with her, then?"

The man's tone softened, the gun lowered from deadly scope, "No."

In sailing, if one tack did not advance you to your goal, you took another. "We would be willing to pay." I saw Tinker's eyebrows rise. He knew the bereft condition of my purse.

"How much."

"One hundred dollars."

"One thousand," the Black Hat answered. He must have seen that deflate me, for he added. "I am not trying to cause offense. We have a client here. A man of some importance. He's in ill health and does not wish to be disturbed. He has…interests in this region. Miss Chastity is in his employ as a nurse. That's all I'm going to say."

A moment passed. We were clearly at an impasse. With his gun he motioned toward our horses.

Tinker snugged his hat down on his head and stepped off the porch. We walked across the snow-speckled ground and untied our horses. The Black Hat then took our place on the porch, tying off his horse to the railing as he headed to the front door. When we were on our mounts he shouted out to us, "When you see Reverend Steadman, tell him Tom Mortenson said we'll definitely be at the church opening. Haven't missed a Sunday yet this year!"

Chapter Thirteen

After our quest to find the girl had failed I came back into town with Tinker to return the horses. We delivered them to the attendant at the Metropolitan Hotel and paid our bill. As he was writing a receipt for me to present to Mr. Stottish we saw an odd sight out the open doors. There was a long wagon train making its way up the hill from the flats. The wagons were driven by the usual core of teamsters—mostly Irish toughs, some of whom had driven mule teams in the war over rugged country nearly as bad as this. But this wagon train had one remarkable difference—there was something terribly wrong with the horses.

"Those horses look ill-used," I said to Henry, the Indian youth.

"They lose their coats in about a week," he answered as they tromped slowly by, the head of one horse overhanging the back of the wagon in front. "They're dead in six."

"It's the grease what does it," Tinker said, nodding his head in agreement.

To me, the horses looked like exhausted soldiers marching on campaign—as if they might drop at any moment. I'd never been all that fond of horses, but it was sad to see the beasts in such pitiful condition, and I said so.

"Won't be for long—they'll be out of work soon," Henry said. "Once that pipeline goes through—"

"That's next week," Tinker said, pointing up the hill to where a small part of the ditch that carried the oil pipeline was visible.

"We could have a small war on our hands then," Henry said. "Teamsters won't give up their share of the oil money without a fight... even I can see that."

"I was in Pittsburg for almost two years and I've seen workers revolt. The iron mill owners always seemed to win those wars," I said.

"I don't know," Tinker said. "The Irish are a feisty bunch. And if the Mollies show up it could get interesting.

"The Mollies?" Henry asked. "Are they Irish women?"

"No. They're Irish axe-handle swingers," Tinker said playfully cuffing the young man on the back of the head. "They mostly defend the Irish if they've been cheated or hurt in the mines east of here, but they've been known to cross the mountains before."

"But the Pinkertons won't back down either," I remarked. "They're on the side of the mill owners and slavers now."

"They were on our side during the war," said Tinker.

"Were they?" I rounded on him. "Think about the information they were feeding McClellan. That's why he was always scared to death of Lee."

"But they protected Lincoln!"

"You mean that fiasco when he took office. When they had him dress up as a washerwoman and sneak into town?"

"They stopped several attempts on his life," Tinker protested.

"Where were they when Beauregard rode into town?"

Tinker's eyes narrowed. "Psssh," he said out of the side of his mouth. But I had planted the seeds of doubt about the Pinkertons.

The wagon train passed, and Tinker and I headed back down the hill to resume working on the well. I had been anxious to ride out and find the girl, and he had been anxious to get back and see if he could get the boiler connected to the steam engine and start drilling for oil. Tinker ranged ahead, dodging around rocks and wading through mud at a quick pace while vigorously explaining how the boiler had passed its pressure test the evening before. I was struggling to keep up, starting to feel that strong thump of pain in my shoulder again, no doubt due to diving for cover at Chastity's cabin and compounded by a jolting horseback ride back to town. I yelled for Tinker to go ahead, I'd catch up with him in a few minutes. I stopped to catch my breath, and I sat for a moment on a big round rock halfway down the steep hill.

I pulled out my bottle of laudanum and lifted it up to the light. Still about two thirds of a bottle left, which was a comforting sight. Up ahead Tinker turned back just in time to see me take a quaff of laudanum—this time without my spoon. He frowned, shook his head, and marched on down to the derrick. I sighed, knowing that he was disappointed to see me reverting to a narcotic to deal with the pain. Aloud, I said to no one in particular, "If I knew I would survive surgery, I'd get this shoulder fixed."

This brought a glance from a lean man in a driller's hat who happened to be passing by, but he made no comment. Up on the hill I could hear the piercing voice of the wild-haired preacher yelling about something, though I couldn't catch enough of it to know what he was saying. From the flats there was a cacophony of steam engine sounds mixed with horses neighing, hammers ringing, drill bits thumping, and just as I stood up, an explosion that sent a jet of fire in the air above a circle of older wells down the valley a ways. Someone had "shot a well" with nitro. I shrugged my shoulders and felt a small twinge, so I took out my bottle and took one more wee swig of laudanum. I wouldn't be climbing scaffolding today, so it shouldn't matter. Or so I told myself.

"'Bout time you got here, you drug fiend," Tinker said when I arrived. He and the smithy, Enos were hoisting a long connecting rod onto the flywheel of the steam engine. In the background the boiler was hissing away, the banked fire giving the room a pleasant warmth. While the men worked on connecting up boiler plumbing, I looked at the piece of paper I had stuffed in my pocket. Spreading it out on a workbench I held an oil lamp close by and read the following:

THOUGHTS ON THE LATE DEFEAT AT GETTYSBURG

As Genrl. Beauregard approaches from the South, and there are rumors that Lee has crossed the Maryland border consider: ~~There were many who warned me I should move the Capital farther North, too late now do I see the wisdom of that course of action.~~ Some 87 years ago, this country was founded on the overreaching principle that all men are created equal. It now appears that no nation, so conceived, can long endure. ~~Instead, we see the tyranny of the few trampling again the rights of the many. It is the same struggle we fought almost one hundred years ago against the king of England and his coterie of lords and noblemen.~~ And that though we have fought to advance this work of liberty, it appears we have failed in that great task. These honored dead gave the last full measure of devotion to that cause. Have they died in vain? ~~Has the dream of a country, where a humble backwoodsman can ascend to the premier spot of leadership, died with those men? Are countries only rightly to be ruled by the wealthy few? Damn them, damn them all!)~~

Written across the entire letter in a bold script were the words: ***Does not scan!***

I could see why Lincoln had crumpled this up, discarded it. I thought of his words *these honored dead*, and *the last full measure of devotion*. I felt the tightness of anger in my belly. I thought again of our futile charge across McPherson's field: the Iron Brigade on the right, the Bucktails on the left, the hail of bullets from behind the fence, General Reynolds falling right in front of us with a bullet in his head. William Jones had fallen in the next moment, James Roberts had been standing with me when the shell landed and we were blown off our feet. We shouldn't have been that far forward! I shouldn't have advanced beyond the first fence… it was all my fault. They'd still be alive…if only…

My fists clenched, and I wanted to crumple up this paper and toss it in the firebox of the boiler. It wasn't just some border-state farmland that we had lost. It was a whole world. A world where now the few lived as kings and the rest of us toiled as if…I looked through the doorway. Daniel was approaching, no doubt to get me to help with the well. Would he soon be found out, returned to slavery? That's all he was, after all. Contraband. Stolen goods.

"Marse Edwards," he said.

Sometimes that slipped out—the deferential tone and appellation he had been trained to use before he became "Daniel Freeman." Back when they used to call him Rufus, a name of mockery.

"Daniel?"

"Don't mean to bother you, sir. But we could use a hand for a moment."

"Could you get Mr. Evans to come here? I want to show him something. Then we can all work together. Perhaps you and Enos could take a break for some coffee?"

"Yassir, Mr. Enos would like that," Daniel said.

As the others drank their coffee Tinker read the *purloined letter,* as Poe would have called it.

"He's right. It was stupid to keep the capital at Washington. He should have moved it North," Tinker said when he had finished.

"That's not the point," I said, trying to tamp down the anger that had grabbed me when I thought again of those killed at Gettysburg.

From under his kepi the gray eyes caught mine, "What, exactly, is the point, Ezekiel? It's been two years. The world has moved on."

"It's the same tyrannical principle—"

"Stop quoting Lincoln."

"But he's alive!"

"So what? Unless he can help us drill for oil, what good is he?"

"He's the one man who can give us hope!"

"He ain't got any left, from what I hear. Not to mention the fact that he can't walk."

"You knew he was alive?"

"The 150th Bucktails dragged him out of Washington. They've been nursing him ever since. If you ask me, I think they should have let him die in peace."

"That's not dying in peace! That's going down in defeat!" I said, my voice sounding shrill even to my own ears.

Tinker rounded on me, "You're right, Ezekiel. But I was the only one who walked off the field that day. I found Daniel lost behind the lines two days later. You were dead. Billy was dead, Roberts was dead, Reynolds was dead, and Lincoln was dead. We were defeated."

"But what we fought for—"

Tinker cut me off with an angry voice, "You missed a lot, Captain, while you were in the hospital. You missed the worst of it. What Beauregard's troops did in Washington before Lee arrived, especially to the women. And then the rounding up of all the coloreds—even as far North as Boston. You missed it all."

I had heard the stories. My imagination could fill in the details of what it must have been like when they sacked and burned Washington.

Daniel and Enos had stepped closer, no doubt drawn by our raised voices. They stood with steaming mugs of coffee in hand.

"No matter what you think of him, we were hired to find Lincoln, and I intend to do so," I said.

"You do that, Ezekiel," said Tinker, turning away. "But leave me out of it. He's not worth one thousand Confederate dollars to me."

After he left, Daniel stood alone at the doorway. His eyes met mine, and he shook his head.

Enos and Tinker went back to fitting a con-rod onto the flywheel of the steam engine. Enos was sweating with exertion, and I realized he had been doing the hardest part of the work—lifting the member into place. I helped steady the long con-rod while Tinker drove a pin home with a brass hammer, still fuming over our argument.

Daniel sat to one side filing a compression fitting that had been leaking when they first tried to get the steam engine to run. Enos wiped his brow, fetched a small stool which he always kept handy and sat down beside Daniel. He pretended to be resting, but what he was really doing was making sure that the filing of the fitting wouldn't damage it.

"Make yourself useful and find some kindling," Tinker yelled, his head in the bowels of the boiler as he tightened the stay bolts with a big wrench. "Take Daniel."

Daniel shrugged, handed the small file he was using to Enos and stood up. I took the coalscuttle and we headed out toward the woodpile, looking for cut-off ends of wood in the mud. The pickings were slim, and most of the pieces I found were half-frozen and muddy. I continued down toward the stream looking for brush or twigs, but finding precious few. It reminded me of the fields around the Rappahannock after the two armies had fought back and forth for two years—there wasn't a stick of wood about anywhere. I found some broken barrel staves near The Confederate States Well. A tall, stout man in new denim jeans and a jacket of Confederate gray nodded to me. He had a thick beard and a weathered face from working out in the cold. "Come here, mate. This'll help," he called to me.

I crossed over to him, walking on some slimy planks and saw he had an open barrel of oil he was just capping for shipment. He took a ladle from a hook on his workbench and poured a heaping dollop of crude oil on my damp kindling sticks. With a smile he said, "She'll burn better with a bit o' the grease on her."

I thanked him, thinking as I did so how the once scrawny Rebel soldiers now seemed to be well fed and prospering—and we were scrounging for handouts. I met up with Daniel and we headed back to the engine house. Daniel had found some charred twigs at an old burn pile near the woods.

"I heard you talkin' about Lincoln with Tinker," he said.

"We disagree sometimes."

"Often, it seems."

"Yes."

"I'd like to go if you searchin' for him." He stopped walking and pulled a pipe out of his worn cotton trousers. He paused and leaned against a nearby tree that had been sawn off halfway up. "Been dyin' for a smoke, but it dangerous near the wells."

"Dangerous to go looking for Lincoln, too."

He eyed me over the brim of his pipe bowl, sheltering it with his hand to block the wind. I noticed he had carved a Union shield on the bowl of the pipe, "Marse Edwards, I ain't got much left to lose."

His deep brown eyes met mine. What did I really know of him? He had been useful in our raids, back in the day. But did I actually know him? A comment from my former wife came to mind, "Ezekiel, you live in your own little world."

"I'd be happy to have you go with me. We'll just have to keep it from Tinker."

He ducked his head in acknowledgement—something you didn't see white men do. It saddened me.

Back at the engine house Tinker emerged from the sooty innards of the boiler to look at what we had found.

"I found some twigs and barrel staves—and a kind Confederate officer lent me some oil."

"Did he look like the virgins who trimmed their lamps with oil?"

"No, he looked like a fat, corn-fed hog," I said sourly.

"Don't be so glum, Captain. By supper we'll be rich. Then you can dine on orsters and New York steaks and put some meat on those bones," He grinned at me, happy as a boy with a new Christmas toy now that his steam engine was about to run.

Tinker took the coalscuttle and pushed most of its contents into the firebox. He lit a fire with the flame from a nearby kerosene lantern, and a roar of burning oil went up. I stepped back, and Tinker stepped closer, peering at the water meter and other arcane instruments of the engine man's trade. I hadn't the faintest idea of what he was doing, but I'd seen him at it before, and he'd gotten results. Nevertheless, when he shoveled a healthy scoop of coal into the maw of the firebox I stepped closer to the door.

"She ain't goin' to blow, Zeke," he said. "I pressure-tested this boiler twicet, she's tighter'n a nun's—"

"Hey, watch the language over there, pard," Daniel said with a nod toward Enos. "We got a practicin' Baptist amongst us."

"Well, now. I am of Amish descent. Amish and Mennonite," Enos said in his ponderous way, "My old pap was Amish, and now my mother."

"Enos! Tighten that fitting. It's startin' to drip. And we need to get the jars and drill bit hung. Hop to it!"

Enos did as instructed, first tightening the big bronze compression nut on the steam line and then heading out with the heavy iron drill bit slung over his shoulder, all the while muttering, "Hop to it, Enos. Shut yer trap and get to work...no rest for the wicked."

Moments later the great fire-breathing contraption sprang to life. It gave a great "chuff!" and the driving rod extended out toward the flywheel, which began to slowly turn with much creaking and groaning. Tinker grabbed an oilcan and darted around greasing the joints, flipping up caps that covered lubrication fittings. He yelled instructions to the rest of us. Daniel and Enos attached the drill bit onto the line that ran up and over the top of the derrick.

To me, Tinker shouted, "Ezekiel, More coal! The wheelbarrow's by the door!"

I ran, grabbed the barrow and pushed it toward the coal pile. A short-handled shovel lay on the pile and I began tossing shovelfuls of coal into the barrow as the noise of the engine rose to a crescendo. I felt jabs of pain in my shoulder as I clumsily wheeled the barrow back over the threshold to the engine room and began shoveling coal into the firebox like a fireman in a train race.

"Ezekiel, we need a hand with the tools!" Tinker yelled from outside now. "Come here!"

I ran to the derrick and saw them struggling with the heavy iron drill bit and the connecting "jars"—big iron hoops that allowed the drill bit to fall and take the shock of breaking rock deep in the earth. I climbed up and steadied the drill bit while Enos wrestled to thread the jars onto the top end. All the while, the steam engine was sitting idle, building up pressure like a teakettle about to blow. Finally, we connected everything, and Tinker jumped down from above us, ran to the engine and let the full force of the piston loose. The flywheel turned, the drill bit raised high in the air, slid down into the steel casing and collided with a resounding "thunk!"

"Yee-hah!" Daniel yelled, "Boys, we're drillin' for 'ile!"

Tinker grinned as he darted from engine to boiler, checking pressure and water levels, eyeballing the alignment of the driving mechanism and flinging open the fire door to add still more coal.

The speed of the drill bit increased. Enos shouted to Daniel, "You need to get up on the throne and start spinning the bit! She'll jam in the rock if not turned!"

Daniel mashed his hat down on his head and quickly climbed the derrick rigging, as I had seen sailors in Salem harbor do when I was a boy. He swung himself up onto the small plank they called "the driller's throne" and grabbed the shaft of the drilling rod as it went up and down in front of him. With gloved hands, he held on to the rod and gave it a turn when it rose free of the ground.

In all the excitement I hadn't noticed that John Wilkes-Booth had slipped into the back of the engine house until he tapped me on my shoulder. Snow lay sparkling against his dark hair as he watched us frantically tending the machinery. Close by, I smelled his cologne: bay rum. I wheeled one more barrow of coal past him, and he motioned me outside.

"Looks like you're making good progress," he said, dancing from foot to foot in the cold. "That boiler man seems to know what he's about."

"I think he's one of the best in the business. Before the war he tended locomotives for the Allegheny Valley Railway. He's a wizard with machines," I said. Not wanting to see our venture halt I started shoveling more coal into the barrow.

"I can see you're busy. I just wondered if you had a chance to look for Lincoln and the girl?"

"I did. We found them."

Booth clapped his hands in glee and danced around pumping a fist in the air. I looked past him to see his slave, Marcus leaning out of his carriage, listening.

"Wait," I said, lifting a hand in protest. "I didn't see them in person. I saw where they have been hiding at a cabin in the woods."

Booth stopped his dance and looking at me gravely said, "But how can you be sure it's them?" Beyond him, I noticed Marcus was now out of the carriage, closer, within earshot.

"Mr. Evans and I talked to the head of their guard. We are not mistaken."

"Well then, you must go and fetch them back!"

"Perhaps you would like me to go to Mr. Prather's bank and fetch you some bags of gold coins, as well?"

"Don't toy with me, Edwards."

"I'm not jesting. Those Bucktails who are guarding him are not fools. We won't simply waltz in there and spirit him away. And the girl appears to be determined to stay with him, as well," I said, noticing that I spoke with Booth as an equal now. Was my confidence because we were drilling for oil and might soon be rich?

Booth paced in a circle. "Will you make an effort to parlay with him? You shall not receive payment from us until you produce results!"

Tinker shouted my name. I paused and said, "Tell Stottish and your Golden Circle friends that I will do my best. But for now I must be about this business here."

Booth pursed his lips, turned on his heel and stomped toward his carriage with his head lowered. For some reason, his slave Marcus was grinning. Perhaps only to see his master rebuffed for a change. None of this mattered to me. I had enough to do at present.

I lifted the handles of the wheelbarrow, which in just a few minutes had been covered with snow. A fresh jolt of pain came from my shoulder, and as soon as I had set the barrow down near the boiler I took a healthy swig of laudanum, which did not go unnoticed by Tinker. Over the clatter of the machinery he said, "You all right, Captain? We been pushin' pretty hard."

"I'm fine," I lied and added, "With this damp weather…"

Tinker glanced out the engine house door where snow flew by sideways, blotting out the view of the creek. "What'd Booth want?"

"Lincoln, dead or alive."

"Figures. Leave me out of it."

Chapter Fourteen

If the truth were told, I was drunk *before* I made it up the hill to Josiah's saloon. Tinker's drive to fire the boiler and force the drilling to proceed caused me to finish off my bottle of laudanum with its potent admixture of morphine and alcohol. And toasting our success at the well with two glasses of applejack had left my head swimming.

Tinker was pouring another round when I excused myself to hike up the hill. Daniel had fixed his usual fare: corn dodgers and sow belly. But the portions had been small, and I let all the others have a second helping. Before the applejack came out Enos was already snoring in the corner of the engine house.

An excess of morphine is no pleasure. My stomach rumbled, and my bowels felt unsettled. I thought the fresh air might help revive me, so I stumbled up the hill. When I reached First Street I realized I had veered off course and ended up several blocks from my intended destination. Damn, it was cold! I leaned into the snow-laced wind and struggled along the icy boardwalk. But in the howling cold I began shivering without ceasing. *Damn, damn.*

A door opened at my elbow, and a shaft of golden light poured out. A man wearing a bowler and a thick wool duster stepped past me, smiling. I ducked in where he had come out.

"Good evening, sir," a woman with what sounded like a French accent greeted me as the door slammed shut behind me. Like the gates of Sheol, closing fast.

"I just stepped inside to warm my hands," I said, extending them to a large Franklin stove that glowed a dull red.

She laughed and replied, "We can warm more than your hands, *monsieur!*"

I looked at her, befuddled for a moment. Above her head was a placard that bore the name of the establishment: "BONNE CHANCE!" I tried to translate it, but my head felt like it was stuffed with cotton. Then, it came to me—"GOOD LUCK!"

"*Allons, Lisette!*" the woman exclaimed.

A wan girl appeared at the door. Thin and blonde, with pale eyes and lips, she wore only a light chemise in the cozy warmth of the parlor. Now it dawned on me that I was being taken for a customer. I backed away from the stove, toward the door. *"Pardonez moi,"* I said in halting schoolboy French.

"No need to be afraid, *monsieur,"* the madam said. "Lisette will not bite!"

Lisette stepped forward, her chemise falling open to reveal pale white skin. I averted my gaze and darted for the door, but not before I had a glimpse of milky white cleavage that descended to her smooth belly. I stumbled out the door onto the porch, hearing the laughter of both women, along with cries for me to return.

As I stepped out onto the porch I almost knocked down a tall, heavyset man with a full beard. To my surprise he stepped close to me and said, "We have laws here, you know!"

His face was close to mine, and I cringed when I recognized him— Reverend Steadman who had served the Bucktails as a chaplain. His beard was flecked with gray, and he was heavier now, but it was clearly him.

"There's a fine of two dollars for public drunkenness, sir," he said, leaning even closer still, and I realized that he was smelling my breath for whisky; good thing I'd only drank apple jack. Then he recognized me. "Gracious sakes, it's Captain Edwards!" He paused to scowl and said, "I would have thought better of *you!*"

He turned on his heel and stomped off, not even giving me a chance to respond. Of course, he had just seen me stagger out of a brothel to the titters of two French prostitutes, so what was I going to say? *I was just warming my hands?* Was this why I had come to the oilfields, so I could make a spectacle of myself on the streets? If my face hadn't been frozen I might have blushed.

* * *

"Pay him no mind," Josiah said when I recounted this to him at the bar. "He's just raising money to pay for the new church by enforcing the drunkenness ordinance. Finding drunks in Pithole of an evening is like shooting fish in a barrel."

Josiah had set a small glass of whiskey at my elbow, which so far I had not touched. He saw me shake from the chill and said, "I've a bit of soup left—mostly broth. But it will help warm you."

He went to the kitchen and returned with a napkin over his big forearm and a steaming bowl of chicken broth.

"Wonderful," I said, taking the first spoonful.

"For five dollars I could have Susanna draw you a hot bath," Josiah said. "You don't want to catch a chill from this weather," he added. An image of the slim girl in the chemise came to mind. A hot bath might lead to something else. But hadn't my run-in with Steadman been a sign from above? The lust of the flesh, the pride of life—that's what the wild-haired preacher had said. I would be ignoring the testimony of two witnesses if I proceeded. Yet a small tremor of a shake passed through me. There remained a chill deep in my bones and an ache in my shoulder.

I took out my wallet and counted out five Confederate dollars.

"Susanna is…occupied, at the moment. But I'll put the big kettle on to get things started." Once again he returned to the kitchen. I glanced around and saw that business was slow tonight because of the nasty weather. Otherwise, Josiah would have been making his money selling whiskey, not drawing water for a bath.

"So, you've started drilling. Any trace in the first sand?" Josiah asked when he came back.

"That's why we were celebrating. We found oil in the sand as soon as we got beyond the casing. I think we have a good chance of making some money."

"Quick wealth and easy women," Josiah said, laughing. "That's the lure of Pithole."

As if on cue, Susanna came through the kitchen door, her skin flushed. Was it from the steam of the kitchen?

"Hey, Suz. We've a customer for a hot bath tonight. Put on an extra kettle, if you would."

Susanna looked at me, blinked and went to the back room. As she said nothing, I wondered if she was tired—too tired to entertain me tonight, at least in the way I hoped for.

When I finished my soup I carried my whiskey glass up the stairs with me to the room. The whiskey was clear fluid, called "white dog"— the first drippings of the mash. But even if it hadn't been aged, it would be a shame to waste it. Wouldn't it?

In my room was a steaming cauldron of water at the foot of the bed. I lowered myself in just a little at a time, the water was so hot. The tub was not as big as the heavy porcelain tub in my parents' house in Salem, but I fit in with my knees bent slightly. Any bath in Pithole was a luxury. I found a cake of white soap on a plate and lathered up thoroughly, washing off all traces of the grease, coal dust and mud I had accumulated over the last few days.

The water had just started to cool when I heard a light rap on the door.

"I've more hot water," Susanna said, opening the door a crack. "May I come in?"

"By all means."

She brought in a large kettle of boiling water and added it to the tub slowly. The warmth on my aching bones was heavenly. She then crossed behind me and said, "I should think it hard for you to wash your back, with your sore shoulder and all."

"That's true. Much obliged."

"Did your wife do this for you before the war?" she asked as I felt the soft sea sponge rubbing on my aching muscles.

I tried to think back to our courting days and the time when we were first married. A carriage parked in a shady grove on Folly Hill. The taste of her mouth. I had to push those thoughts away.

"You're from Gloucester," I said. "I can hear it in your accent."

"Yes. But I have a sister who is married and lives in Salem. And you've gone and changed the subject on me. You were married before the war."

"I'm not married now," I said, reaching up and drawing her forward for a kiss. Her dark hair was curling from the steam of the tub, and her dress was damp from pressing against the side of the tub. My impulse was to climb out of the tub right then, but she put a hand on my chest and pushed me back in.

"Stop changing the subject. Why did your wife leave you?"

"She didn't leave, I did. She thought I was dead at Gettysburg. So, she remarried."

"Many men were thought lost in the war. Most of *their* wives took time to find out for sure."

"The burial detail found a man lying with my jacket, hat and canteen in a pile of dead Confederate soldiers. I was, supposedly, reburied with full honors in my hometown, along with three other men. She had good reason to think I was dead." End of subject, I thought as she reached over me to grab the bar of soap and lather her hands. If not for that, I might have tried harder to end the conversation.

"She had good reason to think you were dead," she said, returning her hands to my shoulders and neck. I felt her breath close to my ear. "Did she also have good reason to remarry?"

"She married the richest man in town. Isn't that reason enough for a woman?"

"Hard to smooth these muscles out with you getting angry."

I had tensed up. It was only natural, though. "Of course it still rankles."

"Did you have any children?" she whispered, closer.

"One daughter," I said, feeling her cheek brush mine. Her hands had crossed forward. She lathered them again. Her cheek brushed mine as her hands changed course.

"You smell like bay rum," I said.

"I'm around men all evening. What else would I smell like? Can't afford perfume."

"I noticed John Wilkes-Booth smelled of that today when he visited our well."

"Who?"

"Booth."

"Don't know him. What is your daughter's name?"

"Abigail."

"That's a pretty name. She's three?"

"Yes."

"The water's cooling off, should I go get more?"

"No. You should help me out of this tub."

Chapter Fifteen

There is a parable in the Bible about a man who had two sons. They were both given a task by their father. The first said, "I go, father." But went not. The second said, "I will not go." But later went. Which of these did the will of the father?

I thought of this as I rode to Petroleum Centre. I had told John Wilkes-Booth that I would not go looking for Lincoln—at least not any time soon. But when I went in to purchase a new bottle of laudanum Jim Christy asked me how my meeting with Stottish had gone. After we talked awhile he told me that the druggist in Petroleum Centre had seen Chastity Stottish at his apothecary shop. I had not yet reported my lack of success in finding Miss Chastity to her father, and I hoped by following up on this lead I might locate her and claim my prize of money.

At the livery stable Henry drew me a map of the road to Petroleum Centre. It was a boomtown on Oil Creek about midway between Titusville and Oil City, in the area that *The Pithole Daily Record* liked to refer to as *The Valley That Changed The World*.

Henry's directions had me follow the freshly laid oil pipeline up and over the hill through the hamlet of Owltown, past a weathered sign for Cornplanter Township and down some steep hillsides to Oil Creek. I crossed Oil Creek on a new plank bridge. It was as slimy as its name, and it shimmered under me as I crossed to Petroleum Centre with a cool drizzle falling on my hat and shoulders.

From newspaper accounts concerning the oil boom I knew that fortunes had been made in this town five years ago. But the rush had now moved on to towns like Pithole, Red-Hot and Shamburg. And just last year a major fire had burned up many of the buildings in Petroleum Centre. Only the core of the town and some mansions up in the hills remained. It wasn't hard to find Stewart's Apothecary. At the rail in front I tied the gentle mare and went inside.

"Can I help you with something?" a stout, gray-haired woman behind the counter asked me.

"Well, ma'am, I'm not sure if you can," I said, adopting a guise that

I had used to good effect in the past: the lonely soldier looking for his lost love. Seeing her dark eyebrows rise I added, "I'm afraid I've lost the girl I love."

"How sad," said the woman, lifting a knuckle to her lips in dismay. "I am so sorry to hear that. Was it illness that took her?"

"Oh, heavens. I didn't lose her in that way. We were separated, and I cannot find her. She was my nurse in Pittsburg when I fell ill from a wound suffered in the war."

It never hurts to mix a little truth in with deception. I could see it was having its effect on this warm-hearted woman. Color had risen to her cheeks, and she twisted her gnarled hands together in dismay.

"She lives here in Petroleum Centre?"

"She has a father in Pithole, but when I sought his aid…" I looked at the floor for a moment, letting my silence speak. "I only found out this morning that she might have come here to work as a nurse to a wealthy invalid."

"Oh!" said the woman, her face lighting up. " Miss Chastity! Oh! She is just the most precious thing."

"You have heard of her?"

"Why, she was here at our shop just the other day," she said as she twisted her hands together again and beamed at me. "She is *such a darling*." She leaned forward, pressing her palms together in excitement. "Are you her fiancé?"

"I must be an open book to you, ma'am," I said, shaking my head. "I was hoping to plead my case to her for marriage."

"Oh, wonderful, wonderful," said the woman, her eyes moistening.

"My problem is she left Pittsburg suddenly to come North. It was the very day I had purchased a ring for her. When I went to call on her, she was gone."

I looked down at the floor again, trying to convey my heartfelt sadness. The odd thing was, the more I embroidered this tale of heartache, the more real it felt *to me*.

"There, there, young man," she said, patting my arm. "I think your journey is nearly over, for if you look up on Stuart Avenue you will see a tall brick house on the corner."

I followed her pointing finger and saw an impressive home on a slight rise. She was right. It was just a short ride from the center of town. I thanked her and pushed through the door to the plank sidewalk, hearing her call out final words of encouragement as I stepped into the sunshine.

I found the house at the corner of Stuart and Jackson Streets—no doubt freshly renamed in honor of those two Confederate devils, Jeb and Stonewall. There was a long approach to the house from the street with a manicured front lawn that even in its frozen and browned state was impressive. The walkway was dark green slate, the stairs were cut granite, the façade of the house hard-glazed brick—not soft brick fired on site. The roof must be slate also, I thought. That's why this house had survived the great fire. I looked up to the tower, and that's when I saw her.

She stood with the curtain parted on the second floor in the bay window of the tower. I stopped walking and stared. She wore the white linen jumper of a nurse with a pale blue blouse with long sleeves. Her hair was lifted up into a nurse's hat with wispy golden curls escaping at the sides. Even at this distance I could see the smattering of freckles and the deep brown of her eyes. There was a crease in her forehead as she returned my stare, a questioning as if to ask, "Do I know you?"

There was a tightness in my chest. I could see her hands lift to draw the curtains closed, and I wanted to shout, "NO!" This sudden emotion surprised me, as if the lies I had told the kind shop-woman were true. As if I could run up the stairs and capture her for my own. My heart sank to see her snug the draperies closed. She was rejecting me without even speaking.

I climbed the remaining stairs to the door, and using the ornate brass door knocker I rapped on the door. It opened to a well-dressed Negro servant. "Yassuh?" he said in a voice reminiscent of house slaves from the Deep South.

"I'm here to see Miss Chastity Stottish." I had rehearsed another elaborate story, but the servant merely looked at me studiously for a moment and said, "I'll fetch her."

He left me alone for a moment, and while looking in the partially open front door I saw something unexpected. A wicker chair with wheels attached was partly in view. Lincoln was here or had been here. My first reaction was selfish—I can tell Booth and collect my money! We can keep drilling!

I tried to peer in further in hopes of catching a glimpse of the man himself. The door was still open a crack, so I sidled in to the foyer. I could hear voices and footfalls from upstairs and then men's voices in the back of the house near the kitchen. Two figures appeared momentarily. First, a stocky, gray-haired man with a full beard, and then I caught a glimpse of Lincoln. His hair had gone pure white, and he was being assisted from the downstairs powder room into his wheeled chair. He looked gaunt and frail, but he stood momentarily before being helped into the chair and pushed toward the back room. Old Abe! He did indeed still live! I felt a strange warmth toward him, as if he were my own grandfather returning from a long journey, and I felt as if I should rush to embrace him. But before I could act on any such feelings I was spotted by his attendant who looked at me with alarm.

"You, there," he said, "What are you doing?" At the moment he spotted me he pushed Lincoln out of sight into the back room. Before approaching me he pushed a pair of French doors shut to close off the back room. An enticing aroma of bacon wafted my way.

I pulled my bowler hat to my chest in an attitude of supplication. "I am here to speak with Miss Chastity Stottish, at the request of her father, Solomon Stottish."

"Who let you in?"

"Your Negro servant."

I heard the stairs creak as the others descended.

"You look familiar," the man said. "I've seen you just recently." He stepped closer to me, studying my face. "I'll have to tell Robert to admit no one unless *I* approve them.

It occurred to me that he might remember me from the night at the cabin, though I had no recollection of that time. He hardly looked like the sort of person who would have robbed me of my money. But if he didn't, and Mortenson didn't—who did? Chastity? Abe Lincoln?

"I'm acquainted with Tom Mortenson," I offered.

"You're that Edwards fellow he saw at the cabin. You were told not to bother us."

"Yes."

"Then, what the hell are you doing here?" he asked, his voice rising.

Another voice came from the stairs, "He works for my father, Elisha. The man won't take no for an answer."

Turning his head up the stairs Elisha asked, "Which man?"

"Either of them," she said and flashed a heart-melting smile my way. I grinned back, lovable rascal that I was.

"He's not to leave the entry nor disturb our…*client*."

"Yessir, Mr. Stiles," I heard Robert say from up the stairs. We were to have a chaperone.

"Speak your business, then and be gone," said Miss Chastity as she stepped toward me at the foot of the stairs. Her imperious remarks were undermined by her lack of stature. Napoleon was short too, though. "Your father was concerned for your welfare and sent me to inquire of you."

"Robert, shoo," said Chastity, waving her hand to the figure hovering in back of her on the stairs. Robert passed behind her to the kitchen shaking his head. A door shut firmly behind him, closing off muffled voices and laughter. "My father's only concern is for his money. I'm surprised he's wasting a penny of it sending you on such a fool's errand."

Before I could answer, her eyes narrowed and she stepped closer to me. "I know you. You were a patient of mine in Pittsburg. And you were snooping around our cabin. You don't work for my father!"

"I am not one of his office workers, no. But he asked me to convey his concern for you, since your mother is not—"

"What do you know of my mother!" she cried, two dots of color forming in her cheeks.

"Your father—"

"My father mentions her to no one! He acts as if she is dead! How did you find out about her?"

I saw no point in lying, "I found an old letter in the cabin."

"You went back there?" She stomped her foot like an angry toddler, which caused me to smile in spite of myself. "Don't laugh at me you— you scoundrel!"

I held up a hand like a conductor trying to slow a speeding train. What did Proverbs say? *a soft answer turneth away wrath.* I tried to reason with her, "Miss Chastity, you are nursing someone who appears to need not only medical care but armed guards. Shouldn't your father be concerned for your safety?" This seemed only reasonable to me.

"My father is not worried about *my safety!*" she said and to my shock, drummed her balled fists against my chest. "He wants you to kidnap me and bring me back to put me under his thumb!"

I dropped my hat and caught her hands in mine. Up close our eyes met, and the color in her cheeks could almost be mistaken for passion. I held her hands for a moment until she struggled free.

"I remember you, Ezekiel Edwards. You got me in trouble in Pittsburg, and now you're up to something here, too."

"I got *you* into trouble in Pittsburg?" I protested as she pulled back. "That's not how *I* remember it."

She looked away. For just a moment I saw a smile at the corner of her mouth, remembering.

She turned back to me, one eye narrowed. Then, she opened her mouth to say something but decided against it. She turned again and shouted at the closed kitchen door, "Robert! Bring me a pencil and pad! I need to write something."

I noticed she omitted saying "please." She spoke as one used to deference.

There was the sound of drawers and cabinets opening and closing, and the servant appeared. He held out a pad and pencil to her with arms outstretched.

She whirled back to me and said, "Now. I am getting rid of you once and for all." She scribbled something hastily on a sheet of foolscap.

I heard something, and I looked through the kitchen window to the back porch—a man mounting a horse. I could not see his face, only the glistening black coat of the horse and the fine cut of his wool trousers. Was it Mortenson or Stiles leaving to go on an errand? I saw the heels of the horse as it galloped away, then Chastity turned back to me.

"Here, I'm finished."

"With this note?"

"With this note, with my father, with you."

"Me?"

"If you're his man, yes."

"I'm guilty by association, then?"

"Certainly. If you're surprised, Mr. Edwards, then you don't know what he's capable of. But I do. So leave."

I saw that Robert was watching from the kitchen door with Stiles a step or two behind him. I replaced my hat on my head, touched the brim and went out the door. No one wished me fare-thee-well.

Chapter Sixteen

I found Tom Mortenson at the top of the hill not far from a place called Owltown. He was off his horse examining tracks in the freshly turned soil of the pipeline. I might have avoided him if I had galloped off to the woods as soon as I saw him, but horsemanship was not my strong suit.

"You're like a bad penny, Edwards," he said and then spat on the ground. "You keep turning up."

"I'm flattered you remember me," I said, drawing back on the reins. Then, to my surprise, the horse stopped and lowered her head to eat some damp clover that the pipeline work had uncovered.

"What are you doing in these parts?"

"Laudanum run," I said, withdrawing the bottle from my pocket. "It's the elixir of life."

"It's a damned narcotic, and you should know better."

Was he angry because he knew Lincoln was just over the hill? I answered mildly, "Watch any surgeons work lately?"

His face screwed up in disgust. No one who had ever marched past a surgeon's tent ever forgot the piles of sawn limbs and the carnage—not to mention the sounds and smells.

"So, you're telling me that was your only reason to visit?"

I was about to answer when an explosion rocked the air. My horse reared up on her hind legs, and I fought to hold on. Mortenson's horse got a wild look in its eyes, and it pranced right and then left while he held the reins and tried to calm it. Like a cowboy, he swung himself up into the saddle and yelled, "They're at it again!" Then, he galloped off in the direction of the blast.

Unfortunately, my horse did the same. She galloped fast up the hill, close on the heels of Mortenson's to where a dark cloud rose in the sky against billowing snow clouds. A sound like sleet filled the air with bits of dirt and rock falling like hail all around us. Mortenson's horse raced ahead to a crater where twisted metal stood starkly against the fading sky.

Mortenson pulled his hat from his head and slapped it against his thigh, his teeth flashing as he laughed, "Those damn Mollies! They're at it again!"

"Mollies?"

"Aye, they're here, all right. They know a thing or two about blasting powder!"

I made no reply, just sat there watching the smoke rise into the sky.

"Uh oh," Mortenson said, suddenly spotting something in the woods. "Pinkertons are coming."

He lowered his head, and we rode back in the direction from which we came. I turned the mare, but this time she followed more reluctantly down the hill. Mortenson motioned for me to take cover with him in some pines on one corner of a crossroads up ahead. But no sooner had we dismounted and ducked into the underbrush than a party of smart-looking riders wearing black suits, with bowler hats like mine, galloped past.

"Pinkertons," Mortenson said and spat again. "Lookin' to shoot some Irishmen."

My eyes followed the riders. If you changed their dapper suits for Confederate gray they could have been Mosby's Rangers—they rode that well. Too bad we never had cavalry like that on our side. The memory of the massacre of Custer's men at Gettysburg still rankled. If only he could have stopped Stuart behind the lines we might have had a chance.

"Whose side are you on?" I asked Mortenson.

"I'm not a fan of the current administration," he replied, standing up and dusting pine needles off his blue wool trousers. "That's who pays the Pinkertons—officially or otherwise." Then, he rounded on me, his dark eyes meeting mine. "How about you? You a Lincoln man? Or will you be lining up with the others to kiss Bobby Lee's feet when he rides in on Traveller next month?"

"I marched a thousand miles to fight him at MacPherson's farm. You Black Hats weren't the only ones there that day."

"Words are cheap. What was it Saint Peter said: *I will go with thee both to prison and to death?* Then, he denied Jesus three times."

"I'm familiar with the story," I said, swinging my leg up onto the mare. But no sooner had I done so than Mortenson grabbed my coat and yanked me off the saddle onto the ground. I hit the ground hard, knocking the air out of me. Then I heard the report of a gun.

I tried to rise, but his strong arm slammed me down again and he said, "Stay down, you fool. He's shooting at you."

The horses, now loosened, ran off in confusion. Mortenson continued to look across the pipeline trail to the trees nearby. There was the sound of branches breaking and someone riding away.

"Mollies?" I asked, still breathless.

Mortenson shook his head.

"I saw him, just for a moment. He was wearing a suit. Must have been a Pinkerton scout."

"Not them, neither," Mortenson said, pulling me up to my feet. "He was black."

"Black Irish?" I ventured.

"Black African."

"Good thing he missed me."

"Not by much."

"What?"

"Look," he said, handing me back my bowler hat. It had a bullet hole just above where my forehead would have been.

"Did you see him clearly?"

"No." He looked back at the woods where the man had disappeared. "Hell of a shot with a pistol, though."

Our eyes met. "What are you doing here?" I asked.

"I'm watching the Pinkertons."

"But why?"

"They're up to something. And it ain't just pipeline mending."

Chapter Seventeen

I caught the mare but didn't climb back into the saddle. The events of the morning had left her skittish and balky. Though it took longer, I walked her the final distance back over the hill to Pithole. As I walked, I dug my hands deeper into my pockets and found the note that Chastity had given me. In all the excitement I had forgotten about it.

Under the branches of some towering white pines I paused and took it out of my pocket. The horse pawed the ground and nibbled at the undercover where some mint leaves with bright red berries were intermingled with grass that yet bore a bit of green. Turkey scratchings and footprints showed that we were not the only visitors to this peaceful spot. I unfolded the letter and read the heading: *Dearest Father*.

I paused, thinking I shouldn't read it, but then thought better of it. Maybe just a line or two...

Dearest Father,
I am writing to you to plead with you to please leave me alone. I am not a child anymore. I have not "run off," as some gossips are saying. I chose to come here and work for an ailing gentleman who wishes to maintain his privacy. He lives in a fine home, and all my personal needs are met. I am not in any danger.
I do not wish to return to Pithole at this time. It is a dirty, smelly place, and the men are crude and insulting. I am happy here. Please stop pestering me. I am neither your servant nor your slave. I want what I want, which is to live my own life.
Love,
Chastity

I noted her words "not your slave" and "I want what I want." It captured her headstrong demeanor well. I also noted the short sentences and simple thoughts. Did she lack intelligence? Or was she just in a hurry? It would be interesting to see what her father made of this. I folded the letter carefully and replaced it in my pocket.

I returned to Stottish's office in the gloomy afternoon haze trying to remember the last time I had actually seen the sun. Was it days ago, or weeks? I was ushered in to Stottish's presence by his cadaverous assistant.

"Ezekiel! Good to see you! Where's my daughter!"

He said all this in a jovial tone, even using my Christian name. It was like Dickens' story of Scrooge on Christmas morning. Had ghosts visited him in the night?

"Good evening, Mr. Stottish," I said. "I have news of your daughter."

"How is she?"

"Stubborn."

"She gets that from her mother! Her mother was always contradictory."

I noticed the use of the past tense.

"But how is her health? Did she appear well-fed?"

If this had been Tinker asking me I would have answered with a more ribald response. Instead, I said, "She appears to be in good health. She's at a mansion in Petroleum Centre tending a wealthy man who is ill."

"Who some say is Lincoln, and others think not."

I merely nodded. That could be a dangerous topic in many ways. "She sent you a letter." I held it forth for his inspection.

His claw-like hand snatched it from me, and he slid a pair of spectacles onto his nose. "Splendid," he mumbled.

I noticed that not only his eyes made it difficult for him to read, but also his hands. They had a pronounced tremor, and in order to read the note he had to lay it on the desk and bend over it like a crow pecking at a carcass.

"Humph," he said at length. "'She'll not be a slave,' she says. Do you think I treated her as a slave while she was with me?" He asked as he turned round to me.

I shrugged. I'd never seen them together, but I could certainly make assumptions.

"Heavens, no. She lived like a little princess," he declared, pursing his lips. "She was our only child. We indulged her every whim—and this is the result." He paused, staring at the letter as if he could erase it with his eyes. "Well, I won't be angry," Stottish continued, stilling his trembling hands on the back of a nearby chair. He nodded his head as if concluding a business deal. "I won't be angry if I know she is well-fed—and not in danger." The hawk-stare again. "You can assure me of that?"

I turned my hat slightly in my hands so the bullet hole was not visible. "She appears to be quite safe. It was difficult for me to even gain entrance to the house."

"Splendid," he said, his air of friendliness returning. "Charles. Come here!" he boomed through the office door.

His assistant appeared at the door, rather quickly I thought. Had he been eavesdropping?

"Charles, go to the safe and remove one thousand dollars for Mr. Edwards," said Stottish. Charles glanced at me sourly. But before he had reached the door again, Stottish added, "Oh, heavens. Make it eleven hundred dollars. He deserves a bonus just for putting up with Chastity, don't you think, Charles?"

I saw Charles' jaw drop in dismay. "If you say so, sir," he said, coloring. And then I realized why he had been so rude to me on my first visit. Not because I was unworthy to gain Mr. Stottish's employ, but because I was a threat. I was a rival for his master's esteem, and at the moment I was winning the contest.

After he left Stottish said, "Oh, I'm afraid Charles is in something of a snit! Hah!"

He seemed to take a perverse pleasure in his assistant's reaction to my bonus. But—a hundred dollar bonus! That was more than a month's wages for most men. The tiredness of the day fell away, and I began to think of what I might do with this bounty. "Thank you, sir. I appreciate it very much. I can't wait to tell my friends and co-workers down at the well. We should now have the funds to easily drill as far at the third sand, if need be." I turned toward the door to see if Charles was coming with my money.

As I put my hand to the doorknob Stottish said, still in a jovial tone, "Oh, I meant to ask you. Do you have tickets to President Lee's appearance?"

"What's that?"

"It's been kept quiet until now, so an ungodly rabble won't besiege him, I suppose. But he's coming to Rynd Farm. Their renaming the town in his honor. Leesburg or Leeville or some such."

"When will this be?" I asked, as if I already had a busy social calendar.

"One week from today!" Stottish said. " Oh, and I almost forgot. Forrest is coming also, and he will address several civic groups. We are quite excited by all this!"

"Sounds exciting, indeed," I said, feigning enthusiasm. But Nathan Bedford Forrest? Why not invite Judas Iscariot? Perhaps Brutus and Marc Antony could come, as well? Or Benedict Arnold? "Keep me posted on the events," I said, forcing a smile as I left the room. But there was a sour feeling in my belly that came from more than an excess of laudanum.

Charles handed me a generous sheaf of brown-back Confederate dollars at the door. I tucked them in my vest and then remembered my mishap on the night I came to the oil region, so I headed to Prather Bank to deposit them. The bank was getting ready to close as I finished my transaction, which meant it was still only mid-afternoon. *Banker's hours,* I was thinking wistfully, when through the glass I saw a commotion out in the street. At first I thought it was the daily parade of the doves—but it was too late in the day for that. When I opened the door I saw the crazy, wild-haired preacher standing in the middle of the street. He had his hands raised wide and was yelling at a teamster who was trying to coax a mule team past him in the mud.

"Stop, in the name of Almighty God!"

"Get out of the way," the teamster yelled back at him, his German accent telling me he was Pennsylvania Dutch, "Och, you'll mire my team. For heaven's sake, get out of the way!"

"Move it," another man in a carriage behind him yelled. A crowd was gathering, including some youths who had a dirty and disreputable look about them—what St. Paul once termed "rude fellows of the baser sort."

I listened from the plank sidewalk as the preacher went into his refrain, "You should not be drilling this oil! You are upsetting the natural order of the world! God is reserving this oil beneath the earth to fuel the fires of damnation. If you remove it you will bring damnation and hell up here onto earth!"

"Shut up, you old coot!" a man in the crowd yelled.

The crowd grew angry, and some picked up clods of frozen mud to throw at him. I thought of Jesus saying *"You build temples for the prophets, whom your fathers slew."* I stepped into the street, thinking to intervene.

As I got closer I saw that though it was still before sunset most of the hecklers were drunk. But I had to admit it was grating to the ears to hear the shrill voice of the preacher all day. At the edge of the circle of men, two teenage boys joined the fray. One tossed a large clod of oily mud at the preacher, who dodged it deftly. He'd been at this game before. But to my alarm, I could see the right hand of the other boy digging in the ooze for something, and he stepped closer. There was a look on that boy's face I had seen before, a look of evil scheming.

Before I could react, the missile came flying from the teen's hand. It was a sharp sandstone rock covered in muck, but still lethal. It struck the preacher right in the face, like a shard of canister shot from a cannon. An incredibly accurate shot—a feat of surprising skill. I had seen similar wounds on the battlefield. The preacher had just lost an eye.

The preacher flew backwards, with blood already spurting from the side of his face. As he hit the ground I saw mud and oil fly in a crescent up in the air, glinting in rainbow hues as it caught the late afternoon sunlight.

"You did it, Nick! You kilt him!" the other teen yelled.

A rage caught me, and I lunged at the two youths. They turned to run, but not quickly enough. I caught them both by their collars, one in each hand, and I drove them down into the slime. They disappeared head first into the ooze. The crowd was suddenly quiet, save for a sickening whimper from the injured preacher. They had come to see blood sport, but not this.

The boys struggled beneath me like gaffed fish, but I did not let them up. It came to me that if I just held them down a few moments more they would be dead. It was damned tempting. It was awfully damned tempting.

My hand slipped from their collars to their filthy hair, and I yanked their heads back out of the slime. They came out snarling and spitting like cornered dogs. But I still had their hair.

"God damn you boys!" I said, pulling their spluttering faces back toward me. "You will tend that man you have injured, or I'll rip your bloody heads off."

They cried out, gasping and choking on the mud they had swallowed and from the pain of having their hair pulled. Still with a firm grip on their hair I shoved them toward the dazed preacher who still lay with the stone wedged in his blood-smeared face. As I pushed them toward him I could smell the whiskey on their breath. Beardless youths, drunk before sunset, accosting a man of God in broad daylight.

They looked back at me with tear-stained faces. I doubted they were more than sixteen. "Take him up the street to McTeague's Saloon. He'll know what to do with him."

They hesitated as if they were thinking it over.

"Get out of my sight, or I'll kill you with my bare hands!"

That settled it. They bent to their task and lifted the preacher out of the mud, the stone falling away to reveal his shattered eye-socket. They began struggling up onto the sidewalk with him toward McTeague's.

I climbed out of the muddy street where the crowd began dispersing, whispering quietly among themselves. The German with the mule spurred his team, and they pulled his wagon of oil barrels forward. In a moment, they stomped over the imprint of the preacher's body that had formed in the mud. Someone gave me a hand up.

"Thank you," I said.

"Your reputation is well-deserved, Captain Edwards."

"What's that?" It seemed an odd comment to be making after this altercation.

"I've heard about you from others, and now I can see for myself why some call you a hero."

"And others a villain," I said, scraping frozen mud off my boots on the edge of the porch decking.

"I would call villains those who stand idly by and let a minister of God be accosted by ruffians."

I noticed his polished speech, as if he were reciting lines of verse. "You're an actor? A writer?"

"I'm a newspaper man. But I do 'write stories' as some put it."

I steadied myself on the horse rail. A throb from my shoulder let me know that I'd overdone it again. I resisted the impulse to reach in my pocket for my laudanum. But that reminded me of something. The writing I had found at the cabin a few days ago. Where had I put it? He looked at me oddly as I patted the pockets of my coat, and then I remembered I had put it in my vest pocket for safekeeping and forgotten it. Lincoln's scribblings.

"Here," I said. "As a newspaperman you might find this interesting."

He carefully unfolded it, peering at it intently. I realized he couldn't read it in the fading daylight, as with an apologetic air he pulled some spectacles out of a vest pocket and said, "You'll have to forgive me. Like General Washington once said, 'I've grown old in the service of my country.'"

"So have I, Crocus," I said, making a guess. A quick glance and a grin from him confirmed I was right; he was the newspaper writer Josiah had spoken of.

"Where did you get this?"

"A little bird gave it to me."

He didn't acknowledge my jest. He was busy reading.

"Can I keep it?"

"Actually, no," I said. "You can take it and copy it. But I'd like to have it back. It's a link to a place and a cause we fought for—some died for."

"I only wielded a pen in that struggle."

"Mr. Lincoln was mighty in both pen and sword. Now, he only has his pen left."

"I would argue that it was always his most potent weapon—even these crossed out lines bear testimony: *that government of the people, by the people, for the people, not perish from the earth.*

"Some of us still think that's worth fighting for."

"We'll always be fighting that war," Crocus replied, and with a tip of his hat he turned to walk away. Over his shoulder he added, "I'll copy this note and get it back to you quickly."

As he walked away I called after him, "Will you be at President Lee's reception?"

"Wouldn't miss it for...*for all the oil in Pithole!*"

Chapter Eighteen

Chastity Stottish

She could hear the voices from the other room. The Ancient's clear tenor could easily be heard above the others. That was how Lincoln had carried debates, they said—with that clear, bell-like voice that seemed to carry so far. But now and then the others, Mortenson, Stiles, even Roberts, pleaded with him. "You must, you must," they said.

And his reply, "I shan't be moved again. If they are going to kill me, here's as good a place as any."

"But they're nearby. Just over the hill," Mortenson's baritone implored.

"They're busy with those pesky Irishmen. Why would they bother with me? I'm as good as dead."

There was a commotion in the room. All of them speaking at once to hotly deny this. But Chastity was distracted by hooves on the road beside the house in the dark. And a shadow at the back door. Marcus had returned.

"What are you doing here? I thought you returned to Booth," she said as he stepped through the doorway, brushing flakes of snow off his dark coat. They sparkled on his hair like stars in the dark heavens.

"I concluded my business in Titusville. I just wanted to see you for a moment—you were not available when I left. I didn't get a goodbye kiss."

He darted toward her, and she held her hands up as if to ward him off. "Nor shall you now! The others are right in the next room…"

"Sounds like they're busy," he said, putting his gloved hands on her wrists and pressing down gently.

He was right, Chastity thought. They were arguing loudly now amongst themselves. And Lincoln's voice had gone silent. As he often did, he got his way by setting them against each other. What was it he had once said: *a house divided cannot stand?* But she couldn't keep listening to the argument for Marcus was busy leading her forward, away from the voices into the front parlor where a fire blazed brightly giving the room its only light.

"We shouldn't," she said as he drew her down beside him on the settee, but she didn't resist very hard. In a moment, his lips were on hers. And she breathed in the rich smell of him—he must have borrowed more of Booth's expensive cologne. He'd get cuffed for that if Booth caught him, but Booth never seemed to.

"You should get back," she said, coming up for air. The firelight gleamed on his silky smooth skin, reflected off his gleaming white teeth, his bright eyes. She would never have thought she could be attracted to an African man, but she was to this one. His hand circled her neck, slipping inside the cotton fabric of her nurse's uniform. She sighed.

"We really shouldn't, Marcus," she said, leaning away from him.

He hopped up from the couch and paced, quick anger on his face. "No Chastity, we should," he said, inclining his head down to her. "We should be allowed the freedom to be together. We should not be forced to live our lives to please the opinions of men. What we share is natural and good. We should not have to sneak about like school children playing naughty games."

He poked at the fire with iron tongs, turning the logs so that the flames rose higher, turning his face golden, his eyes bright red. Then, his expression softened and he moved quickly to seat himself beside her again. "I risked coming back to talk to you for one reason. My preparations are going well. I have some money set aside. We can leave for Montreal soon." His hands clasped hers firmly, insistently. " We can be free there. Free to share our love—which is good and natural."

She tilted her head down, and he kissed her forehead. A deep sadness came over her when he spoke like this. She wanted to believe it could be true—but could it really?

"I want to go with you, Marcus," she said and was about to add a qualifier when they heard heavy footsteps approaching.

"Marcus. Is that you?"

Chastity heard the deep voice of Mortenson coming out of the kitchen. Marcus immediately jumped to his feet and stepped away to the other side of the fireplace, picking up the log tongs in a deft motion. "Yes, Thomas. I'm out here. Tending the fire."

Mortenson stepped into the dim light of the parlor, and his eyes took in Marcus and Chastity alone in the parlor. Was it a look of disgust that crossed his features? Chastity wondered. Would everyone always look at her that way if she married a free black man?

"Where the hell have you been all afternoon?" he asked, his voice even gruffer than usual.

"Titusville," Marcus responded quickly. "It took all afternoon to get Mr. Booth's playbills printed. The print shop is all backed up printing notices for the Lee visit."

Mortenson stared at him with a look that still seemed distrustful, though Chastity could not think why. "You'd better clear out. We don't want Booth coming over here looking for you."

Marcus replaced the fireplace tool and picked up his coat, which he had laid aside on the arm of the settee. His face was totally free of expression, Chastity noticed—the mask a slave put on to hide his feelings.

Satisfied that he had been properly chastised, Mortenson turned away.

Marcus slipped his coat on and headed toward the kitchen and the back entry. "Are you angry at me also?" asked Chastity, catching him by the sleeve at the door.

"No, not you." Marcus said with a flick of his eyes toward the back parlor where the Ancient, as Lincoln's personal staff referred to him, was making one of his jokes, and the rest were laughing along. "It's them. I'll never be one of them."

Chastity didn't know what to say to that.

Marcus leaned close to her, whispering, his bright eyes searching hers, "Come away with me, Chastity. You don't belong here, either." And with that, he was out the back door, which slammed hard in the late winter wind.

She turned back from the door to see Mortenson glaring at her from the front hall. What was *his* problem, she wondered. Jealousy? It didn't make sense. He had never shown romantic interest in her before. Why now?

She pressed past him and went up the stairs to prepare Lincoln's bed. They would be carrying him up for the night soon.

Chapter Nineteen

Ezekiel Edwards

The first thing that caught my eye at the reception for President Lee was Stottish's niece, Lydia. She stood beside John Wilkes-Booth, and for once he was not *stealing the show*, as they say in the world of theatre. She looked stunning in apricot satin that brought out the highlights in her strawberry-blonde curls which cascaded downward, drawing my attention to the daringly low-cut bodice of her hoop-skirted gown.

I noticed that President Lee's eyes also made a quick reconnoiter of that field as he gave his greeting to them when we entered at the receiving line. He stood tall and handsome in the new Federal Gray that dominated formal wear in the Capital at Richmond.

"Ezekiel Edwards, formerly of Massachusetts and the 150th Bucktail Regiment," I said proudly as I shook his hand.

For a moment, he narrowed his eyes. My credentials made me twice a foe—a fire-breathing Abolitionist and a Union raider. He had personally directed the action at Gettysburg the day I was so grievously injured

"Mistuh Edwards," he drawled, emphasizing my civilian status. Flinty gray eyes, a firm handshake, a searching look. He grasped both my hands in his, a gesture of respect. I hated to admit it, but I felt honored shaking his hand, and I said so.

McClelland greeted me next, giddy with excitement. "Captain Edwards! The leader of the great Edwards raid!" he said in a booming voice, and to my surprise he grasped me in a great bear hug that made me wince from both pain and embarrassment.

"General," I said, wheezing as he continued to embrace me, practically knocking me off my feet and making it difficult to breathe. That's how it was with *Little Mac*; you never knew whether to hug him or punch him.

"President Lee," he said. "Captain Edwards truly honors us with his presence," he said, his voice choked with emotion. "For these resolute fighters to come forward, like men, and make peace with our administration—well, sir, it warms my heart."

That, too, was Little Mac. A lot of sentiment—but was he sincere? Next in line was J.E.B. Stuart, the hero of Gettysburg. He gave me a warm smile and the strongest handshake of the evening. "Captain Edwards," he said, having heard my name from McClellan.

"General Stuart," I replied with a small head bow.

I should hate him. It was said that he personally dispatched Custer when they overran the Union cavalry on Hanover Hill. And he helped Rooney Lee drive Hancock off Cemetery Ridge, making Pickett's charge a glorious triumph.

"Nice hat," I said as he gave my hand a bone-crushing squeeze.

"He's more vain than any of us girls," his wife chimed in as she pushed one of the feathers that protruded from his famous hat aside so I could see the shoulder-length curls hidden beneath.

Stuart grinned, still crushing my hand. "The Good Lord put her here to keep me humble."

"We all have our crosses to bear, don't we Mistuh Edwards?" she said with a searching look.

Stuart released my hand, and with a throaty laugh turned to the next person in line. Again, I thought that I should hate him, but I had to admit that his humility made him much easier to admire.

Not so with the next person in line—the surprise guest—Nathan Bedford Forrest. He had been talking earnestly with Solomon Stottish, something about doings in Pittsburg that I couldn't quite catch. And before that he had been enthusiastically embraced by John Wilkes-Booth as Lydia stood off to the side looking like her fiancé was handling a snake.

When Forrest shook my hand, his was strong and cold and firm. His eyes were like hard circles of steel, and I got the feeling that my war with Stuart and Lee might be over, but with Forrest, hostilities continued.

After the receiving line we sat at a round table. Lydia took the chair to my left, Stottish to my right. Other investors from Pittsburg joined us, one of the Mellons and an associate of Frick's from Schenley. The servants brought out fresh oyster stew and warm rolls with butter. My thoughts went to the meager fare of corn dodgers that my mates were probably gnawing on this evening, and I felt a twinge of guilt.

"You seem to have prospered since I first met you on the train to Oil City," Lydia said, dipping her spoon in her soup.

"I took your advice."

"It's a rare man who can find favor with Uncle Solomon," Lydia said, daintily sipping the steaming broth.

Stottish, hearing his name over the din, flashed his niece a smile, an event as rare as the sun breaking through the clouds in Pithole.

"I suffered the loss of some funds soon after I arrived," I said, leaning closer to her so she could hear—or was that just my excuse? "Mr. Booth and your Uncle have been a great help in moving my drilling venture forward." It was not without effort that I kept my eyes focused on her eyes and not lower.

"My Uncle is a genius in business," said Lydia, returning my smile. "He's not only accomplished great things here, but his iron companies are now the talk of Pittsburg. They say he will be a force to be reckoned with in the future. He might be the first in America to make steel!"

"Oh, Andy Carnegie will beat me to the punch, I'm sure." Stottish said, lifting his glass of whiskey and gesturing with it in my direction. "But the new mill will be up and running soon. If you are going to be working for me, you really should go down there and meet my supervisor, Mr. Anton Labeque."

He pronounced the name in the French manner, which made it sound like a line from a children's song. I was about to protest about how busy I was, but he held up his other hand to stop me, downed his whiskey and continued. "In fact," he said, "I insist on it. I'll have Charles procure passage on the new Pithole Valley Railway. You can make the trip down in just half a day."

"If it's just starting to run it will be crowded," I said.

"Oh, just for the first day or so. How about Wednesday, then? Of course, I'll pay you for your time."

"That would be—" I began, but for him our discussion was over. He was already craning his neck to look for a waiter to refill his whiskey glass. I saw a twinkle in Lydia's eye, and she patted the back of my hand. She knew no one disagreed with her Uncle Solomon.

I was going to protest further, but at that moment there was a blast from trumpets by Carnegie's Cornet band. They played a few bars of Dixie, the new national anthem, as President Lee and his wife were seated at the head table. The Episcopal priest from Franklin stood beside him and announced, "Let us pause for a word of prayer before we commence the main course of dinner." In dulcet tones he began entreating the deity. I couldn't help but notice Forrest had sidled up between Booth and Lydia on my left. As they bowed their heads, he scanned the room, apparently not feeling the need for prayer.

"Mistuh Wilkes-Booth," Forrest said when we had lifted our heads.

"We must catch up on old times." But his eyes were already drifting to Lydia and he added, "This must be your lovely wife."

"General Forrest!" Booth said, pouncing to his feet—no chair could hold him. "This is my fiancée, Lydia. I'm afraid I neglected to introduce her in the receiving line."

"Ma'am," Forrest said. He took her hand and bowed deeply, bringing his lips to her hand. Not unlike that scene by the apple tree in the Garden of Eden, I thought.

Lydia blushed.

"What of my proposal, Nathan? Have you considered it?" Booth cut in, trying to get his attention.

"I have, Mistuh Booth. I think I will be able to stay an extra day and address your chapter of the Knights."

"Excellent!" Booth twirled to my right, "Did you hear that, Solomon? General Forrest will be our special guest at the Bonta House. Will you join us?"

"I suppose I could," Stottish said.

Did he lack enthusiasm, or had the whiskey begun to make him sluggish?

"Perhaps Captain Edwards would like to attend also?" Stottish added. "He can come with me."

I noticed a quick glance from Booth to Forrest. They had no intention of inviting me. What went on in their secret society, anyway?

"Splendid, Nathan, splendid. And we must speak, then, of how the new…um… arrangements at my mill are coming along, eh?"

"You will be needing more—?"

"Precisely."

"I'll see to it," Forrest said with an unctuous smile.

I noted his dark, reptilian eyes had returned to surveying Lydia's figure. Perhaps without thought, she lifted a hand to cover her breast. An unconscious way of denying him access? And what did he mean, "I will be needing more—?" Then, I remembered. Forrest had made his fortune before the war trafficking in slaves. But in Pittsburg? That didn't make sense.

Booth, still standing, placed an arm around the taller man and guided him away. They both glanced back at Lydia, and Forrest gave a sharp bark of laughter, echoed by Booth's giddy cackle. I could only guess at what sort of remark had been made at her expense. She colored slightly with embarrassment.

To break the tension I asked, "May I pour you a bit more of this excellent wine?"

"Thank you, Ezekiel," she said, regaining her composure. Her eyes met mine as she reached to take the glass. One hand rested momentarily on my sleeve and she said, "The South claims its soldiers are great gentlemen, but I have found the more humble Northern officers outdo them, by far, in good manners. Thank you."

She smiled at me, and I thought of that great revivalist Whitfield who had met the wife of one of my Puritan forbears and commented: *Would that that Great God might bless me also with such a helpmeet.* As Lydia's eyes sparkled at me over the rim of her wineglass I made bold to comment, "You don't, perhaps, have an unmarried sister by any chance, do you?"

"No, Captain Edwards," she said, her eyes merry, "but I do have a young, unattached cousin—her name is Chastity. Right, Uncle?"

Stottish heard the name and looked over, "Chastity? We haven't got her to return yet. But I hope to have Captain Edwards fetch her back where she belongs!"

Lydia looked at me again, sipping her wine and said, "I think Captain Edwards is just the man for the job."

Chapter Twenty

The next evening I joined Stottish and Booth at their special meeting of the Knights of The Golden Circle. I looked forward to it about as much as having a tooth pulled; I had never been one for men's clubs and gatherings—the Masons or Old Hibernians or whatever. And I had been out of sorts all day. Since I had scuffled with those boys on the street in Pithole my shoulder had been acting up. I thought it would pass, but on this, the third day since, it was red and swollen. I feared it might be infected. I had taken more laudanum than usual to ease the pain, and now my bowels were disordered as well, and I felt sluggish. Stottish had seen me wince when I joined him in his carriage and had made comment.

"Your injury is acting up?"

"Just a bit, sir. It happens from time to time."

"Dr. Miller is an excellent surgeon. They've learned much since the war."

"Thank you, sir. But I'll be fine." I replied, closing the topic.

But I wasn't fine. I was longing to take a heavy swig of laudanum, but I knew if I did I would soon be snoring in the back of the room. Curses! I thought, gritting my teeth as Leonidas Duncan took the podium and introduced Nathan Bedford Forrest. The men of The Circle stood and applauded, and Forrest gave a wave of thanks to Duncan. He started reading haltingly from his prepared remarks.

"Gentleman of the…ummm…North…ahhh…" He peered at a small slip of paper on the podium, frowned darkly and crumpled it up. "Ahh, to hell with it!" He tossed it aside on the floor. There were murmurs from the audience. "Mistuh Duncan, Mistuh Booth, friends: I always fought to the hilt. That's always been my way. If you're goin' to do somethin', do it to the hilt, I say!"

I saw nods of approval from the crowd. But I'd seen men speared with bayonets to the hilt and it wasn't pretty.

Forrest continued, "Some of you know that before the war I was a dealer in slaves." A small ripple of comments passed through the crowd. This part of Forrest's story was not as well known. "That's why I raised a company of men and went out to fight. The damned Abolitionists wanted to destroy everthin' I worked for, everthin' I owned."

Or take everyone you owned, I thought.

The crowd was stilled by this remark and perhaps more so by the color that had risen to the cheeks of the rebel leader. I had heard from those who had seen his visage thus transformed when he was in battle— when *his blood was up,* as they put it.

He continued speaking, "Let me say somethin' I have said in the past. This land was given to us by God to subdue and conquer. It is the destiny of free white men to rule and reign in this new kingdom. This land is for us! Not for the Chinaman with his pigtail, not for the Apache with his pony and tomahawk." The depredations of the Apache and Comanche had been much in the news lately, so these remarks drew the enthusiasm of the audience. His voice rose in pitch, and he slammed the lectern with a club-like fist, "And by God, I say. This land was not to be given over to the Nigra slaves!" His eyes looked wild as he peered around the room. "I dealt in slaves. I'm acquainted with slaves. I've owned and worked with them since I was a boy. And I can tell you that what they need are men like us to teach them, to manage them and to control them."

"Hear, hear!" I heard someone cry out from the shadows—it sounded like Booth.

"Thank you, John Wilkes," Forrest said and continued. "Gentlemen, I am all for the humane treatment of these lesser peoples. But I firmly believe that we have been put here to subdue the earth, *as the Bible clearly teaches.* The sons of Cain live as savages and pagans, and they sow destruction everwhere they go. I have seen Indian raids, I have seen slave uprisin's, and I can tell you that the world they desire is one of anarchy and destruction."

From the side where I had heard Booth's voice I heard men thumping their tables in agreement.

"You Northen men who stood firm during the late War of Northen Aggression are to be commended. They called you traitors, they called you Copperheads. That despot, Lincoln threw you in his jails and prison camps to wither and die. Yet you stood firm!"

A chorus of applause erupted, and Forrest took a sip of water before moving to the main topic of his talk. "In the next few weeks you will be seeing the fruit of your labor. Our party, The Knights of The Golden Circle will be opening several new enterprises in the North. It's a bold move, and it will deal a death blow to the rise of labor unions and immigrant scum in this land."

This brought a flurry of discussion within the crowd.

"I am aware that right here in Pithole you have immigrant teamsters rioting against the establishment of a pipeline to Miller's Farm. Is that correct?"

Freddy Prather, who was sitting at Booth's table replied, "Yes sir! The damned Irish papists, sir!"

Laughter mixed with anger at Freddy's remarks. Forrest raised a hand to still the crowd. "It's the same everywhere, from the iron mills to the woolen mills. Immigrants with no stake in this land are tryin' to tell their masters what their pay shall be. They do no labor but drive horses, yet they steal the profit from your hard and risky work producing oil. What are they charging to transport a barrel of oil now, Mistuh Booth?"

"Three dollars a barrel."

"And what is the goin' price of a barrel of oil in New York?"

"Seven dollars and eighty-seven cents, at the close of business today," Duncan called from a nearby table.

"That's robbery. Highway robbery of the worst sort!" Forrest declared. "And what do they spend it on? Whiskey and whores! That's where your profit is goin'—to the damned public houses and the damned whores of Pithole!"

"Gentlemen, gentlemen!" Forrest said, his voice rising over the din of comments. "Is this the world God wanted? A place where decent women fear to walk the streets of an evening because bands of ruffians would surely ravish and perhaps even kill them? Where drunkards stagger about all hours of the day and night shouting profanities and lewd remarks. I have heard that a minister of the Gospel was *stoned* on these very streets while preaching!"

His logic might be twisted, I thought as he paused for a sip of water, *but he's making some good points about what life in Pithole is like.*

He set the glass down. His eyes were alight and for a moment I saw in Forrest's demeanor a look I had seen before—the same fiery countenance I had seen in the photographs of John Brown at his hanging.

In a quieter, more pleading voice Forrest said, "Gentlemen, friends. There are changes comin' to our country. President Lee is ready to move on Cuba to begin to extend The Golden Circle southward as we have long wished. Laws have been passed this winter that allow us to deal with our prope'ty as we wish everywhere in this fair land. But the forces of lawlessness and evil yet abound."

He took another sip from his glass and looked around as if searching for spies. I was too far back, so he didn't spot me. "And so, we are founding a new organization. It will be similar to the mounted bands I commanded during the war. It will have a simple mission—to strike fear into the hearts of those who still resist our government. Our president, the great General Lee, is a humble and gentle man. But someone needs to deal with the plotters and deceivers hidin' in our midst. There are renegade slaves and renegade soldiers harboring fugitives even in these woods."

People like me and those renegade Bucktails.

"Like Jesus, who drove the moneychangers from the Temple, we must drive these rapscallions from the caves and mountain hideaways where they yet scheme to overthrow God's order for white Christian men."

"Hear, hear!" a voice called in agreement.

"We have named our org'nization the Ku Klux which is Greek for *circle*—as Knights of The Golden Circle you will bear that name proudly." He beamed at them.

I had studied Greek, and I didn't remember any such phrase. What the hell was he talking about?

"I was once called *The Wizard of the Saddle* in my days as a rebel—and I wore that name proudly. But now, I proudly wear the title of *Grand Wizard of the Ku Klux Klansmen.* Are there any among you who will join with us? The fight for our rights and our freedom as white Christian men goes on—who is brave enough to stand with me?"

"I will!" John Wilkes-Booth said, and in a flash he was at the podium standing next to Forrest to sign up for their new club. There was a moment of awkward silence as Booth stood there alone, and then he cried out, "Come on, men! Stand with us! Join with us in this fight!"

That did it. Freddy Prather jumped to his feet and ran to Booth's side. Chairs scraped on the floor as men stood and filed forward, some with what I thought a notable lack of enthusiasm. Looking to my left I saw Stottish was fast asleep in his chair.

"To those of you who might yet hesitate, let me sweeten the pot. I am announcin' a raffle right here in Pithole to raise funds for weapons and uniforms."

He waved to someone out in the hallway, and with a shuffle of feet some oddly-dressed men came in. I recognized them as Forrest's three associates or bodyguards. They wore black uniforms with strange white figures that looked like bones covering them. On their heads were masks of a frightful nature, one having horns protruding like the devil.

"The uniforms of the night riders you see before you have been assembled to provoke fear and submission of rebellious slaves and their cronies. The dark races have a fear of skeletons and ghosts, and just the appearance of these masked riders strikes terror into their hearts. We have found them to be quite effective in quashing the rebellion we have found in some quarters of the Union, especially out West."

I had heard about this, though you wouldn't find it in any newspaper: the whippings, the gunfire at night, the hanging trees. I wanted to shout out: *Take off your masks! Cowards hide their faces!* But one Bucktail against fifty hot-blooded Copperheads was poor odds. I held my tongue.

It looked like Forrest had some sort of gilt ledger to inscribe the names of those joining. Apparently, what had once been The Pithole Swordsmen was no longer. Instead, they had signed on as the military arm of The Golden Circle. As the last of them trudged past Forrest took the podium again.

"Gentlemen, as I said before, we will be holding a raffle to raise funds here. Many of you have heard of my great warhorse Roderick. He has been let to stud and has produced a handsome dark bay foal whom we have named "Star." Like his father, he stands fourteen hands high, and he can run like the wind! He is now in Pittsburg at a prope'ty I own there, but as soon as the rail line opens he can be brought north. And I will provide a further inducement—a fine, stout Mulatto girl named Polly. She's a house servant and unspoilt breedin' stock."

"I bid ten dollars for Polly!" Freddy Prather shouted out to the laughter of those around him.

"Sorry, young man. It's a raffle, so all have an equal opportunity to gain the lovely Polly. Chances at one dollar each."

"Then I'll buy ten. No, twenty," Freddy said.

"I'll buy a hundred chances at Star," cried Booth.

This was enough to distract me from the podium where Forrest had stepped aside. He slipped into the hallway and came back in wearing a special white head covering with a green peak and a cross in a dark-green circle. A hush came over the assembly. "Gentlemen, Klansmen," he said. "Our final order of business is the most important. It is for this reason that I came North to found this chapter. There has been a rumor that somewhere in this northern forest Abraham Lincoln still lives."

There was a gasp from the crowd, though from the back a man shouted, "It's true, I seen him!"

A cold chill went up my spine. Had I betrayed him to this bunch of bloodthirsty killers?

"Mistuh John Wilkes-Booth has told me that you raised a fund for his capture and incarceration, and that steps have already been taken to bring that murderer to justice. Well done, men. Well done."

There were nods of self-congratulatory agreement.

"Two hundred thousand soldiers, both Butternut and Blue, lie in their graves because of him. Let me be clear on this. We don't want him captured. Your first task as a chapter of the Ku Klux is simple: bring me Lincoln's head!"

PART TWO

And did the Countenance Divine,
Shine forth upon our clouded hills?
And was Jerusalem builded here,
Among these dark Satanic Mills?

William Blake, Jerusalem Hymn

Chapter Twenty-one

Ezekiel Edwards

Solomon Stottish's word was, as Dickens put it, *good as change*. Just a day after the Pithole Valley Railway commenced operation I was riding the rails toward Pittsburg. It was hard to imagine that it had been just a couple of weeks since I last journeyed by rail. I had come to Pithole to start my life anew and perhaps make a fortune. Now, with this invitation to visit Pittsburg and my joint ventures with Booth and Stottish, it seemed I might achieve that goal soon.

The train continued south past bleak winter scenery winding its way through the Alleghenies. I took lunch in the dining car and sat alone watching the dun hills and black branches of the woods slip past. The train pulled into the terminal at Station Square not long after lunch, but it seemed like late evening. The darkness in Pittsburg stemmed not from the early setting of the sun, but from the smoke of hundreds of iron mills belching clouds of black soot into the air. *Hell with the lid off* was how some described it, and now I remembered why. When I had been in the hospital at Schenley we were up in the hills above town, and the air was cleaner, brighter and more healthful. Down here at the confluence of the rivers a perpetual darkness clung to steep hillsides as if the city were part of the arctic region during the winter season.

As gloomy as I felt disembarking my spirits lifted by the enthusiastic greeting of Mr. Anton Labeque who found me standing on the platform beside the train from Meadville and other points north.

"Captain Edwards?"

"I'm so happy to meet you," I said. "I was worried I might wander off into the outer darkness and never be seen again."

Labeque laughed, "There's no night and day here, just *dark* and *pitch black*."

He escorted me through the Station Square Terminal to his waiting carriage. We began to backtrack on the cobblestone road along the Ohio River. I had seen the smoke-belching mills along the river when the train passed this way, but now we were right in the midst of the iron-making district. Barges on the Ohio brought ore; what seemed like an endless series of hopper trains slowly churned along the riverbank carrying coal and coke to be made into iron and steel. The sky grew darker, and I couldn't tell if the sun was setting or the smoke was closing in around us.

"You were with the Pinkertons during the war?" I asked Labeque. It was his manner of dress that made me think so.

"Yes, as a matter of fact I was. That was how I met Mr. Stottish."

"Was that during the first workers' strike?"

"Rebellion is more like it," said Labeque, raising a hand to twirl the end of his moustache. "Mr. Stottish was pleased with the, uh, *firmness* with which I managed the response to that first wage rebellion."

"I was in the hospital in Schenley then. The nurses were all talking about it. Pittsburg felt like a city besieged in those days."

"The deaths were unavoidable. That's not likely to happen again," he said and then smiled. "Even a modest wage is better than the alternative."

I had heard that what the mill owners now termed a *modest wage* was not enough to keep meat on bones for one man, much less a family; but I let this pass. I tried to keep to the role of guest, not inquisitor. "So, you are the overseer of all Stottish's laborers now?"

"Oh, my goodness, no. We have hired others to do that. Our new manager ran a large plantation in Mississippi before the war."

As he said this he indicated with a sweep of his hand a tall fenced enclosure of unusual size. Wrought iron fencing taller than our carriage led to a gate several hundred yards down the road. The high fencing alone marked this as a different sort of place than the other mills we had passed along the river. We arrived at a guardhouse in front of a pair of large swinging gates. The title STOTTISH STEEL WORKS stood in wrought iron letters on the header above the wide gates which now stood pegged open. Two guards armed with Colt pistols flanked the open gates.

A man in an ornate guard house with a ledger took down our names and time of arrival. With a cheery wave he said, "Morning, Mr. Labeque."

"Afternoon, I think it is, William. All quiet today?"

"Yes, sir. I am happy to say so, sir."

"Wonderful. We shall be an hour or two, at the most. Good day."

The carriage continued on. As we passed under through the gate I noticed that the fence was topped with pointed iron spikes ground to a sharpened edge. Climbing over this fence would be difficult. Next, we came to a row of buildings constructed of tarpaper and slab lumber. They reminded me of the barracks at Camp Curtin. My stomach tightened, not only at that memory, but as I realized what I was seeing. "The workers' houses?" I asked as we passed through the neatly ordered rows.

"Yes. Note the tin roofs to prevent sparks from catching!" Labeque said proudly. "We provide clean and comfortable housing for the workers. Most say it's the best living conditions they've ever seen."

I saw children playing a game with a stick and ball on an icy, cinder-covered field— colored children of many shades.

"Recreation facilities. So they grow up healthy and productive."

"Very enlightened," I said and smiled. Say little, maintain a front of sincerity and good cheer. That's how I had been taught to behave when behind enemy lines during the war. I never would have thought I would have to employ such deception in civilian life, but if I revealed my outrage the tour would be over, and I would not know just what was going on in these new Confederate States of America. I swallowed hard and pointed to a large building we were approaching.

"You have medical care for the...workers?"

"Oh, yes," Labeque said, his eyes twinkling. "But not here. This is a different sort of factory here."

I shook my head in confusion. Weren't those nurses exiting on the grand stone staircase?

He slowed the carriage, and I could see it was a fairly large complex. It looked partly like a hotel and partly like a hospital. A couple of young slave men bounded up the stairs and went inside, laughing. A young African woman, quite obviously great with child, stepped out through the doors as the men went in.

Labeque saw my expression and laughed, "It's a Baby Mill."

I looked at him, not sure what he meant.

"Forrest thought it up. The man's a genius, in spite of what some say about him. Instead of importing slaves, which still is against the law, we produce them."

A second young woman came out the front door. A middle-aged man went in. It dawned on me what was going on. "So this is kind of like a..." I searched for a polite word for *whorehouse* but could think of none.

Labeque grinned and punched my arm in a good natured way. "Come, Mr. Edwards. I've been to Pithole. You have many similar establishments there. But..." he held up a finger like a schoolmaster making a point. "here, the purpose is nobler. Procreation! Bully idea, I say. Keeps the young—ah, workers' minds off causing trouble. And it will soon provide us with a whole new generation of workers to take their places."

He flicked the reins and the horses moved on. We passed a side door and a slim white woman, also pregnant, stepped down some side stairs.

"Do some of the neighboring women also come here to deliver babies in the infirmary?" I asked.

"No. The white women who are, ah, *servicing* the workers, have been sentenced for helping escaped slaves. It's put a real damper on the Underground Railroad in these parts. Of course, this has been fully endorsed by the current administration."

Meaning Robert Lee, I inferred. He had been known to be especially vengeful with his slaves who tried to escape before the war. This seemed an extension of that policy. I stared out the window, my anger rising. I hid my face, clenched my hand, which made my shoulder throb anew with a sharp, lancing pain. Anything to keep from crying out the rage and impotence I felt at this moment.

Labeque went merrily on, "The African women, too, are wives and daughters of slaves being punished for one reason or another. Attempted escapes, rebellions, thefts."

I tried to regain my composure by shifting the subject, "You mentioned Forrest. Did you mean the General?"

"Oh, yes. The former Confederate cavalry officer—*The Wizard of the Saddle*, I think they used to call him."

Most of my compatriots used other names for him, but I didn't mention them.

"Look," Labeque said, pointing a chubby finger toward the rail yard, "there's one of his trains now."

I saw what appeared to be a train of cattle cars pulling in at the fence. In a meat packing town like Chicago this would have been a common occurrence. But it was an odd sight in a Northern river town. The train stopped at a series of platforms with fences. "You must bring in your own beef to be slaughtered. Very efficient, I must say."

"No. We're still receiving shipments of workers from one of Forrest's plantations."

As we neared, I saw lettering on the cattle car's wooden placard. The logo read THE GOLDEN CIRCLE PLANTATION. Well-armed overseers, with shiny pistols and riding crops for tools, unlocked the doors to the first car. Filthy and poorly-dressed slaves came tumbling out of the boxcar shielding their eyes from the meager daylight. The boxcar emptied, and I saw that the floor was covered in straw like a stable—not fit for human beings. A grief-stricken woman bowed over a child that lay unmoving on the floor. Her wails could be heard over all the commotion of the nearby factory and the stomping of hundreds of bare feet on the icy planking boards of the human stockade.

For the first time, Labeque seemed slightly embarrassed.

Chapter Twenty-two

With a sharp metallic clank, the iron gates pulled shut. Then, the guards brought out chains and padlocks to further secure them. Not to keep intruders out, I surmised, but to keep the slave workers in. I had seen similar arrangements at prisoner-of-war camps, both North and South. I didn't mention this to Labeque, but I did say, "Very efficient. Is this the wave of the future?"

"I should think so. Times are changing. The discoveries of our modern industrial age demand it. For society to move forward we need a dependable class of workers. It is clear that not all races are equal."

"It is?"

"We're not in Boston."

"I thought Boston was the cradle of liberty. And it was a Virginian, Thomas Jefferson, who penned the line: *All men are created equal.*"

Labeque remained unruffled. "Some's just a bit more equal than others, as we say here in the West. But I shan't debate philosophy with you, *Professor Edwards.* I'm a practical man, and I'm paid well to oversee Mr. Stottish's operations whether I agree with them at all points or not. But let me say this. I think a professional worker class is a good thing. The workers here are clean, well-fed and healthy; none of the squalor that you find with the workers of the other mills' living quarters."

He waved a hand as if to bat away my objections and then changed the subject, "You do know why Stottish sent you here, don't you?"

"To see his new steel mill and the Bessemer Process at work, right?"

"Yes and no. He's building an identical mill in Cleveland, Ohio. He needs a manager there. Someone with the brains to understand the process, someone who is used to giving orders and seeing men obey. Someone like you."

I hesitated. Labeque turned my way as he reigned in the horses in front of our hotel near the train station. "The pay is excellent. I have improved my situation immensely from what I used to earn as a Pinkerton operative."

I tried not to let my warring emotions show in my face. I was both elated to be considered for such an honor, and yet my heart sank when I considered that the nature of the job would be Slave Master. I remembered a quote from Cotton Mather: *Piety hath begotten prosperity, and the daughter hath devoured the mother.*

"You have not responded?"

"I have just started my life anew in the oilfields."

"There are side benefits," Labeque said with a raise of his eyebrows.

I pondered this, thinking he meant free admission to the women of the baby factory, but he surprised me by adding, "Stottish said you might be interested in taming that unruly daughter of his. She's quite a little beauty."

"Aren't you single and perfect husband material, Mr. Labeque?"

"I've known Miss Chastity since she was a child—an only child, I might add." This last bit made me think he meant a *spoiled* only child."

"And her mother?"

"Unfortunately, she's in a sanitarium up in Schenley, across the river."

"I've not met her," I said. "Miss Chastity gave me a letter to deliver to her."

"Oh, I often drop in with her correspondence. I can take it there next week."

"Is it near Schenley Soldier's Home?" I asked, as if it mattered. In truth, there was a rumor that Mary Todd Lincoln was there also. I had heard that seeing the murder of her youngest child, the irrepressible Tad Lincoln, had pushed her fragile mind beyond endurance. She had been committed to an asylum by her eldest son, Robert.

"It is not far from the Soldier's Home. I suppose we could take a ride up there tomorrow, after our visit to Stottish's offices and warehouse facility."

I answered with another fabrication, "I have several friends who still are recovering at the Soldier's Home. It would be good to see them again…they are scheduled to be released soon."

* * *

The next morning the sky was fair and sunny. I would not have known this if I hadn't accompanied Labeque up through the city to the newly constructed elite sections of town called Squirrel Hill and Schenley. Here, the air was clear and the sky was bright. Small wonder the captains of industry built their mansions here. After a brief yet depressing stop to greet fellow soldiers still recovering at the Soldier's Home I followed Labeque into the Sanitarium, anxious as to what we might find.

"I don't think you really want to see Mrs. Stottish," the brawny nurse said to me as I stood with Labeque at the entry desk.

"*Au contraire!*" Labeque said with gusto—the clear weather had seemed to lift his spirits. "Mr. Edwards has traveled a great distance just for that express purpose."

The nurse glanced at me doubtfully, then back to Labeque, "If you feel it is necessary…"

Off to one side, a pretty and fair blonde haired girl lifted her pen off the page where she was writing notes. I wondered why a girl like her was working in a place like this, and then I remembered Chastity and her nursing work. She didn't have to work at all, yet she chose to do so.

Labeque pressed his case, "It is of paramount importance that Mr. Edwards see her. It pertains to a serious matter concerning her daughter, Chastity."

The nurse narrowed her eyes at Labeque and said, "I have always thought you a rogue, Monsieur Labeque. An *unmitigated* rogue and a *roué* of the worst sort."

I was shocked at such harsh words, but then I saw that a faint smile creased the corner of Labeque's mouth; an eyebrow darted up with pleasure. I also noticed the arctic beauty was smiling at their jest.

The nurse continued her tirade, "A *scoundrel* and a *wastrel*," she said. "Your goals are despicable, your intentions detestable—"

"Ah, but you exaggerate, Nurse Collins…my intentions are good!"

The nurse shook her head, reached into a drawer and pulled out a large ring of keys on a metal hoop. She shot a quick glare at the pretty Slavic girl who was smiling shyly at me in a most flirtatious manner and said, "I suppose I can't have Mr. Edwards standing here all day tempting my assistant. Let us go see Constance."

We walked down the corridor to one side of the nurses' station. The walls were white tile, the floor was white marble squares, and the plaster ceiling was painted glossy white—all very modern and sanitized.

"Has she made any progress since my last visit?" Labeque asked, his demeanor more serious now.

"Not that you would notice." She stopped at a door and knocked lightly, then sorted through the worn skeleton keys for the correct one. She opened the door a crack and said, "We're about to come in, Constance. I hope you're presentable. I have two gentlemen with me today."

I heard a muffled response of assent, and the door fully opened. I followed Labeque and Nurse Collins inside. They stepped forward and I saw a frail-looking woman sitting on the bed near a window. The room was clean and airy, but I couldn't help but notice a whiff of vinegar in the room—soured urine. It was a familiar smell to anyone who had been injured in the war and had convalesced in a hospital or infirmary.

"Constance, you remember Mr. Labeque. He's brought a friend with him to talk to you," said Nurse Collins.

"I don't want to talk to any more doctors," said Constance firmly. In the harsh winter light her face looked much older than Mr. Stottish's, her skin mottled, discolored.

"Now dear, you like Mr. Labeque. He works for your husband."

"It's the doctor he's brought I don't want to speak with."

"Oh, Mr. Edwards isn't a physician, Constance," said Labeque, pulling me forward. "He's a…journalist. He's with *The Pittsburg Gazette*. He's writing an article about the eligible young ladies of Pittsburg, aren't you Mr. Edwards?"

His nudge pushed me closer, and I responded to his leading, "Yes, yes, I'm writing an article about the most coveted young ladies of Pittsburg who stand in need of suitors. I've already written a piece about Miss Frick and the young Mellon girl."

"Eustice," Nurse Collins added from behind me.

"Correct, Eustice Mellon. I was thinking it would be splendid to include your daughter, Chastity in this series."

I glanced at Labeque, wondering if I were laying it on a bit too thick. But what was the saying the Germans have: *porridge cannot be ruined with too much butter?*

Labeque gave me a quick nod of approval. Constance stepped toward us. She moved slowly, and I wondered if she might suspect something. She paused for a moment then began to speak, but in a different voice. I'd heard that sound during the war. It sounded like a Virginia Tidewater drawl, very cultured.

"We-ell," she began, drawing out the word to an extra syllable. "She was just the *cutest* little baby you ever saw. That beautiful hair, with all those ringlets."

She paused and Labeque interjected, "Mr. Edwards, your notebook." He thrust a pad and the stub of a pencil toward me.

"Thank you, Mr. Labeque," I said, glancing his way. Over his shoulder, on a peg on the far wall, I noticed a thick white cotton strait jacket. A feeling of unease came over me.

"You were saying, Mrs. Stottish," I asked, my pencil poised over my notepad. "something about Chastity as a child?"

"Oh, yes," Mrs. Stottish said, leaning closer still. "She was the prettiest child anyone had ever seen. Very, very pretty. My, yes."

I smiled in response, but my eyes searched her face. There was something odd about it. What I had thought were lines of age were something different. In this light, they appeared to be more like scars. Healed scars from an injury some time ago. "She was pretty then?" I asked, leading her on.

"Yes, yes," she said, her voice seeming to change again. "Pretty and happy." And now I thought I heard a different tone of voice, higher pitched. "She was always happy!" Her voice rose higher still. "Happy, happy, happy! Always happy!"

From the corner of my eye I saw Nurse Collins step forward.

Constance continued, "That is, of course, until he broke her doll. Right in front of her, he broke her doll's face. He hit it over and over again. Right in front of her! He broke that pretty doll's face! *Her own father!*"

The nurse went to her, withdrawing a syringe from her pocket—and that's when I knew. The scars on her face, the hysteria, and her daughter's odd behavior toward her father. Stottish must have done this.

Constance wailed and thrashed. Labeque stepped in and helped restrain her as she cried out, "No more medicine. No more medicine! Ohhh!"

She flailed out at us trying to strike me or the nurse, but Labeque's strong grip held her still. She stepped backwards and crumpled up onto her bed, sobbing, still repeating, "No medicine, please no more medicine."

Labeque took my arm and pulled me away as the nurse tended to her. I looked back as we departed the room. Nurse Collins, her face sad, tucked the drooping figure with the ravaged face into her bed. My stomach tensed, and I yanked away from his hand.

"I'm sorry you had to see that, Ezekiel. Perhaps we should go." He pointed down a different hallway that I assumed would lead us more directly to our waiting carriage.

"Stottish did this," I said, trying to keep my voice calm but failing. "He paid to have her put away."

Labeque's face became stony, "Mr. Stottish pays me well. So, my aged parents who struggled their whole lives, can now live in comfort,

Mr. Edwards."

"Judas got paid well also, didn't he?"

Labeque looked at me darkly, and for a moment I thought he might actually strike me for I saw him clench his right hand into a fist. But then I realized it was more frustration than anger for he stopped at a junction of two hallways, and with a glance to see that the staff was not in sight motioned for me to follow him, "There's someone else here I think you should see."

We stopped at a room off by itself at the end of that hallway. It was different than the other rooms; a private suite. There was a small, crisply-lettered placard on the door. It bore a simple legend—*Mrs. A. Lincoln.*

Chapter Twenty-three

The Bucktail guards had called her *Hellcat*. Even those of us not in the presidential guard detail had heard of her mercurial temper. Like a wildcat that had been purportedly tamed, she was de-clawed now.

I thought about her as the train slowly worked its way out of the smoky city and up into the hills to the North. She had not said much when we visited her, and I wondered if they kept her temper under control with the same *medicine* that Constance Stottish abhorred.

"A Bucktail captain!" she had said with delight after Nurse Collins introduced us. "And dashing handsome too! Abraham will"—she paused. I think she had been about to say, "be jealous."

To my surprise, the light in her face showed that she had once been pert and pretty, the most desired young woman in Springfield. But her face was now clouded and she said, "I think he yet lives. I can't see him."

"Ma'am?" I asked.

"Oh, I see Edward and Willie and Tad, and I speak with them. They miss their father so—"

"He does not join them?"

"No. It is quite sad," she said, and her face lost its youthful vigor. "You Bucktails must still have him somewhere."

I saw Labeque's eyebrows rise. I thought I knew what he was feeling; it was spooky. I could tell that she was deranged, yet her delusions had a certain rational consistency to them. Not unlike the sermons of the crazy, wild-haired preacher.

"If you see him, Captain Bucktail, give him my love. Tell him that Edward, Tad and Willie send their regards, also."

I tried to imagine myself giving such a message to the former President—that his dead sons send greeting. I smiled politely, which encouraged her to reach out her hand to me and grasp it firmly, "Tell him not to lose heart. Tell him I am sure we will be one day reunited—one day soon. I'm certain of it."

Labeque eyed me carefully. Was he looking for some slip on my part? Once a Pinkerton detective, he had just this morning introduced me to

Pinkertons on his staff who kept watch on the mill workers, both slave and free. When they learned I once commanded Bucktails the air in the room had turned cool.

"If I should ever have the honor of meeting him I will surely let him know."

Labeque's eyes met mine. I could see he clearly thought the woman a lunatic—the influence of the moon had upset the balance of her mind. Nurse Collins came forward with a draught of laudanum for her, which confirmed my suspicions. It was a dose that would have knocked me out for hours. But Mrs. Lincoln drank it down like a sailor quaffing a cold ale on a summer's day.

"Mrs. Lincoln and Mrs. Stottish seem to suffer from similar delusions," Labeque had said as he guided our carriage down the hills to the train station.

"She lost three young children and her husband, and she is quite estranged from her eldest son who had her committed to an asylum. Perhaps it is her only way to cope with the tragedy of her life," I said.

"I find it simply amazing that some still cling to the belief that her husband survived. Some of our Pinkertons up North are actually hunting for him when they aren't guarding Van Syckle's pipeline from the depredations of the Irish." He gave one of his short barks of laughter to show the insanity of such behavior. Or was he trying to draw me out? "Some say the Bucktails guard him still."

"Could be. But my Company never did guard duty. There's only a handful of us left…two of whom are helping me drill a well in Pithole." I didn't mention the fact that I'd led the charge into that withering fire. I pushed that thought aside and instead, I quizzed him, "What are your former chums doing chasing Old Abe?"

"They are happy to work for anyone with cash. Greenbacks, gold, or Confederate dollars, they have always been coveted by Mr. Pinkerton."

"Even during the war?"

"Especially during the war, though you didn't hear that from me."

"So, when he wildly inflated the numbers of the enemy . . ."

"I'm buttoning up my lip," Labeque answered. He paused and caught my eye, "Not sure if you've been around them much. But they're pretty damn good shots, those Pinkertons. Not to be trifled with."

That settled it for me. I would have to keep a close eye on the Pinkertons when I returned. I thought of Tom Mortenson on the hills above Pithole, already keeping vigil.

* * *

The train crept north through forest and farmland. No snow this far south, though it wasn't that far. Yet it seemed a world away from Pithole. The sun had set, and I was thankful I would be riding a train all the way this time. No more midnight climbs on icy cliffs, thank you.

I thought of another train ride north from Pittsburg just a few months ago. That excursion had taken me all the way to Salem, for all the good it did me. I had gone back to receive my inheritance, to see my daughter and to deliver the divorce papers to my wife.

In the time I spent recovering in Pittsburg I had become estranged from my family completely. Intellectually, I could understand it. There were many cases of men who were presumed dead during the terrible carnage of the war. Some, like me, had been wounded and ended up in the hospital far from home. And with an unreliable postal system and the upheaval after the war, many returned home to the astonishment of friends and relatives who had attended their funeral. I wondered how that would have felt walking up to my own house and seeing my tombstone at the family plot. At least they were warned that I was coming.

I found Elizabeth rocking her new baby on the porch of her palatial new house. Or should I say, on the porch of Seth Winchester's mansion on Chestnut Street, Salem's most impressive address. It made a pretty picture. The beautiful young mother with the darling infant, his wispy blond curls blowing in the warm spring breeze while the young sister stood to one side smiling. The only problem was it was my wife, but not my baby. That much was certain.

"Daddy's home!" my daughter shrieked when she spotted me walking slowly up the sidewalk. She ran to me and flung her arms around me. I would have swept her up in my arms and danced, if not for my injury. Instead, I knelt and felt her small arms encircle my neck. It struck me that I had missed her much more than I had missed her mother.

"Abigail, you must be gentle with your father. He was injured in the war," said Elizabeth, in a voice remarkably lacking in compassion.

"She's fine," I said, lying.

Abigail leaned back and eyed me with her dark eyes, making sure she wasn't hurting me. Then she said, "Daddy, you must come and see our new house. Papa Seth got me my own room! It's beautiful, and I've ever so many things to show you." Suddenly, her eyes brimmed with tears, and she choked out a very small sentence, "Daddy, I *missed* you."

That was like a dagger to my heart. I pulled her close to me again, not wanting her mother to see my emotions so close to the surface. I felt the warmth of her, the fresh smell of her hair. Then, I heard her mother's voice again, "Abigail, go upstairs and get that new doll. The one you told me you wanted to show to your father."

Was she trying to separate us?

Abigail looked up at me, and her eyes lit with excitement. She held up one small finger and said, "Wait!" Then, she turned and raced nimbly up the stairs and into the great house, her feet echoing on the hardwood floors.

"Did you bring them?" asked Elizabeth, her expression stony.

"Yes," I said through gritted teeth, handing her a large envelope. "Your lawyers seem to have been quite thorough in their fabrications."

I heard a gate close on the side walkway and saw Seth Winchester come from the back. His carriage house was bigger than the house I had inherited from my parents. He tugged off his riding gloves and tucked his riding crop under his arm. His posture reminded me of a pugilist readying himself for a fight.

"I hope you haven't come to make trouble. Things have been going well since you were gone."

"Why would I make trouble?" I countered, "Who wouldn't be thrilled to come home from the war to find his wife in the bed of the richest man in town? How many substitutes did you have to hire to fight in your place so you could stay home and seduce my wife?"

Dots of color came to Elizabeth's cheeks. Seth crossed to the porch, as if to defend his bride from my advance. He put one hand on her shoulder when she made to rise and shook his head, "I didn't have to seduce her. She came to me before you left."

I looked at Elizabeth, and the shame on her face told me it was true. They were lovers even before I left. Now I knew why so many of my letters home went unanswered. It was not just problems with the postal system; she was with him, even then.

This filled me with such a rage that I charged the porch, thinking to pummel him with my fists. But it was a foolish gesture in more ways than one. He was younger, bigger, and not only due to my injury, stronger. He swung the heavy leather riding crop at me like a whip. The first strike hit my upraised hand, and it stung like a swarm of stinging bees. The second strike smacked into my ear, and I heard a cry. Abigail burst through the front door and with a high, wailing cry, flung herself between us.

"Stop it, stop it! Don't hurt, Papa Seth!"

Something in the way she said it gave me pause. I looked from Seth, who stood panting from the exertion of beating me, to Elizabeth, who stood behind him, her jaw jutted out in anger. She said, "That's right, Ezekiel. These are both Seth's children. So just go away."

This brought a fresh wail from Abigail. Her mother grabbed her arm roughly and jerked her away. The doll she had brought down to show me clattered to the porch, its porcelain head cracking on the bricks, pieces of clay clattering down the stairs. The door slammed behind them, and I was left alone with Seth who still held his riding crop aloft, ready to bludgeon me again.

I looked him firmly in the eye and thought of comments I might make, but I decided none of them could convey the loathing I felt for the two of them at that moment. I turned and stepped to walk away. Big mistake.

That was when he hit me the third time with the riding crop. He aimed it perfectly, hitting me at the exact spot where my shoulder had been stitched together. It felt like a fresh shot of canister had struck me from behind, full force. The pain was a searing heat deep in my shoulder, as if a blacksmith had poked me with a dull red shaft of steel.

I should have crumpled in pain to the ground. Instead, I did something I had seen men do in battle but had never done myself. In spite of the pain, I acted with strength far greater than normal. In one motion, I turned and ripped the riding crop from his hand sending him backward, falling on the steps and crying out in pain. Through the glass I saw Elizabeth's face in abject terror. Seth lay prone, one arm raised to fend off the blows he was sure I would inflict on him. I pulled the crop up and brought it down sharply with two hands, breaking its wooden shaft on my knee and snapping it in two. I threw the pieces at Seth's face and said, "Vengeance is the Lord's—He will repay."

That was the last time I had seen any of them.

* * *

On the train back from Pittsburg I must have drifted off to sleep while remembering my trip to Salem—the rocking of the coaches and the dark, starless night conspired to increase my weariness, and so I dreamt:

I was in a tall house, a mansion of many rooms, and I climbed the stairs all the way to the top. The stairs looked familiar, and an internal voice said, "See, it's the mansion at Petroleum Centre."
As soon as I realized this, I was somehow standing on the third

floor. *There was someone there with me, looking out the windows. Not a man, but a sort of man-beast, covered with fur.*

"If he turns, he will chase me," my inner voice said.

And he did turn, and he chased me down staircase after staircase. We raced further and further down, and I shut each door on the landing as I went, hoping to slow him. Finally, I found myself out on the grand front porch, and I slammed the double-doors shut to keep him in.

But the next thing I knew, he was beside me breathing heavily. We stood side-by-side on the edge of the porch for a moment. Then, I stepped behind him and planted my feet firmly on the floor. With two strong hands I began to press on his back to will him away from me. The fur on his back curled up in coarse tufts between my fingers as I pushed harder and harder. Finally, like a stump being torn from the ground, he toppled forward and fell from the porch.

That was when I heard a voice calling out, "Oleopolis! Change trains for Pithole City!"

And then I woke up.

Chapter Twenty-four

The train to Pithole arrived at the new station down in the flats, and I had only a short walk to our well. When I was still several rods away I was accosted by a white dog. He raced forward through the dark of the evening, lowered his head and made a low growling sound as I cautiously approached.

"Bobby Lee! Git back here!" Daniel called out from the shadows.

The dog glanced back, lowered himself even more and continued his low, odd growling sound. When I passed by him he leaped up and raced to Daniel, a streak of white in the dark.

"That's Bobby Lee, so-named on account of his hair bein' white like *You know who's*," said Daniel, collaring the dog and bringing him inside the engine house. "Found him last week when I was gatherin' wood."

"So, you found a pet, but have you *struck 'ile* yet?" I asked as I came in from the damp evening air to where they huddled around the warm boiler. No one was drinking cider—not a good sign.

"Captain, we're havin' a bit of a problem," said Daniel in his mild drawl.

Tinker stood glaring at the boiler. From the set of his face I could see he was angry.

"Damn, dammit all to hell," said Tinker, kicking at the greasy floor with his boot.

I looked from him to Enos, whose face was smudged with mud and his hair plastered to his head from sweat. "Tools are jammed, Mr. Edwards. Been tryin' and tryin'. My apologies, sir."

"So what do we do now? Start drilling in a different spot?"

Tinker kicked at the dirt again, but said nothing. Enos filled the void. "Well, yes. I suppose we could do that. We have the engine running well, and most of the supplies we would need. We could do that, yes."

"You said you could get them out!" said Tinker, his voice rising. "If they're stuck, you'll just fish 'em. That's what you said this morning!"

"Well, now, I did say that," Enos replied. "I said I might be able to fish the tools if they were stuck. Not easy, my no!"

"For gracious sakes, Enos you just told us we should drill another well. What is it, drill a well or fish the tools?"

I held up a hand like a referee in a boxing match, "Wait, let's discuss this. Enos, have you ever fished for stuck tools before?"

"Not on an oil well," said Enos, his eyes downcast.

"But you—" Tinker interjected.

"Wait just a second, Mr. Evans." I raised my hand again and turned to the blacksmith, "Enos, have you fished for tools on salt-drilling wells?"

"Well, yes. Me an' me old pap done that a number of times. The tools will often get jammed in a crevice—all twisted and such. Then you have to back off the bit and try to grapple the end with fishing tools. We done it a few times down Tarentum way."

"Well, then that's what we ought to try first," I said, looking from one to the other.

"We'd have to buy fishing tools," Tinker said, his voice still tight with anger.

I nodded.

"We're out of money, Captain. I couldn't even pay Daniel and Enos this week."

Now the real problem had come out. "We spent all our capital, already?"

Tinker nodded sadly. "Fuel for the boiler. And the bill for some pipe came due. And we have to eat…especially Enos."

Another point of conflict, I could tell. Daniel and Tinker were accustomed to getting by with short rations—not so, Enos. "How much for tools?"

"Around three hundred dollars, just for the tools."

"In the morning you and Enos find the tools," I said. "I'll go talk with Mr. Booth and see if we can get one last advance."

* * *

The next morning I followed the muddy track up the hill to the Metropolitan Theatre. When I arrived at the hotel, Marcus was outside with a hammer in one hand posting a notice beside the main entry door. In bold script it declared:

EDWIN BOOTH—AMERICA'S GREATEST ACTOR
HERE ON STAGE IN MACBETH
A THREE-DAY ENGAGEMENT!
STARTING APRIL 12th!

Marcus gave me a cursory glance as I stepped past him and approached the door. "Mr. Booth has not yet arrived for the day," he said as I placed my hand on the thumb latch to enter.

I looked back at him. His eyes projected distrust, if not outright hatred. I wondered why, "Do you know when he'll return?"

"I believe he's at McTeague's saloon this morning," he said this in an airy tone that made me think he was either being evasive, or he really had no clue where his master was.

I paused for a moment before placing my hand on the rough, unpainted oak of Josiah's saloon door. I had the same queasy feeling in the pit of my stomach I had felt when I'd gone to the Salem bank to try and borrow money for my first home. I looked through the dirty glass of the door window and saw Booth sitting with Susanna. There was something odd about their posture. Were they holding hands?

I pushed in through the door in time to see Susanna pull her hand back, holding a cup of tea. Perhaps that was it. Booth had been pouring her a cup of tea. But why were they together so early in the day? What had changed since I had gone to Pittsburg?

"Why, look Susanna, the prodigal has returned," said Booth when the door slammed shut from the breeze.

Susanna eyed me over the brim of her cup and smiled, but said nothing. Her lips looked redder than usual. Were they chapped or bruised? I wondered.

"How was your trip, Captain Edwards? Did you meet that rogue Anton Lebeque?" Booth asked in that booming stage voice of his.

"My trip was fine. I enjoyed my tour of the mills," I answered. Booth grinned—right answer. I swallowed and said, "But there has been a difficulty at the well since I left. The tools are jammed."

"I'm sure your men will free them up, perhaps in a few hours?"

"It's been a day and a half already."

"So you want more money," said Booth quietly, then louder. "You want more of *my* money!"

"Yes," I answered quietly. "I want more of your *Goddamn* money."

Susanna dropped her teacup onto her saucer with a clank. Droplets of tea flew in an arc up into the air and then landed as tan blemishes on the pure white of the fresh linen tablecloth.

Booth shot his wrists out of his jacket and leaned forward in his chair, "No servant of mine shall speak to me in such a haughty manner. I will stop funding of this project immediately, I swear it!"

I noticed as he waved his fist at me that there was an odd tattoo on his wrist. As his fist got closer to my face I was able to read the inscription. *J.W.B.*—his initials. I should have felt menaced by his theatrics, but I didn't. I had been shot at with cannons.

"You can strike me down if you will. But it will not resolve this problem. Do you wish us to purchase some fishing tools and attempt to salvage this well, or shall we forfeit what we have invested so far and go our separate ways? It really doesn't matter to me, Mr. Booth."

Booth slammed his fist down onto the table, whether in frustration or anger I didn't know. He jumped up from the table and paced about. From the side I could see Josiah pause in his washing of dishes at the bar and watch. Would he intervene if Booth got violent?

I waited.

Booth spun on one heel and threw himself into a chair, "All right, fine. I'll advance you more money. But you'd better pray that this well flows like the Allegheny River, as much money as we've thrown into it.

Then, he pulled a large billfold out of his vest pocket and counted out the money. "One thousand dollars, Mr. Edwards. Not a penny more. And that's the last dollar you'll ever see from my pocket!" And with that he rose, pulled Susanna by the wrist and said, "Susanna and I will be upstairs, Josiah. We are not to be disturbed."

Chapter Twenty-five

I returned to the well with Booth's money, but his strange behavior troubled me. Was he purchasing Susanna's services just to spite me? He had shown friendliness to me prior to my trip to Pittsburg, so what had changed? The last time I had seen him had been at his Golden Circle meeting. I thought I had hidden my feelings of disgust for his hero, Nathan Bedford Forrest, but perhaps not as well as I had thought. Maybe this was his revenge. Surely, he would know it would poison our business dealings if he chose Susanna over the many other prostitutes in the town. Moreover, wasn't he engaged to be married to Lydia? St. Paul had said: *It is better to marry than to burn.* I shook my head at the thought. The man was an enigma to me.

Then, it occurred to me that later in the day I could quiz Josiah about Booth's strange behavior. So, I decided to drop the money off at the well to enable the men to purchase the fishing tools, and then I would return to speak with Josiah.

I was just about to put this plan into action when something stopped me. I had come back up the hill and was nearly to McTeague's Saloon when I spotted a dark rider on a horse on the cleared pipeline right-of-way. He was silhouetted against the gray noon sky, and he looked familiar—was it the dark rider who had tried to shoot me? I don't think he saw me because he turned his horse and cantered off along the pipeline heading east toward Petroleum Centre.

I quickly obtained a mount from Henry and hurried after him. It occurred to me partway up the hill that there wasn't much I could do if I apprehended him. All our weapons were down in the flat with Tinker. It made little sense to go charging after him unless I planned to unhorse him by throwing rocks. Perhaps I could shadow him and find out who he was and what he was doing. It wasn't long after I'd passed Owltown that I spotted him again. It had started to drizzle, and he was stopped with a trio of riders sequestered under a tall pine. I tied the mare at the side of a shed containing supplies for the pipeline and crept forward on foot until I could see who the other men were—Pinkertons.

"When do they change shifts?" I heard the taller of the three Pinkerton men ask.

"Usually around three. The big one, Mortenson, has been coming up to the ridge and posting a lookout to keep an eye on you."

"We've seen him. He appears to be the most dangerous one," said the tall man.

"Black Hat from the Iron Brigade. He'll need to be neutralized if we're to succeed in capturing Lincoln," said the smaller of the Pinkertons. Other than height, they all looked the same: wool suits, bowler hats, thick beards, dark eyebrows, large revolvers on their hips—all lean, lined faces, hard looking.

My horse snorted and shook her head, and I saw their heads turning my way. My anger rose. I wanted to strike her, to tell her to be silent. Then, I remembered that in my pocket were some apples. Henry had given them to me, as the horse had missed her afternoon feeding. I tiptoed back to where she was tied and rolled one to her, holding my breath, listening for footsteps. In a moment I heard the voices again.

"Fine, then. At sunset. If you can do something to draw away Mortenson that would be good."

I scooched back to where I could see who had just spoken—it was Marcus! He was taking an envelope from the tall Pinkerton, looking inside. "You're a hundred short. I need twelve hundred."

"You lead Mortenson away, there'll be another five hundred."

"Another four hundred—the deal was for twelve hundred now. The four hundred will be a bonus. But I need the twelve hundred now, or it's no deal."

"We could just shoot him now," said the smaller one with an evil sneer, "then go get Lincoln. Save twelve hunerd that way." He spoke as if Marcus were not standing there.

"Good idea. Then you'd have John Wilkes-Booth to contend with. He's jealous of his property."

"Meaning you," the tall one said pointedly to Marcus.

"Twelve hundred, or you can take your chances alone," said Marcus brazenly.

For a slave, I thought, he was a canny bastard.

There was an exchange of more money, and they began to part ways. As the Pinkerton men turned their mounts to head back to Owltown, Marcus yelled after them, "And don't shoot the girl, she's mine!"

"She's Stottish's daughter, for chrissakes!" the smaller one said. "Do you think we're that stupid!"

Marcus didn't wait for an answer. He galloped off toward Petroleum Centre.

After the others had left and they were out of sight, I slowly led the mare out from beside the shed. I looked at the inclination of the sun in the sky. Perhaps three hours until sunset at the most. I would have to act quickly. I followed Marcus at a brisk canter as he descended to the busy valley of Oil Creek. When he reached the bridge I saw him wave to Mortenson who was sitting at the far end of the bridge watching an oil pipeline crew at work extending the line up the hill from Miller Farm. When Marcus had left the bridge and entered some trees on the far side I crossed to where Mortenson sat.

"Edwards, what brings you out on such a damp and dreary day?"

"Your friend," I said, with a tilt of my head toward the barely visible figure of Marcus ascending the hill across the valley.

"Did he take another potshot at you?"

"You knew it was him?"

"I confronted him last week. He said he was just trying to scare you off. He thinks of Miss Chastity as his personal plaything."

I shook my head. I wished I could pursue the topic further, but I was in a hurry. "That's not why I'm here. I saw him up the hill talking to some Pinkerton operatives. They're planning to come and steal Lincoln at sunset tonight. We must act!"

"I find it hard to believe Marcus would be in league with them," he said with a tilt of his head to the two Pinkertons on the hillside where the workers toiled on the pipeline. "They don't own slaves, and they didn't hire Negroes, even when it was legal."

"They gave him twelve hundred dollars. Told him they'd arrive at Lincoln's mansion at sunset."

Mortenson's eyes bored into me, and I saw a change come over him, "Go get help! I have some Bucktails I can call on. Bring anyone you can find who can handle a firearm." He swung himself up into the saddle and pointed toward town. "There's a railroad spur behind Lincoln's house. You follow that spur of rail line in the woods there. It'll bring you in the rear of the house. Go quickly!"

Chapter Twenty-six

I raced back to the well as fast as the mare would carry me, which I feared would not be fast enough. The sun had broken through a scrim of clouds at the horizon, and shadows were lengthening down in the flats when I reached the well.

"Daniel, Tinker," I yelled when I reached the derrick.

"We're busy," Tinker yelled back. "We're trying to clear the line so we can fish the tools when Enos gets back."

"I need your help," I yelled up to them. They were both up on the driller's throne twisting at the cable that ran down to the tools. "The Pinkertons are threatening to snatch Lincoln!"

"They can have him! We have work to do!" Tinker shouted back, annoyed.

I looked up at him in disbelief and replied, "Surely you don't mean that? We must help the Bucktails defend him. They want to turn him over to Lee for trial."

"That's his problem."

"Tinker, I don't have time to argue. Come on!"

"I don't have time to spare, go yourself!"

"Daniel?" I called out.

"Don't go, Dan. I need you here," said Tinker.

Daniel looked from Tinker to me, and then back again. Finally, he said, "Gotta go, Mr. Evans. I gave the captain my word."

"He's not our captain anymore, for crying out loud. He's a…dag-gone civilian."

"I gave him my word," said Daniel.

Nevertheless, I could see it pained him to break with Tinker. I remembered now Tinker's words, "I found him wandering, lost on the battlefield." Daniel climbed down. But I could see Tinker's face—it was like stone. We left him behind.

Up at the livery stable Henry got Daniel a mount and a fresh one for me. The mare was about clapped out. Outside, the sky was growing darker.

"Are you about to close?" I asked.

"Yes, Mr. Edwards. You'll have to return your horses in the morning."

"We could use a hand. Do you have a gun?"

"What?"

"There are some bad men, Pinkertons. They're going to try to capture Lincoln. We're riding to stop them."

"I'll come. I've got a gun here in the cabinet," he added, pulling an old derringer out of his money drawer. He locked the drawer, stuck the gun in his belt and then headed towards a small roan in a nearby stable. To my surprise, he didn't even bother with a saddle or a bridle, he just jumped up on it and grabbed its mane. Riding bareback, he soon proved faster and more agile than either Daniel or me. We raced against sunset up and over the hill.

We galloped over the bridge on Oil Creek, our horses lathered with sweat, and then we circled on the railroad wye in behind the house. No sound of a pitched battle, though it was almost full dark. Perhaps we were too late.

But our horses were grabbed by several rough-looking men in homespun behind the mansion and spirited into the carriage house. They beckoned us to the back porch where a small group of men crouched in the shadows—Mortenson and his Bucktail friends.

"Edwards, great to see you made it. Where's Tinker?"

"Couldn't get him. Got Daniel and Henry."

"They'll do. You three follow me. The others are going with Elisha around the other side. We'll give 'em a warm welcome."

Daniel, Henry and I followed Mortenson around the north side of the house. There were prickly bushes there and icy patches of snow against the stone foundation. We waited, pressed close to the house as icy water slowly chilled our feet right through our boots. I wished we'd drawn the south side of the house where it was warmer, but no such luck. I was beginning to wonder if I hadn't been like the little boy who cried wolf as the sky grew darker and darker and no Pinkertons appeared.

And then, the first gunshot. A Sharps repeater, from the sound of it, well hidden in the woods. Then, they appeared at the tree line—a row of riflemen, blazing away.

For a moment, I was back at MacPherson's farm, and it was Jubal Early's skirmishers coming out of the woods pouring fire across the fields like poisoned darts, and I was calling, "Come on, you Bucktails!" and hearing the cheer as we made our charge and the withering fire of shot and canister that mowed us all down…but I held my tongue now, though every inch of me wanted to jump up and charge that exposed line. Then, smoke and fire poured from across the yard and there was a sharp scream, and one of the Pinkertons toppled forward, mortally hit in the head, and still they poured fire from their carbines, not needing to ram shots home like in the old days, the good old days.

But an exposed position is yet an exposed position, and when a second Pinkerton fell, this one with a rifle bullet that I saw Mortenson calmly aim, fire and strike with lethal accuracy, their line began to crumble. They stepped back to the cover of small trees and bushes, and we stepped forward, firing constantly, driving them off. We were winning, I thought with a wave of excitement. And then we stepped further into the open, which was a big mistake.

Across the yard, standing with the others, was Marcus. He must have led them here and then joined in the shooting with his handgun. I had not seen him before. But as we came into the clear I saw him raise his gun and fire, and Daniel cried out and was blown backwards from the impact.

Something terrible came over me. A frightful anger, an overwhelming frustration. I screamed in rage and charged forward. I saw Mortenson's shocked face as I ran by, but in an instant he was with me. As was Henry, as was Stiles and the rest of the grubby Bucktails. We were firing, yelling and running like men possessed. At the sight of our advance, the Pinkertons broke and ran. They raced to their mounts and galloped away firing over their shoulders until all had mounted and run off, leaving two men writhing on the ground from their wounds—but not for long. Mortenson motioned to me, took my handgun, and with a look of profound sadness, shot them both to death.

I didn't have time to contemplate this. I ran back to where Daniel lay in the icy water beside the house, fearing the worst. I leaned down, my face close to his. There was a trickle of blood coming from his mouth and a grisly looking hole in his chest.

"Cap'n" he whispered. "D'you get 'em?"

"Yes," I said. I tried not to let my grief show on my face; he would need all the courage he could muster to survive. "Hang on Daniel, we'll get you inside."

Henry helped me drag him quickly around to the back porch where a shaft of light poured out of the open kitchen door. Chastity came out of the door, her face knit with concern. "How bad?" she asked, looked closer and then said, "Oh my."

Her hands went straight to his wound to stanch the flow of blood, even as we dragged him further into the warm kitchen. Mortenson appeared at my side, pulled out a formidable Bowie knife and sliced away the remnants of Daniel's jacket, "Let's get him up on the table."

I swept cutlery and crockery off the table and onto the floor, and we hoisted Daniel up onto the heavy oak surface. My hand came away drenched in blood. "Hold this compress," Chastity said, and I put my hands hard on his chest. Too hard. Daniel started to gasp and choke.

"Ease up! You're killing him!" Chastity yelled at me. She was at a basin rinsing her hands, and she ran down the hallway to the pantry to fetch more bandage linens.

"Let me do that," I heard a voice beside me say.

I looked to my left and did a double take. It was Lincoln. He placed his broad hands on Daniel's chest. They were brown and gnarled, with lines of ancient scars.

"He's stopped breathing," Mortenson said from the other side of the bed.

"Blow a breath in his mouth. That's what they did for me," Lincoln said.

Mortenson hesitated, so I leaned in and parted Daniel's lips and blew breath into his lungs. He shook, gasped and started breathing again.

Chastity returned and shoved me out of the way. She motioned to Lincoln, and in a swift movement they swapped compresses, the dirty for a clean.

"Will he live?" Henry asked me. I could see there were tears in his eyes.

"If—" I began, but Lincoln cut me off.

"We're all here for an appointed time," Lincoln said. "If God wills it, he shall live. If not, then it is his time to depart."

Chastity managed to get some laudanum past Daniel's lips, and his breathing slowed and became more regular. He ceased to struggle on the table against the pain he must be feeling.

"Mr. President, we should consider leaving," Mortenson said. "Our safety here has been compromised."

Lincoln's sad eyes took in Mortenson and the rest of us who were crowded into the room, "I am tired, Thomas. Tired."

"Perhaps you would wish to rest while we prepare your carriage, sir."

"Tired of living like a refugee. What I just said to our young Indian friend is true. We each have an appointed time. I feel I have overstayed my welcome. If it is time for me to meet my creator, then so be it. I will not hide any longer. What was it Saint Peter said? *I am ready to go to prison and to death.*"

"You cannot sacrifice yourself, sir, if I may say so, sir," Mortenson replied.

"I cannot live in hiding any more. If we have the funds, get me a hotel room."

"We would need more guards…" Mortenson said, looking at me and raising an eyebrow.

"There are more Bucktails around here drilling wells," said one of the drillers from where he stood warming himself by the fire.

"Perhaps we could take turns," I said, expanding on this. "Have teams that stay with Mr. Lincoln for part of each day and then switch off. With you and Mr. Stiles present on a regular basis, that should be sufficient."

"He's right, Thomas. An excellent suggestion, Mr.…?"

"Edwards, sir. Captain Edwards of the 150th, sir."

The eyes caught mine, "I've heard of you. You were the one who lead that charge at MacPherson's farm. When Reynolds went down."

"Many of us went down, sir," I said, and then had to look away.

"And here is another of your comrades—fallen defending me. That is why this must end, Captain."

"We thought it had, sir," the grimy Bucktail said, "We stacked our weapons two summers ago."

"I'm afraid that was only an uneasy truce," Lincoln said, "The struggle continues."

Chapter Twenty-seven

Chastity Stottish

The next afternoon found Chastity still sitting with Daniel, keeping watch and reading a book of poetry given her by Lincoln. She heard a rap on the door and to her surprise saw a dark face at the window—Marcus. He must have been watching and known that all the guards had gone with Lincoln to Pithole.

"Chastity," he whispered, "let me in."

"No," she said, opening the door a crack. On the table behind her, Daniel stirred.

"I've come for you. We can go now."

She looked at him through the partly open door. God, he was handsome. Those jet-black eyebrows, bright eyes, sparkling teeth. In a different world Booth would be his servant, his slave.

"Marcus, I can't come now. They are to transport Daniel after Lincoln. Then, possibly I could come."

"When?"

"Tomorrow, at the latest."

She saw Marcus look aside, as if even now eyes were watching him from the woods. He grinned and said, "You make it tough on a man. If I'd known you would be delayed I wouldn't have shot him!"

"What!?"

"Edwards' slave. If I had known you'd stay just to tend him I wouldn't a shot him!" Marcus laughed

He was the one who had shot Daniel? If they had told her, she must not have been listening. Why hadn't someone told her? Good lord! Chastity felt a sharp, cold pain in her stomach, as if she had fallen on a spear of ice. Marcus had no heart. He had beautiful eyes, but he had no heart in his chest. She'd had inklings of this before, but it was not confirmed until now. She closed her eyes and shut the door.

"Chastity! Girl, you open that door!"

I'm not your *girl*. She thought. I'll never be your *girl*.

"Chastity, listen. I gained more money! Look, I have booked passage to London!" He waved some sort of scrip in the air and continued, "It's no longer safe in Canada! So I booked passage to England. I have friends there!"

She turned the latch, locking the door. The glass steamed up where he shouted at her through the thick glass. He raised his fist and pounded on the glass, his breath causing the window to fog, obscuring his remarkable features.

"Damn you, girl! This was all for you!"

Shooting Daniel was for her? Taking money from those killers was for her? Had he ever done anything *for her?* With a sinking heart, she realized the answer was *no.*

"Chastity! I demand you unlock this door!"

She turned back where the noise had stirred Daniel awake. Still, he pounded on the door and yelled angrily at her to obey him. But she no longer heard him. She placed her hand on Daniel's forehead. He was hot with fever. Most likely it would consume him, and he would die. She had seen it over and over again in Pittsburg. Handsome, fair young men— some boys, really—dying right before her eyes.

She sighed. It had grown quiet in the kitchen once again. All she could hear now was Daniel's rasping breath—the prelude to the *death rattle* she had heard so often before. She glanced out the window at the shadow of Marcus riding away. But the only thing she felt was relief.

Chapter Twenty-eight

Ezekiel Edwards

We made two trips over the mountain along the pipeline road that day, first using the good carriage, which had a spring suspension, to take Daniel to Josiah's Saloon and up to the room I had shared with Susanna. Then, we waited for reinforcements before transporting Lincoln. The fellows I called "The Grimy Bucktails" joined us for the second trek, but they'd had time to redd up and don clean clothes by then–and they brought with them some new Sharp's carbines for each of us. We crossed the Pinkertons' territory cautiously, but deliberately, and only saw them peering at us sullenly from their shack near Owltown. Two white wooden crosses already marked the fresh graves in the mud outside their headquarters.

Even with the good carriage Lincoln looked haggard as we traversed the rutted landscape. I once caught a glimpse of him looking out and scowling at the snow squalls that had kicked up on the mountaintop. For just a moment, he looked like those angry posters of Uncle Sam that had been so *in vogue* during the war. He was Uncle Sam in the flesh—the embodiment of the *United States.*

We arrived at the Danforth Hotel in late afternoon, though the gaslights had not yet been turned on. A crowd formed along the street, most in disbelief that this could actually be Lincoln. A couple of hecklers yelled obscenities. Two men in spotless Confederate gray officers' uniforms fingered their shiny black holster straps as we approached, but we met their gaze, and they stood down. To my surprise, the crazy wild-haired preacher, now with an eye patch over his damaged left eye, broke into exclamations of joy when he spotted our entourage.

"Blessed is he who comes in the name of the Lord!" he shouted, his voice as strong and piercing as ever. "Hosanna! Hosanna!"

From inside the carriage I heard Lincoln laugh, a rich, throaty sound I had not heard before and exclaim, "I knew I should have rode in on a donkey!"

Waiting on the sidewalk was a man in a crisp, brown wool suit with matching Trilby hat— Crocus, the reporter. That was no accident. I had sent Henry to alert him when we came into town with Daniel.

"Mr. Lincoln, could I have the privilege of an interview, sir?" Crocus asked as the wagon came to a stop.

"Come back this evening, if you would, Mr. Crocus."

"You've been reading my stories!" Crocus responded in a bemused tone.

Lincoln nodded with a pained smile and said, "Later, later."

We helped get Lincoln into his wheeled chair, dusted snowflakes off the wicker seat and guided him into it carefully. Like King Saul of Israel, he towered head and shoulders above all of us when he was upright and his arms were on my shoulders and Mortenson's. The strength in the grip of those gnarled hands astonished me—I was happy he wasn't gripping my injured shoulder or that vice-like grip would have had me in tears.

Crocus had his notepad out and was rapidly scribbling his impressions of Lincoln's arrival as we rolled him to the large double-doors. Across the way, a familiar-looking team of African railway workers, with their tools beside them, stood waiting for their master to come out of the hardware store. They gazed with wonder at their one-time hero, Abraham Lincoln.

Lincoln held up a hand before we wheeled him through the doors, "Just one minute, gentlemen. I want to read this."

There were handbills posted on the sides of the entry to the hotel. One said:

RAFFLE
DARK BAY HORSE: STAR
MULATTO GIRL: POLLY
TO BENEFIT
KNIGHTS OF GOLDEN CIRCLE!

He scowled at this one, prompting more scribbles from Crocus. Then, a broad smile creased his face, and his eyes lit up when he saw the handbill next to it that read:

THE GREAT EDWIN BOOTH!
APPEARING AS!
MACBETH!

There was more writing beneath that, but a crowd was pressing in against us, and we had to continue on. But his expression of joy at that poster reminded me of stories some of the Bucktail guard had told of him reciting portions of that tragedy from memory. I could also see his eyes light up at the name of Edwin Booth—no doubt it brought back happy memories of performances from Ford's theatre in Washington when he still was president and the war was not yet lost.

To get him over the threshold we had to turn him around backwards. When we did so, he spotted the slaves shackled together across the street, and they saw him. To my surprise, the one I had heard singing along the train tracks suddenly broke into song.

"O, *sometimes I feel like a motherless chile...*

Lincoln's hand gripped mine on the wheel as the others joined in with hauntingly beautiful harmonies and he said, "Please."

...sometimes I feel like a motherless chile,
O, my lord sometimes I feel like a motherless chile;
din I gi'down on my knees and pray,
pray gi'down on my knees and pray."

We paused as the slaves sang their mournful song of loss and despair, and I could see it touched Lincoln to hear it. He had lost his mother as a child, I remembered, and that made the words have an even more special meaning to him.

As we watched, however, the slave master came out of the hardware store with a bundle of shovel handles in his grip. "Stop that infernal moaning!" I heard him shout at the slaves, whose attention was not on him, but on our party across the street. "Stop it, I say." Then he swung a shovel handle at the tall, strong Negro who was the lead singer. His first swing missed, but his return swing caught the lead singer squarely on the back, silencing the music and dropping him to the decking of the sidewalk where he dangled from his chains between two other slaves.

I recognized the slave owner in his dapper Confederate gray from the day I had seen him at the railway grade. All I had with me that day had been a satchel of clothes. Today was different. I grabbed one of the Sharp's carbines from the Bucktail guard standing beside me, aimed it at him and fired.

The report of the gun in the silent street was tremendous, and the round I fired slammed into the hardware store sign right by his head. The ash stave he had in his hand clattered to the porch deck, causing the other shovel handles to tumble down the stairs into the mud. Before he could respond I worked the mechanism of the carbine, and the spent shell ejected, steaming with smoke onto the ground beside me. Then, another blast of sound echoed down the main street and for once, Pithole came to a stop. People stared in shock at what was happening. The slave master raised his hands to cover his head, a reflex that would do him little good against a .30 caliber rifle bullet.

"What the—" he began.

"Stop beating your servants, and I'll stop shooting," I said. "That might be fine where you come from, but up here we don't countenance that behavior. Next time we see you doing that, there won't be a warning shot."

The slave master gave me an evil look, spat a brown tobacco stream into the mud and muttered under his breath, "Pick up them shovels, boys." The shackled slaves did as he said, and as he picked up their chains he began to lead them away toward the rail line. But the least of them, a thin youth with fairer skin and a hint of red in his hair, shot me a buck-toothed grin as they shuffled away.

I turned back to see that the other Bucktails had already wheeled Lincoln away. As they went I heard him comment on the song. "*A Motherless Child,*" he said, "that reminds me of the story of the youth who murdered his parents and then asked the judge for mercy at his sentencing, saying he didn't deserve to be hung since he was 'only a poor orphan.'" I heard Lincoln's high laugh, joined by that of Stiles and the rest of his guards.

After Lincoln was shown to his room, Tom Mortenson arrived to take over his shift watching the president, and I was free to go—sort of.

"We need someone to pick up Miss Chastity and her luggage and transport her here. It would be good if you could do that while we still have the carriage."

"I was going to go visit Daniel and see how he's doing," I said. Overnight, Tinker had borrowed a flat wagon and had moved him to an upstairs room in Josiah's hotel. I could see from Tom Mortenson's expression that he hoped for a different answer, so I relented. "Perhaps I could stop by on the way, just for a moment."

I moved the carriage to Josiah's and went up the stairs to the back room. I was not surprised to find Tinker there, but I hadn't expected to see the white dog with him.

"He's here to cheer him up," said Tinker, indicating Bobby Lee who sat beside the bed with his head leaning against Daniel's hand.

"Will he recover?" I asked.

"If he can overcome the infection. He's running a low fever now. They gave him morphine to get him to rest. The doctor left just a few minutes ago."

There was a pause, an uncomfortable silence.

"I should have been with y'uns, Captain. This might not have happened."

"Booth's slave did it purposely. There's something wrong with that man," I said.

"You mean Booth or the slave?"

"Both. I don't trust either of them."

"Still, I should have been there."

"I was there, and I wasn't able to stop what happened." I paused, looked at Daniel struggling for life against the effects of the wound and said, "I wish it were me. That might be better than living with this guilt."

Tinker eyed me and replied, "We all carry guilt for things we've done."

"I've been getting people killed. That's different."

"Yeah," Tinker said. "Some people just kill with words. Is it really that different?"

"I took Daniel— "

"Daniel wanted to go. I saw it. And what you did brought Lincoln back to public life. Like I said, I wish I'd gone. We all have regrets, Ezekiel."

A door slammed downstairs. Someone was coming.

"Susanna's been with him most of the time," Tinker said. "She'd make a good nurse. Josiah said it was her that nursed the old preacher back to health."

Daniel moaned softly and turned in his sleep.

"How are things going at the well?" I asked.

"It's flowing ten barrels a day without pumping. We'll prob'ly get fifty, if I can get the pump going. That's what I'm working on."

"Wouldn't take long to pay off Booth and Stottish if it keeps flowing oil. We'll make our investment back in a couple weeks."

"If Daniel recovers, we can drill another," Tinker added.

There were footsteps on the stairs outside. Susanna came in with a steaming bowl of hot, soapy water and cotton cloths draped over her arm.

"I best be going," said Tinker.

"I'll stop down later."

Susanna sat down by the bed and gently drew back the covers. She began unwrapping the bandages on Daniel's chest. He moaned and stirred again, not waking up. The dog looked anxiously at him and then at me.

"Don't worry, pup. He'll be okay."

"It doesn't look good," said Susanna, lifting away the last of the bandages.

She was right. The wound where he was struck by the bullet was swollen and red, the edges of the bullet hole puckered up like a child getting ready to spit.

"Nasty."

"Dr. Miller said if he lives the day he may recover. It's all up to him," said Susanna. She reached out a hand and touched his brow.

"We appreciate you nursing him. I will pay you for your services here."

"That would be a first."

"I have offered to pay you previously at your customary rate."

"Your generosity knows no bounds," said Susanna, applying ointment to the wound and spreading it about.

The dog stood up, with its paws on the bed and looked at Daniel's wound and then at me. He barked, and I pushed him aside. "First, you complain that I haven't paid for your services. Now, you complain if I offer you money."

"I guess I just expected more from you, Ezekiel," she said, eyeing me coolly from the corner of her eyes as she continued to wrap Daniel's wound.

"It would not be seemly—"

"What? To take a prostitute as a wife? It's only acceptable to bed me, not to wed me?"

"You've been practicing that line."

"Have not!" she snapped, but I could see her smile.

I grabbed her by the neck and pulled her to me for a kiss. She resisted me for a moment, then put both hands on my chest and pushed me away. Small spots of color brightened her cheeks.

"Do you love me, Ezekiel?" she asked. I could see sadness,

apprehension, even fear in her eyes. "*Would* you marry me?"

I looked away for a moment. Answer enough that she pushed me away. I stood and paced, "I do care for you. But is what we share enough to make a marriage work?" I paced more. The dog followed me looking anxious. " I already failed at marriage once."

"I have a sister in Salem," Susanna said, her eyes on Daniel as she pulled the covers back up over him. In his sleep, a small smile creased his lips.

"Oh?"

"Well, she lives across the bridge, in Beverly. She knows your ex-wife. She told people in the church there that you were sparkin' with a student."

"We were not *sparking*," I said, feeling the warmth of embarrassment rise to my cheeks. "I was her teacher and she had an inordinate affection for me. That happens, sometimes."

"You never kissed her?"

"Only once. When I was leaving for the war."

"And your wife saw it, or found out about it?"

"Not that I know of." I paused. How could she have? And then I knew. "One of her friends. She had seen me with the girl that day, and I confessed the great temptation I had felt and how I thought I had mastered it. But I had asked for her prayer."

Susanna looked at me, shook her head and said, "And you thought it wouldn't get back to her; a juicy tidbit like that? For someone who *studied at Harvard* you can be quite dense at times, Ezekiel."

But I was not listening carefully. Her words had made me wonder again about the silence from home when I sent letters. What really had gone on there? Had Elizabeth believed I was having a romantic affair with a student? Is that what had made her flee to Seth?

"She told me that Abigail was not my daughter," I said to Susanna who had risen from her stool and put the soiled cloths in the basin to carry out. "She said it was Seth's girl—that they had been lovers before I left."

"That would help smooth things over in Salem, wouldn't it?"

I shook my head at the thought. But still, she had a point. One I had never considered before, "The last time I saw them I resorted to fisticuffs with Seth."

"I'd a shot him," said Susanna. "Right in the crotch!"

"You're a bawdy person, there is no doubt of that," I said, trying to catch her for another kiss.

But as I leaned closer, she said, "Not like Miss Chastity, your little princess?" She dodged away from me and headed down the stairs.

"I was hired to go find her, nothing more," I said as I followed her to the foot of the stairs where she poured out the dirty water of the basin onto the slimy ground.

"And where, pray tell, are you going now?" she asked with a nod to the carriage.

"I am to fetch her so she can nurse Lincoln," I said, pleading my innocence. But the truth was when Mortenson had asked me to go get her in the carriage I had been secretly pleased.

"Why am I not convinced?" she asked, tossing her hair and turning away to go back to Josiah's saloon. Then, she turned back and said, "Don't forget to close the door up there." She pointed upstairs to a sliver of light where the door stood ajar. "And take your little white friend with you, too," she added, referring to Bobby Lee who was sitting right behind me. "Josiah don't allow animals to stay in his rooms." And with that, she spun away from me once again and entered the back door to the saloon kitchen.

The white dog watched me as I went back up the stairs and latched the door to Daniel's room. He continued to watch me as I passed him and went to untie the carriage from the railing.

"What are you looking at?" I asked him as he stood mutely eyeing my movements. "Come on, then."

With a happy "woof" he raced to the carriage and jumped in— muddy feet and all.

Chapter Twenty-nine

By the light of a full, early spring moon I helped Miss Chastity up into the carriage. She made a face at the dog that was sleeping there, and I pushed him aside so she would have a place to sit. For just a moment, as she hopped up onto the carriage seat, the swaying movement of her bell-shaped crinoline exposed her dainty lace bloomers, with a generous view of her shapely, milky white calves—the very sight of them made my heart catch.

"You traveled to Pittsburg for my father and spent time with Anton Labeque, that swarthy brute," said Chastity after we'd started our journey.

"I visited Pittsburg."

She narrowed her eyes at me. I thought of how Labeque had all but called her a brat; she now called him a brute. There was some history there, but I didn't pursue it. Instead, I broached a more delicate subject and said, "I visited the Soldier's Home."

"Just the *Home*, or did you go to the *Sanitarium*, also?"

"Labeque took me there," I said, not a lie, but not quite the truth either.

"And how is my mother?"

"Not good."

She sighed and looked out the window at the glistening branches. The snow was slowly melting, and the tree branches glistened, wet and shiny in the moonlight.

"Did she go into her routine about Father beating her?"

"Yes."

"It's true, he did. But she provoked him."

"How?"

"Trying to claw his eyes out with those fingernails of hers. They were fighting. She was the one who lost control—at least, at first. The whole thing was horrendous. I screamed and screamed until the servants came and pulled them apart. It was the worst night of my life."

"So, he had her committed for a family fight?"

"That was just the final episode. She had been teetering on the edge of insanity all that winter. That day, she fell." She paused and looked into my eyes and said, "I hate them both."

"You don't mean that," I said, thinking of her mother's letters, her father's emotion when he asked me to get her.

"I'm not a child, Captain Edwards!" she huffed. As she said this, she pushed the dog away from her, toward me.

"Your parents both care deeply for you. Even your father expressed to me how much he cared."

"He doesn't approve of me."

"He spoke highly of your abilities as a nurse."

"That's not what I'm talking about."

"What *are* you talking about?"

"You know."

What am I? A mind reader? I shrugged.

"Marcus. He didn't approve of Marcus."

"You mean the guy who shot Daniel?"

She nodded, "I took a liking to him."

"I can see why. He seems like a decent fellow, other than being a murderer and a traitor to his own people."

"You Yankees are all hypocrites," she said and shoved the dog toward me again.

I glared at her. "Don't take your frustrated love life out on him," I said, putting an arm around Bobby Lee and pulling the dog toward me. He leaned affectionately against me, his head resting on my shoulder.

"I'm not frustrated!" She slid further away from me, still in a huff.

A trio of deer suddenly darted out of the woods on our right. I reined in the horses.

"Why aren't we moving?" she asked as we continued to pause on the Plank Road.

"I'm waiting for you to stop carrying on."

"Don't think you can try anything on me out here in these woods!"

"I wouldn't think of it."

"You're just jealous of Marcus, that's why you're tormenting me," she spat, glaring at me and gathering her skirts with one hand, holding them to one side in a protective manner. "You Boston Yankees talk about how the coloreds should be equal, until one shows up in your town and starts threatening what you feel entitled to yourself."

"It's one thing to have one in your town, another thing to have one in your bed," I retorted.

"See. You talk about men being equal, until one tries to act as your equal."

"No, you aren't getting it. I am talking about that specific African man—he's bad. He can't be trusted, and you know it."

"Get out!" she yelled.

"Happily," I yelled back, handing her the reins and hopping out of the carriage, causing Bobby Lee to be jostled out of his sleep. He looked confused and then jumped out after me. We started walking down the Plank Road toward Pithole, keeping to the side of the road in case she should spur the horses down here to run us over. Bobby Lee trotted alongside me contentedly, his nose darting this way and that as he smelled the scent of game in the forest.

I then heard a clatter of hooves behind me, and for a moment I thought she was going to stop and pick me up. I smiled happily to myself. We would ride together to Pithole, our love would blossom, and soon we would marry. With her father's approval, I would become a respected man in the community, running a vast empire of oil and steel interests. But while I pleasantly mused on my future estate, I heard her crack the buggy whip, and the horses hastened past me on into town.

Bobby Lee excitedly ran after her, and then he stopped and looked back at me. We had reached a fork in the road. One side led to town, the other down to the flats.

"It's up to you, pup. You can go to town with her, or come down to the flats with me for some supper at the well. Choose whom you will."

He barked again in the direction of the carriage that bore Miss Chastity away. I headed down the road to the right, which took me to the flats. I had only gone a few steps when Bobby Lee nearly bowled me over, racing past me, brushing hard against the back of my leg. He bounded down the road to the well and skidded to a stop just a few yards ahead. Apparently, I had a new friend. The Lord giveth, and the Lord taketh away.

Chapter Thirty

The next morning it was my turn to help guard Lincoln. We had agreed to have four Bucktails on guard at all times. Mortenson knew some of the Iron Brigade who would also pitch in to help to keep the former president safe. I didn't know which might be more dangerous: Lincoln's enemies or Chastity's anger. She had her hair up and her nurse's uniform on, and she looked very professional. She eyed me with cool disdain and left the room when I entered.

After reporting in to Mortenson I took a copy of the day's paper and sat in a chair outside Lincoln's room. I had not been there long before I was interrupted by a man coming down the hallway stating, "If you want good reading, turn to page three."

"Good morning, Crocus," I said. "Here to see the boss?"

"Yes, Captain. His majesty granted me an audience at ten o'clock."

I knocked on the door and led him into Lincoln's presence. Lincoln was sitting at a table with a pen in hand. He pushed his spectacles up onto his forehead, pushed aside his pad and replaced his quill in the inkpot.

"Thanks for coming, Mr. Crocus, though I would guess you have another name."

Crocus nodded, "Thank you for favoring me with an interview, sir. This will give me a leg up on Mr. Thomas of the Franklin rag."

"Getting a leg up was something of a specialty of mine, once upon a time," Lincoln said. "In fact, you might find this hard to believe, but my nickname as a youth was 'Shanks.' Most likely on account of my *jambs,* as Molly would put it."

Crocus grinned and pulled out his pad, "And if I may be so blunt, how is your wife?"

My hand had been on the knob to leave, but I paused.

"I'm afraid she has not been well for some time. Robert, ah, suggested she receive care in Pittsburg at the sanitarium in Schenley."

The sadness with which he said this touched me, and I found myself blurting out, "I saw her there just last week."

"Really?" Lincoln said. "Come join us and tell me about it."

I stepped further through the doorway and said, "I was there to deliver correspondence to my employer's wife, who is also there." Seeing Crocus's surprised expression, I said, "I was delivering letters to Constance Stottish from her husband Solomon, a local investor."

"The Tycoon, some of us call him," Crocus interjected.

"At any rate, I happened to see Mrs. Lincoln, who is also there."

"Did you speak with her? Was she well?" asked Lincoln.

"She seemed quite healthy and full of spunk, I must say."

"That's my *Molly!*" Lincoln said fondly. "But tell me honestly, was she lucid?"

Lucid? I thought. "She was quite alert and responsive. But to report honestly—she does still seem to have delusions about Tad and Edward and Willie."

I noticed that Crocus was noting what I said, and I hoped I hadn't spoken out of turn.

"She always had a strong belief in communicating with those—those who had passed," said Lincoln. "Robert said that she just got carried away with it after they attacked Washington and Tad died—and my injury, of course."

"She knows you're alive," I said, still speaking out.

"I had hoped to visit her this spring, since I have been feeling better. Before I was sunk—I was, ah, not well and wished not to trouble her fragile mind."

"Do you hope to reunite with her, then?" asked Crocus.

"If she is well enough to take the shock of seeing me with white hair," said Lincoln, smiling, and then more seriously. "Yes, sir, I would like to see dear Mary once again." He glanced out the window, the depth of emotion showing in his glistening eyes. Then, to me he said, "Perhaps, Captain, you could get word to her. It would be wonderful for her to join us at the little get-together I have planned."

"What have you planned?" asked Crocus.

"Oh, a reunion of old soldiers, I guess you'd call it. I've been corresponding with a few friends out West."

"Oh, really?" said Crocus. If he was interested before, he was even more at attention now.

"Yup. Friends from out West. A certain shopkeeper from Galena and a runty, red-haired injun fighter."

"Grant and Sherman," said Crocus. "They are coming here!"

"Yes," Lincoln said. "Last time I checked, free white men could assemble peaceably in this country. Grant is coming in a couple days, Sherman hopes to follow soon."

I shook my head at this news. The telegraph wires would be burning up when word of this got out. But I thought for a moment of Forrest and his call for vengeance on Lincoln. A chill went up my spine. Did we have enough men?

Even Crocus seemed concerned, for he said, "There is supposed to be free speech in the Confederate States, but in reality, since the war—"

"Bullies and hoodlums have frightened into submission those who oppose the policies of the current administration," said Lincoln, with some of his old fire showing. "I, for one, will not hide any longer."

I swallowed hard at this declaration, fingering the Sharp's carbine I was now carrying with me while on duty.

"When will this convention take place?" Crocus asked when he looked up again.

"Next week. We thought we'd gather on April 16th, Easter Sunday. Seemed like a good time for new beginnings."

"For coming back from the dead…" said Crocus, mostly to himself, writing furiously. He looked up and cried, "Good Lord, Mr. President. You're going to make me famous!"

"Blame the good Lord then, not me."

Crocus rushed away to get the word of these developments out on the wire, and I supposed there would be a special edition of the *Pithole Daily Record* today. In fact, the Franklin reporter and the gent from *The Oil City Derrick* were next in line, but Lincoln would not see them. He knew that those papers had Copperhead sympathies, so they would have to get their news from Crocus second-hand.

After the newsmen had departed to get their stories out, one of the other Bucktails brought Reverend Steadman in to see his old charge. I had not seen him since he had reprimanded me on the street for imbibing spiritous beverages. He had not warmed to me in the meantime, for he brushed past me without a word of greeting to go meet Lincoln. They stayed in consultation in the room for some time, and I heard laughter from inside the room. But when he left he passed by me again without a greeting. In fact, without so much as a friendly glance my way. No doubt thinking of the prophet's word: *thou art of purer eyes than to behold iniquity.*

Chastity came by just moments later, her pretty chin lifted so she didn't have to acknowledge me either. She walked past and slammed the door to Lincoln's room as she entered, just in case I hadn't noticed she was still angry with me. If I had come to Pithole to make enemies, I was doing quite well.

Chapter Thirty-one

John Wilkes-Booth

Booth picked up the horses at the Metropolitan Hotel and walked them down the hill to the train station. He had to pass the Danforth Hotel on the way, and it raised his ire to see two Bucktail Rangers idling on the porch, Sharp's carbines slung over their shoulders. Damn them! He should have struck at Lincoln when he was skulking in the woods. Now it would be much harder to get rid of the old fool.

He tied the horses at the rail near the waiting platform, but didn't stray too far from the sight of them. Stealing one horse made a man a criminal; stealing two made him a teamster—which reminded him of that horse-thief Marcus, the reason he was here standing in the cold April weather waiting for Stumpf. Booth smiled when he saw the man disembark from the first coach. He wasn't hard to spot wearing a canvas duster and tall boots, with a Kentucky long rifle in one hand and a saddlebag in the other.

"John Stumpf!" Booth called out to him.

"Mr…" he pulled a folded telegram from his pocket. "Wilkes-Booth?"

"In the flesh!" Booth declared, vigorously shaking Stumpf's hand. He liked the look of this slave-catcher. Tall and lean, with a hard cast to his eyes. Just what he needed.

"Gotta get my dogs," Stumpf said, picking up his bags again and heading back to the open doors of the baggage car.

"You're from near Frederick?" asked Booth.

"Yup."

"I'm from near there. We might have even been neighbors, at some point."

The slave-catcher looked at Booth dubiously and then replied, "Never seen you before."

"Perhaps you've heard of my performances at the theatre in Hagerstown?"

"I heard of an *Edwin* Booth," Stumpf said, cocking his head to one side. "But I don't attend theatres. My wife's a Methodist."

"Ah," Booth nodded. Well, that explained a few things.

"Now this here Marcus fellar," said Stumpf, reading the name from the telegram. "You think he's headed north on horseback?"

"Um hum. Stolen horse. Took money from some Pinkertons to get his start. Shot another slave while escaping."

"That'll be an extra hunerd," said Stumpf. "Hazard pay."

Booth met his eyes. They were a strange blue, reminding him of one of his mother's sayings: *lit with demon fire*. Yes, exactly what he needed. "I don't mind if it costs more. He's a valuable town slave."

"Might be more money if I have to bring him back unblemished."

"I'm not opposed to you using the lash," said Booth, nodding to one that was coiled on top of his satchel. "Just don't overdo it. I plan to sell him next week, as soon as I acquire his replacement." With a twinge of anticipation, Booth thought of how he intended to gain the mulatto girl at the raffle…

"I use the lash sparingly, but well," said Stumpf, picking up the whip and running it through his fingers. "Just takes a little practice."

The baggage handler unloaded two ash crates with yelping dogs of an odd breed. Stumpf apparently anticipated Booth's unspoken question and volunteered, "They's blue tick hounds."

"Handsome beasts."

"It ain't their looks what matters. They never tucker out. They could run down the devil hisself, if needs be."

With that, Stumpf unlatched the gates to their cages, and the two dogs began leaping about and barking. Booth leaned back away from them and their prominent teeth.

"You have the cloak?"

Booth handed him one of Marcus's shirts from a Gladstone bag, as well as a crisp white envelope containing five hundred dollars Confederate.

"Thank ye," said Stumpf, mounting up and tucking the money in a vest pocket under his long, tan duster. "I'll start at Petroleum Centre and head north from there."

"How will you find his trail?"

Stumpf looked at him with disdain. "It's what I do," he said, flicking the reins of his horse. "I'll send you a telegram when I've got him treed."

And with that, he galloped off up the hill, the hounds in hot pursuit.

"Treed," Booth said aloud and clapped his hands together. "Splendid!"

Chapter Thirty-Two

Ezekiel Edwards

After my shift at Lincoln's room, I returned to the well. One reason I wanted to return was because Tinker was to have delivered our first barrels of oil to the railhead to be transported. He thought we might obtain a thousand dollars or more for our first batch—more than a year's wages for most men. All in three days time!

"Hey there, moneybags," Tinker said when he spotted me coming down the hillside at sunset.

"I wish. How'd we do?"

"Fifteen hundred," Tinker said, grinning and pulling out the cash from inside of his jacket. The black walnut butt of his revolver was nestled in right beside it in his coat. "Price went up since yesterday!"

"What are last week's bills?"

"Four hundred," he said, with a tilt of the head.

"Give me a thousand. Then you can pay our creditors and Enos."

He counted out ten Confederate hundreds, with Jeff Davis's gaunt face on each. I tucked them in my pocket, right beside the small revolver Mortenson had given me yesterday.

"It will be with pleasure that I pay off Booth. If things go well over the next few weeks we can be free of him *and* Stottish."

"I thought you were quite taken with those gents."

"More taken in, than taken with. Not sure I trust Stottish, and Booth's a Copperhead through and through."

I put my hand to the plank door of the engine room. Tinker placed his beside mine to stop me. "Daniel's in there resting," he said.

"Josiah kicked him out?"

"Too much noise and commotion at the saloon. He asked to come here."

"Shhh," Tinker said, pushing the door open. He looked in, "That Susanna has been a real blessing. She's hardly left his side."

True enough, as Tinker pulled the door open on creaky iron hinges

I saw Susanna dozing beside Daniel. She was leaning in, with her head resting on a pillow beside his, her hand reaching forward to clutch his hand. The creaking of the hinges woke them both. Daniel's eyes fluttered open, and he smiled briefly mouthing the word "Cap'n."

"I'm sorry for what happened, Daniel. We all are," I said with a nod to Tinker.

Susanna's dark eyes met mine. Was she still mad at me for causing this whole mess?

"Thank you for all you've done for him," I told her.

"In awhile I have to go up to Josiah's to work. He's hiring a new girl, and I have to help train her…" she said, her voice drifting off.

I wondered what training a new girl entailed? But then, I wasn't sure I really wanted to know, "I won't tarry. I intend to go into town to see Mr. Booth. I owe him some money."

Susanna caught my eye. I thought of the last time I'd seen them together, heading up to her room. I chose not to bring that sore subject up. Tinker, still nearby looked from her to me, not comprehending. Daniel had already drifted back to sleep. I tipped my hat to her and Tinker and headed to town.

* * *

At the Metropolitan Hotel, I walked in on a dinner party in progress.

"Ezekiel, so nice to see you!" Booth said when he spotted me at the door. A warm reception was not what I had expected, and then I saw that he had one of the side rooms of the theatre set aside for a sumptuous repast.

"May I have just a few moments alone with you, Mr. Booth?" I asked.

"Later. Come, there's someone I want you to meet."

The smell of chowder and roasted meat assailed my senses. Well, perhaps I could stay, just for a spell. He shepherded me into the small conference room where a fire blazed before a group of well-dressed people who were crowded around a tall, handsome man holding a glass of bourbon.

"Edwin, this is my associate, Captain Edwards!"

The small circle turned to me as one, and I spotted Lydia looking radiant in a dark green satin dress. Booth's brother turned as well, and with a gleaming smile extended his hand.

"Captain Edwards! Such a pleasure! John Wilkes speaks highly of you, which is quite a feat considering his warped political views!"

"He is a strong supporter of our new president," I said.

"Yes. Our sister, Asia and I have had to quite disown him. He is an absolute boor with his prattling about the Confederacy. We haven't the faintest idea where he gets his notions!"

I noticed John Wilkes' smile had become a bit strained, and perhaps so did Lydia's for she interjected, "Mr. Edwards, I must introduce you to Edwin's lovely child, Edwina. Come with me."

I looked longingly at the buffet of oysters and a joint of juicy red beef as she pulled me along to Booth's side-office room. I did notice that the room seemed somewhat disheveled— Booth had no servants to tidy up after him. In the midst of strewn books and papers, Lydia's son Jesse and a pretty little girl were playing a game of jacks on the floor.

"Edwin lost his wife two years ago," explained Lydia. "He dotes on little Edwina and takes her everywhere with him while he's on tour. She's the same age as my Jesse."

Both children smiled at me and then returned their attention to the game. Through the door there were peals of laughter about something John Wilkes was saying. Edwin stood off to one side, smiling but not joining in the gaiety.

"Those two brothers look very much alike, but Edwin is much more well-mannered." She paused and then whispered to me as we entered the buffet line, "I hate to say it, but I wish I had met him first!" She laughed then, but I wondered if she were jesting or serious.

I filled my plate as Lydia continued to accompany me to the dessert section where a variety of cakes and bread and plum puddings tempted me sorely.

"I appreciate you bringing Chastity back to town. Her father is grateful."

I shrugged. I wasn't sure Stottish still held a good opinion of me since I had fought with the Pinkertons, but I didn't mention this.

"You should invite her to see *MacBeth*. Mr. Booth has reserved a block of seats in the balcony."

"She currently is not speaking to me," I said, studying my food.

Lydia laughed out loud.

"What?"

"She's smitten!"

I shook my head in disbelief. Lydia reached her hand to me across the table and said, "Trust me on this one, Captain Edwards. I know Chastity. Ask her to go see *MacBeth*. You can join John Wilkes and me in our private box. It will be the event of the spring season."

When I had finished eating dinner I managed to nab Booth out in the hallway away from the guests. His tone held a touch of irritation as he finally turned his attention to me. "Yes, Ezekiel, what do you need? I hope you don't want more money to keep drilling your well."

"No," I said, relishing the surprise of my response. "I need to give you back some of the money I borrowed. The well is flowing."

"Flowing? Not being pumped?"

"Flowing, about fifty barrels a day."

"Tremendous! That is wonderful news!"

"Here's the thousand dollars I borrowed last week. There'll be more coming. We intend to pay a dividend on shares soon."

Booth riffled through the stack of bills and smiled, "Ah, the Golden Grease! There's nothing quite like it!"

"I appreciate your patience. I hope this is just the first-fruits of our labor."

Booth grinned and stuffed the money into his trouser pocket. He slapped me on the back, causing me to wince sharply. But he took no notice and said, "I have just the thing to invest this money in! Wonderful!"

And with that, I went back to say goodbye to the other guests, spotting Lydia in the back room. She stood silhouetted against the back window, her head tilted down reading a small book as the children picked up their toys and put their wraps on under the supervision of Edwin Booth. I was just about to cross the room to say goodbye when something about her countenance gave me pause. Her mouth opened in a round *O* and the book fell from her hands. She looked right and then left, like a deer trapped on a snowy lane when a sleigh approaches. She stepped quickly forward and roughly grabbed Jesse's arm, hard enough to make him cry out in pain. And then she dragged him off with her through the dining room, past a startled John Wilkes-Booth and right out the front door.

Edwin looked after her and looked at me, then took his daughter's hand and pulled her away. There was a commotion in the dining room over Lydia's sudden departure and several of the guests went out on the porch to see what was happening. I stepped further back into the office and retrieved the small, leather-bound brown book she had dropped face-down on the floor. I leaned back into the lamplight and noticed that the cover bore a simple legend: CONQUESTS OF J.W.B.

I opened the front page, which had the opening title *Teenage Years*. And there followed a list of girls' names, starting with *Heather*. In Wilkes' flowing hand I began reading:

long, dark hair; dark eyes; skin like white parchment, smooth and unblemished; first kiss—by the old bridge; after two glasses of some port wine she allowed me to remove her outer garments; enjoyed tickling and love play.

It continued on in that vein, and I soon saw that it was a journal of his *amorous* experiences, to put it politely; page after page of names and dates. I tuned out the cacophony of noise as I skimmed the book. Many were of very young girls seduced after performances. One engagement of *Hamlet* yielded several such trysts. Many of the listings were of brothels attended and the quality of the prostitutes and accommodations. There was even the remarkably young daughter of a Senator from Massachusetts named therein and an account of the young woman in Baltimore who had slashed his face with his own razor when she found him with another girl the same night he had taken her virginity.

I flipped toward the end of the book and found Lydia's name. *Lydia, Stottish's niece* it began. I didn't read that account. Two pages later I saw Susanna's name, and I was just beginning to read about her when he grabbed the journal and shoved me back against the wall. But not before I had seen one last name—for a conquest not yet completed—*Chastity Stottish*. A cauldron of anger began boiling up inside me. He had his sights set on Stottish's daughter next.

"That's mine," he said in a hoarse voice. Apparently, he had been shouting at Lydia outside. "Damn that Marcus for leaving it about."

"Obviously," I said, unable to hide the scorn in my voice, "should make for interesting reading come Judgment Day."

"God will judge me—and I fear Him not. At least *I* have not broken my wedding vows with young women. Susanna confided to me what *you* have done," Booth said, leering at me.

I pointed at the book he held, "No. You just seduce foolish women into breaking *their* vows to *their* husbands–and rape underage girls in their parents' beds."

I didn't even see the punch coming. The next thing I knew, time had passed and I was being helped up by Edwin Booth who was holding his handkerchief to my damaged nose. "Tilt your head back, if you would be so kind, Captain Edwards."

My eyes were blurry. I had been knocked back, first into the brick fireplace, and then I must have fallen forward onto the floor, unconscious. There was a bloody smear where I had landed, and I bled from the nose until helped by Edwin.

"My apologies, Captain," Edwin sighed. "I'm afraid my brother's behavior prematurely ended the evening's festivities. Perhaps he has gone off to sulk with one of his floozies at the New Idea brothel. We won't see him again tonight."

"I hope not," I said, rubbing my jaw, which hurt even more than my shoulder. "I only have a limited supply of laudanum."

We both sat down on a settee beside the door to the dining room. All the other guests had gone, and Edwina must have been taken away, as well.

"My brother has long been a source of…" Edwin searched for a word, "*consternation* to the rest of the family."

"He seems to have found success on the stage and in business," I said, trying to be civil.

"You know, Captain Edwards, I think that is at the root of his problems. Things have always come too easy for him. Money, fame," and with a nod to the small brown book he added, "women."

I nodded, which hurt. But it also hurt to speak, so I just listened.

"He takes after our father, Junius Brutus Booth. You've heard of him?"

I nodded again, wincing as I did so.

"A marvelous thespian. A great, great man, in many ways. But…I must say it…his character was deeply flawed. He was never faithful to any of his wives, my mother included—and his rages!"

I noticed that Booth clenched and unclenched his fist at the memory. "Like father, like son?" I ventured, though it hurt.

"I pray not, at least in my case," Edwin Booth said sadly.

Not without a struggle, I got to my feet and took my leave. I saw Edwin on the sidewalk, his hand clasped by his fair young daughter who was skipping along beside him and smiling. I thought back to Lydia's comment, "Hard to believe they are brothers." But I disagreed, for I remembered the story of Abel and his brother, Cain.

Chapter Thirty-three

As I stumbled down the hill, I felt as if my head were a bell that had just been soundly rung. I drank a glass of whiskey before I departed, but it did nothing to dull the pain in my nose and upper front teeth, and I thought that this must have been what it felt like to be kicked in the face by a horse.

I paused at a derrick partway down the hill to take a bit of medicine. In the pale moonlight I read the sign *Rebel Yell Well* crudely lettered with charcoal on the pine-slab siding. I shuddered, remembering that sound, the image of crazed, bloodthirsty rebel soldiers charging toward us with muskets blazing, and the cannon being unlimbered at the edge of the trees…and the canister being loaded…and…I took another swig of the tonic.

I had been doing a bit better on my consumption lately, but the damp weather of the coming of spring seemed to make it worse. And the whiskey I drank with Edwin hadn't touched that pain in my face and head. I sighed and sipped from the bottle again. I had a familiar emotion, one I remembered from my days at the hospital: *I wish I were well.* I wanted to be free of the constant toothache pain in my shoulder that so often woke me at night and was like an unwanted companion by day. I wished that I had my health back.

I shoved off from the mooring of the derrick and went down to the well. If things had been going badly up in town, they were going worse down in the flats. Tinker met me grim faced at the door. I could tell from that look that something bad had happened.

"He didn't make it?" I asked as the dog added to the confusion by barking and putting his feet up on me in greeting.

"No, he left us," Tinker said.

I clenched my fist in anger, "It's all my fault."

"No. It's the water that done it," Tinker said, "It was the last straw for Enos."

"What? Fluid in his lungs?"

Tinker looked at me like I was deranged, "Hell no, Captain. Though

Daniel does seem more feverish again since sunset. I'm talking about the well. It's flooded."

I stepped into the engine house. Susanna was applying a damp cloth to Daniel's forehead. She looked at me anxiously.

"Where's Enos?" I asked.

"Don't you listen to nothing? The well's flooded! He skedaddled. I paid him off, and he's gone."

"So what now?" I said, thinking, my head must be foggy from laudanum. This was very bad news, but I could barely comprehend it.

"Well, if we had some more money, we could start again. Just move the derrick over and try to miss the groundwater. Or, we could buy a lease somewhere else—this valley might be getting played out."

"I'm not on the best of terms with Booth or Stottish at the moment," I said, thinking of my sore nose and head.

"I'd say we're in a tough spot then," said Tinker.

"I'll stay and work for shares," said Daniel, his eyes now on us.

"Don't be working for nothing," Susanna said, a comment a wife would make. Or was she alluding to my habit of not paying for "services rendered?"

Tinker had been drinking from a large mason jar of applejack. I took a swig; it was stronger than Booth's whiskey, so I took another one.

"I'm not asking anyone to stay and work for nothing," I said. "I'd be willing to split the shares in the well three ways once Booth is paid off."

"A three-way split of nothing is nothing," said Susanna.

"Who asked you?" I asked, starting to lose my temper. What made it worse was she was right.

"Now, wait a second," Tinker said, stepping between us. "Captain Edwards has paid us for a month now and bought all the tools and supplies. He's the one that owes Booth three thousand dollars. Still, I say we salvage the derrick and drill again over at the corner of the lease."

"The Clancy boys have a dry well right by that corner," said Susanna.

"How'd you get into this discussion?" I said. In the back of my mind was the way she'd betrayed me with Booth. I still held a grudge.

"Fine. I'll just leave, then. Josiah wants me up the hill, anyways." It took her only a moment to don her coat, grab her bag and brush past me to the door.

"You comin' back?" Daniel asked. But she was gone.

"She has been a big help around here, Captain. She's cleaned Dan's wound twice a day," said Tinker.

"We were talking about starting over. Who's for it?" I said, ignoring the subject of Susanna for the moment.

"Well," said Tinker. "The weather is improving. Be a lot easier to rebuild the derrick in warm weather."

"We'll just have to do our best," said Daniel, his eyes drifting closed. "I do hope Susanna does come back, though."

His words struck at my heart. He had nearly given his life for this venture, and how had I repaid him? I set down the mason jar Tinker had given me, noticing it was now empty. "I'll go talk to her," I said, though I hated the thought of leaving the warm comfort of the boiler room and climbing that hill again tonight. "I'll come back down tomorrow after my guard duties. We can get started tearing down the derrick."

But as I stepped out into the damp cold I thought, *who am I kidding?* A one-armed man and a Contraband with a chest wound. Tinker couldn't build a fifty-foot derrick by himself! It seemed our mission had failed for good this time.

I followed Susanna's steps up the hill. If I could catch up to her before she reached Josiah's, perhaps I could reason with her to return to Daniel and keep nursing him—at least in the morning. Perhaps I could calm her down, and we could share our old room again. The thought of spending another night alone and hurting from aches and pains seemed too much to bear. Perhaps, if I spoke comfortably to her? Isn't that what Isaiah had said: *Speak ye comfortably to Jerusalem?* That might work. And if not, I still had one fifty dollar bill left in my pocket.

The flats were as quiet as a grave, but the town above was as raucous as a Saturday night in hell. Streetlamps glowed, Irishmen walked arm-in-arm singing bawdy songs, Booth's theatre had just let out, and doves cried out for patrons among the rowdy male crowd heading back to their hotels and boardinghouses. From one corner I heard the thin, reedy voice of the crazy, wild-haired preacher crying out his jeremiads. I caught up with Susanna near the foundation of the new jail, just across from the Danforth Hotel.

"Susanna, wait up," I said, still out of breath from the climb up the hill and from too much laudanum and alcohol. "I wanted to speak with you a moment before you reach Josiah's."

"You said enough down there. I don't need to hear any more of your schemes."

"My request is for Daniel, not myself," I said, though that wasn't quite the truth.

Her tone softened. "I like Daniel. I would like to see him get better, but I am still obligated to Josiah. I need to work if I want to eat."

"Well, I'd be happy to pay you for this evening," I ventured. Looking at her in the streetlamp's glow she was *pleasant to the eyes,* as Eve said of the apple.

"What?" Susanna said, her voice rising. I could see color forming in her cheeks. She was feeling it too—the first stirrings of passion.

I leaned closer, noticing that my balance was slightly perturbed, and I whispered, "I'd like to procure your services for the evening. I greatly—"

"What!" Even on the noisy streets of Pithole, her voice carried above the din.

"Shhh!" I said, noticing with irritation that I was slurring my words. Damn that Tinker and his apple hooch! "Look," I continued. "I have some money still." I pulled the fifty from my pocket and held it out for her to see.

She grabbed if from me, like an owl snatching a mouse from a field, and I thought: *Good, she's taken the bait.* But in one swift motion, she ripped it in half and tossed it in the air.

"I wouldn't do that with *you* for all the money in the world, Ezekiel Edwards!"

Curtains stirred in some of the rooms above us in the Danforth Hotel. I noticed a dark figure cross the street and head our way. But mostly, I noticed that the very last of my money was being trampled into the mud. I couldn't restrain myself. I lost all control, and I reached out and slapped her.

She immediately launched herself into me, kicking and screaming, pulling at my hair. We both toppled over into the dirty and muddy snow on the roadside. She was actually getting the better of me with her nails when I felt a strong arm pick me up and drag me away. Susanna rolled to her feet, blew her hair out of her eyes and stomped away to Josiah's place. I was startled to see that it was Reverend Steadman who had me by the collar.

"Well, look who it is. The drunken lout, Ezekiel Edwards accosting a woman in the street. Too bad the jail isn't finished—I could drag you right in the front door."

"Fuck you, Reverend Steadman!" I yelled at him, shocking myself almost sober at my own words.

Lanterns now illuminated the windows of the hotel above, and I heard gasps of horror at my shouted imprecation. Even Susanna flinched as she hurried away.

I expected him to strike me down or stomp me into the mud. But instead, he leaned close and in a quiet voice he whispered, "You're not angry at me, Captain Edwards. You're angry at God."

And with that, he let go of my collar, and I slid back into the icy mire.

Chapter Thirty-four

Chastity Stottish

Chastity Stottish watched the scene unfolding in the street below, having just finished preparing Mr. Lincoln for bed. She had heard Captain Edwards shouting, his queer New England accent unmistakable, and had looked out to see some floozy launch herself at him. That hussy must be trying to drag him off to some brothel, she surmised. The nerve! Chastity left the window, still hearing the screaming and yelling from the street below as she slipped into her winter coat and pulled on some slippers. She ran down the stairs and out into the street just in time to see the dark figure of Reverend Steadman saying something quietly to Edwards before hurrying after the prostitute; probably to arrest her and get her off the streets—the witch.

"Ezekiel, are you all right?" Chastity asked as she ran across the road to offer him assistance.

He looked up at her, appearing stunned, lifting a hand as if to ward off another attack. Then, he realized it was her and not that evil cat that had scratched him mercilessly. She pulled out her handkerchief and dabbed at his face. Why, it looked as if the wretch had even bloodied his nose!

"Chastity?" he said, sounding confused.

"Oh, Ezekiel," she said, leaning down and putting her cheek next to his. She lifted him as she had been trained in nursing school, cradling his lower back with her hands and pulling him gently upright, "I'm sorry I was so rude to you in the carriage yesterday. You didn't deserve that."

He just looked at her, not seeming to comprehend. Had he been hit on the head?

"I regret it also," he said as he regained his feet, looking about for his hat. "Lately, I'm afraid I've had too much to drink—and far too much laudanum."

"Your shoulder still pains you. You can't fool me."

"Thank you for your kindness, Chastity. I'm afraid I've made quite a fool of myself this evening. I should be going."

She noticed he looked around as if he were not sure which way *to* go. She wondered again if he had been struck on the head. He might be disoriented and not be aware of it. "Ezekiel, come inside and let me dress those scratches. You really look a fright!"

He smiled, but his injured face made him wince. She took his hand and led him inside and up the stairs to her room. As she opened the door to let him in, the older married couple who shared the room next door appeared. They had attended the program at Booth's theatre and were returning; but when they saw her leading the dirty and disheveled man into her room the matron gave her a disapproving glare.

"Sit down while I get some warm water from the stove," she said, paying them no attention. In the lamplight of her room he looked even more beat up than on the street. Her heart went out to him. He was too much of a gentleman to strike back at a woman. If only her father had lived by the same code. "She not only scratched you badly, she nearly broke your nose!" Chastity cried as she gently washed away the blood.

"I got in a fight with John Wilkes-Booth earlier in the evening. Then, there were some problems at the well."

"What did you fight with Booth about?"

"I got caught between him and Lydia." He paused as she brought another warm cloth to his face. The water in the basin was turning pink.

"They were brawling?" Chastity said, shocked.

"She found…evidence of his infidelity."

"I could have told her that."

"Oh?"

"He's tried to charm me."

"Did it work?"

"No."

"Women seem to find him irresistible."

"I resisted," Chastity said. She had him looking quite a bit better now. The scratches were not deep and with the crusted blood removed he was looking like himself again. In fact, looking quite good, she had to admit. "Lean forward so I can inspect your scalp."

He obliged, and she ran her fingers through his thick, wavy hair feeling his scalp. No damage she could find. But she let her fingers continue—she could tell he liked it.

"Ahhh. You're doing it again."

"What?"

"Going a bit beyond the call of duty as a nurse." He caught her hand.

With his other he circled her waist and pulled her to him, "Will you also resist *me?*"

She felt his hand reach up to her hair. It must be a mess! But if it were, he didn't seem to notice. She leaned toward him, her resolve weakening. He must have sensed it because he pulled her gently in to him and his hand drew her mouth near for a kiss. She should draw back, but his breath smelled of apples and when his eyes met hers he drew her further in. Then, he kissed her gently, and she sat on his knee and leaned forward and let him hold her. He lifted her chin for yet another kiss, but they were interrupted by a sharp rap on the door.

"Chastity, open up! It's your father!"

She gasped, jumped away from Edwards and hissed, "Hide!"

Chapter Thirty-five

Ezekiel Edwards

I awoke the next morning to a pounding on the door of the engine house and the sound of Bobby Lee barking like a crazed wolf. I had curled up in the corner close to the boiler and had slept fitfully after what had been one of the worst nights of my life—except for the brief time near the end when Chastity had taken me to her room. But even that was spoilt when her father stopped by on his way home from the theatre. She'd quickly gotten rid of me then and had given me an embarrassed *adieu*. My head pounded, and my face felt like a bobcat had clawed it; and now, someone was demanding my attention at the crack of dawn. Damn them.

"You know someone named Stumpf?" Tinker asked.

I arose from my pallet and went to the door. Tinker had to grab Bobby Lee because the man at the door had two hounds tethered to his horse, and they strained at their leads wanting to attack him. The tall stranger turned to them and snarled, "Hush!" and the two beasts whined and lay down.

"John Stumpf, slave-catcher," the man said, extending his hand. He was taller than me; lean and grizzled looking, with deep-blue eyes like Pennsylvania slate. He extended a coarse, dry hand and asked, "You Edwards?"

"Yes."

"What's your address in Salem, Massachusetts?"

"Fifty-four Derby. Why do you ask?"

"I've got something with your name and address on it. Taken off a slave I cotched."

I shook my head, knowing I wasn't dreaming, but my foggy brain struggled to make sense of what he was saying. From his cloak he pulled out two ratty-looking envelopes—stuffed with old greenbacks and newer Confederate notes. I looked at them for just a moment before it dawned on me what he had—my inheritance!

"Where did you get this?"

"From the satchel of the man who took it. Not sure how much of it he pilfered or when it was stolen from you. But he was a liar and a thief like his father, Satan."

"I greatly appreciate your honesty in returning it. This was an inheritance from my mother, who died while I was away at war," I told him.

"People shouldn't take what ain't theirs," Stumpf said, an odd glow to his blue eyes. "That's why I return slaves." With a nod, he indicated Daniel sleeping on a pallet behind the stove. "That darkie there. Who owns him?"

"I do," Tinker spoke up from behind me. "Purchased by my father," he added, with a slight drawl. It was a ruse we had employed behind lines during the war. Tinker could pull it off, but I couldn't, not with a Boston accent.

"Keep an eye on him. If he takes off, send me a wire." He handed me a card that bore the name **John Stumpf—Slave-Catcher** in bold letters. Beneath his name was a telegraph station number and a mailing address. "Good day to you, gentlemen," he said and with a low whistle, his dogs leapt to their feet.

"Wait," I called after him. "Can I give you a reward for your service?"

"Been paid for my service already," he said, saddling up. "And my reward shall surely be a mansion in the heavenly realms."

I would have laughed if he had not been dead serious.

When he was gone Tinker said, "That is one strange man." He looked at me as I riffled through the bills. "Good lord, Captain. Those are all hundred dollar bills." He grinned and slapped his thigh.

"There's more here than I inherited," I said in surprise.

This exchange caught Daniel's attention. He sat up in bed, coughed once, then held his hand to his mouth for a moment and said, "Captain, that's enough to drill a new well, ain't it?"

I finished counting the bills, nodding as I did so. "Enough to drill again and pay off both Booth and Stottish! Boil some coffee boys, we're back in business!"

* * *

I was in a jovial mood when I returned up the hill to serve my shift guarding Lincoln. But Lincoln was not. He shoved the morning's paper my way, and I read:

A WINTER'S MORNING RESPONSE FROM PRESIDENT LEE

The ever-gracious and gentlemanly President Lee has tendered his response to the remarks of Mr. Lincoln first printed in The Pithole Daily Record and later in The New York Herald Tribune:
My esteemed former colleague: I have read with interest your late remarks on the topic of Emancipation. May I offer first my regards to you and your family and our delight in hearing that so great a voice has not been stilled by the serious injuries which you so unfortunately suffered during the sack of Washington, D.C. Let me share with you some of my thoughts on this topic.

Part the First: Natural Rights: My policy has always been that the African and American Indian races, though inferior, are yet God's children. As such, they are entitled to many of the natural rights which all people strive to attain.
Part the Second: That co-mingling of the races is not part of the natural order—that is why our forefathers made clear in our country's Constitution that this was to be a nation of Free White Men.

Conclusion: That the native Indian races and the African races should be settled elsewhere and that our government, therefore, shall vigorously pursue and fund a POLICY OF MANUMISSION to end these seemingly endless conflicts that inter-mixing of the races cause.

"Manumission?" I said looking to Lincoln who was slumped in his chair, a hand splayed at his temples in consternation.

"What makes it so damn galling is that *I* could have written that ten years ago. But not now—not after what we've been through."

I looked down and continued reading:

Therefore, I am proposing not an Emancipation Proclamation, which can only result in anarchy and disunion, but a different solution, which I have entitled THE MANUMISSION PROCLAMATION. My proposal is that all Native Indian people be granted lands in the Great American West. For there they will be productive and happy to live amongst their own.

*Likewise, I propose that a fleet of ships be prepared by my government
to transport all African slaves back to Africa and to replace them
with Immigrant workers of the white races of Europe—transported
to these shores by the same ships and at no expense. These new workers
will each serve an appropriate period of time of indenture and…*

"He's trying to steal our thunder!" Lincoln said angrily. "He must
have spies that know our plans."

Our plans? I wasn't sure what he meant. What secret plan had he
concocted? I thought of the letters to the West he had been composing at
the cabin in the woods. "You're referring to Grant's former army?"

He looked at me oddly, as if actually noticing my presence clearly, "I
forget you're a new member of our team. But yes, Grant's men are already
on the move. They will soon be positioned to strike the new capital at
Richmond."

"A military coup? You would attempt that?"

"Not exactly—though with God's help we will overthrow them. But
we must do it quickly, before Lee has the chance to implement his plan
to deport all the Africans. If he can get that underway, all hope is lost."

"Yes, but begging your pardon, sir. Wouldn't that solve the problem?"

"No! It's the whole rotten Southern system that's the problem—
that there are to be two classes in America—the indolent aristocracy
and the workers. That's the problem. They just wish to perpetuate it.
Permanently."

"But what of their *Golden Circle* of prosperity built on the slave
trade?"

"First, it will be built on the backs of slave labor; then, using
indentured servants; and then, mere wage slaves toiling for barely enough
to keep flesh on their bones. But always the aristocrats at ease in their
mansions—*and the rest of the world be damned!*"

There was fire in his gaze, and he flailed his great strong hands about.
And then, I realized who was talking—the rail-splitter—the man who
had lifted himself out of poverty with a strong back and two strong
hands. He rested his hands on the arms of his wheeled chair and gazed at
me intently, "Captain, I need your help. We must send a wire to Grant to
speed the process along. Time is of the essence now. Could you fetch me
some writing materials?"

From a nearby desk I brought him a pencil and pad. From his pocket he withdrew a penknife and sharpened it to a better point, his hands quick and skilled. He touched the tip of the pencil to his tongue, his brow furrowed in concentration, and I noticed him write *Attention: General U.S. Grant* and in clear, block letters he continued with his orders.

"Take this to the telegraph office for me, and make sure it's delivered," he said. The act of writing seemed to have calmed him, his speech now gentle.

I reached down to take the pad, and he noticed something else.

"Is it your arm that was shot?" he asked, those gray eyes searching my face.

"Canister, sir. At Gettysburg—the first day."

He nodded. Something in that look bade me continue.

"I led an ill-advised charge. Lost most of my Company, 'bout the same time General Reynolds fell."

"Let that guilt go."

"Sir?"

"I said, *let that guilt go.*" His eyes met mine. He was used to being obeyed without question. He looked out the window into the harsh winter light, as if surveying distant battlefields. "Captain, how many men do you think I sent to their graves in ill-advised charges?" he turned his head back. The pale eyes bored into me.

I wanted to respond, but the frustration and shame of that day rose up in me, and I struggled to control my emotions. My eyes teared up, but I thought: *I can't let him see.*

He reached out a coarse hand, crusty with calluses from rolling the wheeled chair, "I wish I could shed a tear for each one lost. For each widow, for each orphan…but they are beyond numbering."

I looked down at the note clutched in my hands, still feeling ashamed.

"Soon, more men shall die—but these are not lives wasted. These are lives spent in a worthy cause. Think on that as you go."

I was heading down the stairs to go out when Chastity came up the other way bearing fresh linens. At the moment we met I was folding the telegraph message to place in my pocket, so I didn't see her immediately. I almost knocked her down the stairs.

"Well, that's not much of a greeting!" she said in surprise as I caught her arm with my free hand to keep her from losing her balance.

"My apologies. I was distracted for a moment."

"Last night?" she said, those deep brown eyes of hers just inches away.

"Yes?"

"I wish we had not been distracted then," she whispered and then gave me a quick, sisterly peck on the cheek before running past me up the stairs.

Chapter Thirty-six

My duty hours guarding Lincoln seemed to fly past that day, and soon I was heading down the hill. The sun had made a rare appearance in early afternoon, and there was a balmy, southwesterly breeze melting the snow under the trees and from the piles shoveled against buildings. Rivulets of water ran forth to join the larger Pithole Creek.

I forgot my fight with Booth, Susanna and Reverend Steadman and thought instead of the fresh smell and velvety smooth skin of Chastity as she had leaned forward and kissed me. It warmed my heart like the sun warming the cold hillside of Pithole City.

Down at the well, Tinker had set up his scaffolding and was removing planking from the derrick. To my surprise and relief, Daniel sat outside the boiler room on a bench, leaning back to let the sun warm him. His color was much improved.

"I would like to start de-nailing those boards, Captain. I feel much better today."

"What did Tinker say?"

"He said don't!"

"I agree. Give it another day or two. Let that wound fully heal."

He nodded and closed his eyes to soak up the sunshine. I donned a tool-pouch and hammer and climbed up to lend Tinker a hand. When I reached the top level of scaffolding, I spotted a lone rider working his way gingerly around the rocks and melting snow: John Wilkes-Booth.

"What are you doing to my well?" Booth asked in an impudent tone when he arrived, our quarrel from last night coloring his speech.

"Good afternoon, Mr. Booth. Pleasant day, isn't it?" I said. If he wasn't going to apologize for his violence toward me yesterday I wasn't going to kowtow to him today.

"I asked you a question. I expect an answer!"

"Pretty obvious, isn't it? We're tearing it down. It's flooded with water and useless."

"I heard it was pumping oil, and I was due a dividend! Where's that damn driller and that blacksmith? I want him fired!"

"I'm afraid you're too late," I said, avoiding his legitimate request for money. "Our driller is injured and can't work. Our blacksmith quit the job and left the area."

"Well, then this partnership is dissolved, I say! No more loans! Do you hear me Edwards? No more loans!"

"Then, I suppose you'll be wanting your money back?"

"Absolutely. And if I don't get it *immediately*, I will commence litigation."

"Immediately?" I asked him. I turned to Tinker who was prying on a plank siding board. "Did you hear that, Mr. Evans? Mr. Booth demands that I pay him *immediately!*" Out of Booth's sight I smiled and raised my eyebrows, so only Tinker could see me, and I showed him the corner of the envelope I had tucked away in my vest.

"Well," I said, turning back. "If you must have it *immediately*, then I guess I must comply with your wishes." And with that, I opened the envelope and began dispensing one hundred dollar Confederate notes. They wafted down on the warm spring breeze, floating this way and that, most of them landing in the oily mud or puddles and rivulets of the spring thaw.

Booth started scurrying around, mouthing obscenities as the flood of money began drifting all around our lease. A crew of teamsters laboring up the hill stopped in their tracks and approached eagerly. "Look, Ned," one of them shouted, "it's raining money!" Then, Bobby Lee got loose and began tearing around in circles barking wildly with excitement. When he got too close Booth lashed out at him, and the dog yelped.

I held up one bill, looking at the images engraved on it and yelled down to Booth, "You know, I never liked these bills with their loathsome images of happy slaves working in fields." I held one up to examine, "You can have all of them." And with that, I threw the last twenty or so of them in the air, and they spread out widely on a gust of wind, blowing all over the hillside.

"Damn you, Edwards! Damn you! You'll pay for this! You'll see!" Booth snarled up at me as he raced about grabbing his muddy prizes away from the boisterous crowd that had gathered. Bobby Lee circled close.

Tinker looked on, amused and said, "Guess that's what they mean by filthy lucre, eh Captain?"

Booth filled his pockets with the mud-encrusted money, then mounted his horse to the jeers of the oil field workers who, for once, saw a town dandy get the worst of it. "There'll be hell to pay for this, Edwards!" he shouted at me and raising a muddy fist in a convincing imitation of *Simon Legree* in *Uncle Tom's Cabin,* he galloped off up the hill.

I watched him go, not without a certain sense of satisfaction, I must admit. *Hell to pay,* I thought with a sense of foreboding. I no longer owed him money, and our friendship and business relationship was dissolved. What further vengeance could he possibly extract? Then, I thought of the last name in his little brown book—Chastity Stottish—and I wondered.

Chapter Thirty-seven

I was supping on corn chowder and biscuits at Josiah's when I heard the explosion. Josiah had just been telling me that he thought he might have lost Susanna for good now that she had taken a shine to Daniel.

"Perhaps that's for the best," I said. "I seem to have a talent for getting her riled up."

"I've noticed that—" Josiah said and was about to continue when a resounding boom filled the air, and the whole building shook.

"Someone's takin' a shot in the dark," a nearby driller said. He was slurping soup without even removing his hat.

"Didn't sound to me like gunfire," I said.

"No, you greenhorn," the driller replied, "shootin' a well with a nitro torpedo to make it flow. Roberts holds the patent—he shoots wells during the day. But there's other outfits do it at night so's they don't have to pay him—it's called *a shot in the dark*." He grinned, displaying a crooked set of bright, yellow teeth.

"Sounded too loud for that," Josiah said. "Sounded like a nitro wagon blowin' up."

At this, the driller with the yellow teeth smiled. "Too bad fer them fellars. Prob'ly got blowed to kingdom come."

Someone shouted from outside, "Fire! Fire in the flats!"

Those words killed the driller's smile. He stood, tossing his napkin aside and in a couple of long strides was out the door. I looked at Josiah, and my thoughts went to my own well, to Daniel, Tinker and Susanna down in the flats. I followed the man out the door and into the street. Men ran shouting, "Fire! Fight the fire!" Some had buckets and shovels, but most raced toward the bright light of the blazing inferno.

I caught up to the driller from Josiah's on First Street. "Lord Jesus, don't let it be my well!" he shouted. I made the same prayer as I raced alongside him, almost carried along by the throng of men pouring out of the town and into the valley. We ran past a banner that read SMOKE AND BE LYNCHED!, a grim reminder of how dangerous a fire could be in a place filled with oil, flammable gas, and wooden derricks. The spectacle of the flaming derrick up ahead lit up the night sky.

The scene of the explosion itself looked like a battlefield. Men ran everywhere, screaming and shouting. Smoke shifted about with the swirling wind and heat. Men were cursing as they flung shovelfuls of mud and bucketfuls of water at the burning ground.

I spotted Tinker's tall form off to one side. Next to him, Bobby Lee faced the fire and barked furiously. Men were throwing up earthworks to contain the flood of burning oil that flamed out at them, causing men to cry out and dive backwards into the mud. One man got flamed, and his clothes ignited. His companions tackled him instantly, rolling him sideways into the steaming slime, the flames guttering out as he was covered with mud and water, but not before he began screaming in pain from the burns.

The burned man's shovel lay unused on the ground, and Tinker darted forward and tossed it to me. We began shoveling like madmen, like soldiers trying to build a wall of dirt when the enemy was advancing fast. I tried to ignore the fresh pain this brought to my already-aching shoulder—but it would have hurt much worse if this had been *our* well, tools, derrick, boiler. Above us, the sky was illuminated by the flaming derrick, a jet of burning gas spewing from the top.

The dramatic scene ended as quickly as it had begun. The earthworks stopped the spread of flames to other wells, and the derrick was quickly consumed. With a resounding crash the remains fell down into the blackened mud. Men with shovels heaped slushy mud onto the last pockets of the fire. In the fading light of the embers I saw the charred carcass of the horse and nitro wagon that had blown up right beside the well.

The driller of the burned well walked around in shock muttering, "I'm ruined, I'm ruined." He tugged on Tinker's sleeve and turned his blackened face to us, "They done it on purpose! Why?"

"What?" Tinker responded.

"They yanked on a rope, tipped over the wagon and made it blow up!"

"Who did?"

"They was dressed up like ghosts!" The man said, running a black hand through gray hair slick with oil and soot. "Why the hell would they blow me up? I done nothin' to them ghosts!"

But I did, I thought, seeing the money floating down from the sky and Booth's face red with anger. They were Night Riders, come for revenge.

I grabbed the man's arm and said, "Which way did they go?"

He pointed toward our well, where Daniel was alone.

Tinker saw my fear and concern. He knew, too. We turned that way and ran.

We ran through the slick mud as fast as we could, but we were too late. Already, a circle of men stood mute at the foot of our derrick, looking up. I felt like someone had kicked me in the stomach as I looked up and saw a body dangling from the open lattice of our derrick—Daniel. Booth had extracted his vengeance. A wave of shock and dismay swept me from head to foot, and I sank down on my knees in the mud.

Tinker arrived just then, but said nothing, only put his face in his hands. Bobby Lee, black from the fire, sat beside him looking this way and that. Then, he spotted the body and began howling. I reached out to him, drew him to me to quiet and comfort him.

"It was during the fire," someone in the small circle said. "The Rebs used the explosion to cause a diversion—so they could hang your Contraband."

Behind him, another voice called out, "We oughta shoot us a few Rebs! Even the score!"

"Yeah, an eye for an eye!" Someone else shouted, to the approval of the crowd.

Tinker turned on them, tears showing on his blackened cheeks. "No!" he cried. There was silence for a moment. "This wasn't the Rebel soldiers. I fought them. They fight. They don't dress up like ghosts and come by night."

"Well, who was it then?"

"Men from the town," I said. "The ones who were too chicken to fight in the war."

The men grew quieter and moved closer. Tinker said to them, "All our property is in danger. Vengeance won't help him," he said, pointing upwards. "But if we band together, post guards, next time might be different for those cowards."

There were nods of agreement. A plan was made to provide for defense. A couple of the younger, stronger men volunteered to help us with the burial. They climbed up and untied the rope that bound the body to the tower and began slowly lowering it to the ground.

Tinker and I watched as the body descended in the dim moonlight.

"Hey, Captain," Tinker said, when it was halfway down.

"Yes, I see," I answered.

"Where do you think he went?"

But I had already left the circle of men and gone to the engine shed. Inside, a chair was turned over and beside it a woman's shawl lay by the door. A cup, which had been filled with cider, was tipped over, its contents a damp circle on the floor beside the boiler door.

Tinker followed me to the doorway and said, "He ran?"

"Yes."

"I wonder if they caught him up the hill."

"Let's not wonder. Let's find out."

Chapter Thirty-eight

I still had soot on my hands from the fire when we reached Freddy Prather's place up on the hill. He wasn't hard to find because it was common knowledge that he lived above his daddy's bank, Prather Savings and Trust.

Tinker followed me up the side stairs to the door of his second-floor apartment. A pair of tall, mud-encrusted boots stood beside the door. I lifted one and put a finger to the side of it. "Pithole crude, I'd say. Fresh."

Tinker nodded, "Good guess, Cap'n."

"Not hard. He always hollered the most at the Knights' meetings. Figures he'd be one of 'em." I borrowed Tinker's pocketknife and slipped it into the door latch. Only a slight twist popped it open. It was not locked, "Either drunk or stupid."

"Both," Tinker replied.

We slipped inside. Even an oaf like Freddy could sleep with a revolver and be deadly at close range. We moved cautiously through his apartment to the bedroom door. We posted ourselves at the door jambs and stood still. I extended a hand to Tinker. He placed his heavy Colt Navy revolver in my hand. We stood silent, our eyes adjusting to the dim light. I heard a reassuring sound—snoring.

Nevertheless, my heart pounded in my chest as I used the butt of the gun to push the door open. It made a loud, screeching sound as the hinges protested. No time to lose now. I dove in and grabbed the bedclothes away in one quick motion. There was a cry from the bed, and a figure rose quickly, sitting up—a stark naked girl who cried, "Oh!"

In an instant I was to her, one hand over her mouth, the gun in my other hand coming in from behind to silence her. Her eyes were wide with fright, and I whispered in her ear, "Be still." Freddy snorted and rolled over, muttering in his sleep.

She nodded to me, her eyes wide with fear at the sight of the gun. She was familiar, a chubby, doltish girl they called *Ball O' Fat*. She slowly got off the bed, her pendulous breasts swaying, and I handed her off to Tinker. He gave her a dressing gown and then led her away into the outer room. In spite of the tension, I almost smiled to hear her say, "Your name's Tinker. I remember you."

When she spoke, Freddy turned again, reaching for the covers. I opened the revolver to be certain I hadn't chambered a round. Then, I leaned in and placed the muzzle against his neck.

He woke with a start, his piggish eyes opening wide.

"Hi there, Freddy. Remember me?"

"I didn't— " he started.

"Freddy, ever see someone who got his jaw shot off?" I asked, twisting the tip of the gun upward. "Hardly anything more pitiful in the world than a man who has his jaw shot off. His tongue hangs down loose, like a necktie."

Freddy's eyes met mine, and he began to shake, and his breath came in rasps.

"Someone hung a man at our well tonight, Freddy. I want to know who."

"We didn't, I didn't find—"

"Find who, Freddy? The Contraband you came looking for?"

I pulled the hammer back on the gun with my thumb, and his eyes widened even more, the whites prominent. "What did you do with them, Freddy?"

"We didn't find them, him or the girl. Just the dog. He barked and barked at the door, and when I tried to go inside he bit me!" Freddy held up a hand that showed bite marks on the back, crusted with blood. "All we saw was a white dog. He bit me, then he run off."

"Booth put you up to it?"

His eyes widened again, and then he replied, "We took an oath. If he finds out, I'm dead."

"You're dead for sure if you don't answer my questions. Booth's only killed men in stage plays. I've killed traitors like you in their beds for years. Don't bother me a bit to rid the world of trash like you."

"Booth led us down there to make an example of the niggers. But we couldn't find your'n. And a crowd was comin.'"

"You killed Booth's slave?"

"No. That slave-catcher delivered him dead. We wasn't goin' to kill nobody."

"We found two ropes at the well, Freddy." He squirmed against the headboard, looking for a route out. "I wouldn't go jumping out of bed. Tinker Evans has your whore on the other side of that door with a knife to her throat."

Freddy hesitated, so I ground the barrel of the gun harder against his jaw and demanded, "You're sure Booth didn't catch my slave or his woman? You're sure?"

"No, sir. We had a drink at his place, then split up."

"How much did he pay you?"

"A hundred Confederate."

For just a moment I saw the Brownback dollars floating in the sunshine that afternoon. "Who were the others?"

Freddy hesitated again, his fear diminishing a little.

I yelled to Tinker, "Mr. Evans. Come here."

Tinker appeared at the door. The girl watched from over his shoulder, her arms crossed over her breasts that had been visible through her thin lace nightgown.

"Cut his Union suit off him. He's not a Union man no more."

At the sight of the knife coming toward him, Freddy grew talkative. "Andrew Hingston and Merle Adkins and Joshua Cramer."

"I'll tell you something, Freddy. These woods are thick with Bucktails, Black Hats, even Zouaves from New York City. You go night-riding around these parts, it ain't the colored folk you have to fear. It's men like me who will hunt you down in broad daylight and shoot you like a dog in the street." And with that, I pulled the trigger, and the gun made a loud *click* as the hammer struck home.

A small cry came out of Freddy's mouth, and I heard a slight hissing sound followed by a horrible stench. His bowels and bladder had betrayed him out of fear. I put the gun back in my pocket and shoved him away from me. "Tell your friends about this—and remember, if you plan on killing any Bucktail Raiders it's a good idea to get them all. We take care of our own."

We left Freddy with his frightened companion. I'd seen cowards before—how they acted, how they looked. He was one. I had no fear he would seek retribution.

"We should go roust Booth, too," Tinker said.

"An eye for an eye?" I asked, echoing something we had heard earlier in the day.

"He's the instigator."

"He won't be sawing logs with his door unlocked."

"We could get Mortenson, Stiles."

"I'll deal with him in due time."

"Don't go alone. That's all I'm saying," said Tinker.

We continued on down to the well in silence. It had been a long day. But partway down, I couldn't resist. In a high, girlish falsetto I mimicked the voice of Ball O'Fat, saying, *"Why, I know **you**! You're Tinker Evans!"*

For that, I got a sharp elbow in the ribs.

Chapter Thirty-nine

Tinker told me not to go after Booth alone, so I decided that I was only going to Josiah's in the morning for breakfast, not to confront Booth. Nevertheless, I still borrowed his gun.

"I provided them with horses and money for the road," Josiah told me as he set a steaming mug of coffee before me.

"I'm obliged. Have they gone to Canada?" I asked, leaning forward so only he could hear.

"Not sure. They'll lay low for awhile, 'til Daniel's fit to travel," he said, reaching under the counter. He pulled out a bottle of amber liquid and raised it to my glass.

"No need," I said, putting my hand above my mug.

"Captain, those lines on your face beg to differ." He poured a splash of whiskey into my cup, just as Reverend Steadman came through the doors, heading straight for me.

"Oh, Christ," I said under my breath as Josiah whisked the bottle away.

"Amen," Josiah said, as Steadman took his seat.

"What's that?" Steadman asked.

"Mr. Edwards was just blessing his food, Parson."

Steadman smiled at me through his thick, black beard. Did he approve of my blessing, or was it because I was sober for a change?

Josiah looked over his head and yelled, "Peanut, fetch some eggs and toast for Captain Edwards."

A young boy darted into the kitchen and Josiah said, "No more serving wenches. They call the lad Peanut because he sells bags of roasted peanuts to the patrons at Booth's theater when there are shows." Josiah lowered his voice and said, "Reverend Steadman told me it would be best to change my ways, now that Susanna has gone."

Steadman turned his gaze on me and remarked, "Trafficking in women taints a man and leaves a tincture of carnality on the soul."

"So, no more whores!" Josiah declared loudly, causing Steadman to blanch.

"Doesn't seem to have hurt business," I said, looking around.

"Don't you know? Today's the raffle," Josiah answered as the boy came with my food. "Booth 'n' Forrest are already setting up the platform."

"Only thing worse than trafficking in women is trafficking in slaves," Steadman said, his dark eyes smoldering.

"That won't stop half the town from coming to gawk. They've already paraded the girl and the horse around town," said Josiah.

I had to admit, there was a certain prurient attraction in being able to purchase a pretty slave girl to do with as one may. However, I didn't say that aloud in front of the preacher.

"Well, I best be about my business—my father's business," Steadman said, standing up and wiping his mouth with a napkin. "Come with me, Edwards. Be good to have an armed accomplice."

I took the last bite of my breakfast and downed my coffee. The healthy jolt of whiskey spread a warm glow as it went down. I had to step lively to catch up to him as he headed up the hill toward the reservoir where the crowd was gathering.

"Right in sight of my church," he said with disgust as we approached. "I would that God would strike them down right now!"

The wild-haired preacher, whom we could hear from the back of the crowd, echoed this sentiment. But mostly, it was the clear voice of Nathan Bedford Forrest that rang out over the crowd. A beautifully groomed stallion stood tied in the center of the platform, pawing the wooden planking and snorting out clouds of steam in the brisk morning air. On its forehead was the white, star-shaped patch that gave him his name.

"Gentlemen! Please line up for tickets for this raffle, being sold at one dollar each! This is to benefit the benevolent society of The Knights of The Golden Circle!"

"Humph!" Steadman snorted.

Men were lining up to reach the desk where the Pithole Swordsmen sat at the table doing a brisk business in raffle tickets. Now and then, one of them would ask for tickets in his name. Soon, I heard, "Twenty dollars in tickets for Mr. Prather."

I spotted Freddy Prather, with a grinning face and a blackened eye, descending the platform stairs. I didn't remember hitting his face—had his fellow Swordsmen learned of his piggish squealing?

Booth approached the table, and then I heard Forrest shouting, "Ladies and Gentlemen! Ladies and Gentlemen!" The crowd quieted. A glance around confirmed my suspicion that there were no ladies present.

"We have sold the last of the raffle tickets! Mr. Booth has purchased one thousand dollars in chances on my fine bay horse—Star!"

Some gasped, some cheered, some hissed at this news. Leonidas Duncan stood and waved a raft of Confederate Brownback dollars in the air. Some looked muddy and oily, suspiciously like the muddy dollars I had given Booth yesterday.

"And now, we will draw the winning ticket," Forrest called out in his deep, Southern accent. He looked to Duncan, who reached into a dry oil barrel and came out with a ticket.

"Number nine hundred seventy-seven."

"Whee-ooh!" exclaimed John Wilkes-Booth, and he went bounding up the stairs to the platform. Forrest grinned and handed him the reins, but as he did so, the horse reared up and pawed the sky with its front hooves.

"You couldn't *pay* me a thousand dollars to ride that beast," I said to Steadman, who shook his head as we watched the diminutive Booth lead the animal down the back ramp.

"And now!" Forrest said excitedly, "Tickets will be sold for a chance to win this stout and comely slave girl—Polly!"

There were shouts and jeers from the crowd as men pressed forward to buy chances. She was brought forward with her head down, her cheeks pink with shame. I thought of how I had lustful thoughts myself when I contemplated this in my mind over the last few weeks. But the crowd of men who saw a chance to purchase a slave girl for a dollar had no such scruples; they shoved and fought forward to purchase tickets.

"She's a clean, healthy girl free of disease!" Forrest said as the line of ticket buyers moved forward. "She's a hard worker who can cook, sew and do laundry!"

At that point, Booth stepped forward again, pulling another sheaf of dirty bills out to present to the ticket sellers. But I was surprised to see Forrest say, "No, Mr. Booth! Only one prize per customer. That is the rule!"

Booth stiffened and kicked at the planking in anger. Then, it seemed an idea appeared to him. He grinned, stepped back to the slave girl and shouted, "I know what will increase the bidding!" And with that, he reached to her back and in one strong motion, tore off the flimsy cotton dress she wore to cover her nakedness. "There you go, boys!" Booth continued. "That's the prize you're bidding for!"

I didn't hear a response from Steadman, but I saw it. Like Moses parting the Red Sea, he moved forward through the crowd of men, clearing a wide swath. I followed after him as he strode up the stairs, shoving men brusquely out of the way. A silence came over the crowd when it became clear a preacher in his collar had gained the platform. I saw the grin leave Forrest's face, and Booth stopped clowning and stepped back also.

Steadman reached the girl, who now had tears streaming in rivulets down her face, to her chest and down to her breasts, her fine light-brown skin mottled with goosebumps from the cold. He whisked off his coat and draped it around her. Then, he pulled his handkerchief out of his pocket to dry her tears as I stepped up beside him.

Behind us, a lone heckler near the front cried out in a drunken drawl, "Hey, you're spoilin' the show. I wanna see them titties!"

My coat was open and the revolver out and pointed at him before anyone else could add to that sentiment. The crowd grew quiet all of a sudden.

To one side, I saw Booth moving toward me, and I said to him, "Come a little closer, Mr. Booth." And then I flicked the point of the gun his way and added, "I've got six rounds."

Chapter Forty

With the detour to the slave raffle, I was late for my shift at Lincoln's side. Mortenson, who was still taking the nighttime shift, was drowsing in a chair out in the hall when I reported for work.

"'Bout time you showed up. We were about to send out a search party," he said.

"My apologies. A lot has happened since I left yesterday."

"So I heard," came a voice from behind me. It was Solomon Stottish. My stomach tensed. I figured I was about to hear his opinion of my rift with Booth.

"Mr. Stottish," I said, trying to keep my tone cordial.

"I heard you won't work for me in Pittsburg, and that you've broken with John Wilkes-Booth, as well."

"I have not said I would not work for you," I said. That much was true.

"Lydia told me you got in a fistfight with Booth."

"Not exactly," I said, honest to a fault.

He leaned in to fix me with his direct stare, "Don't equivocate. Charles was up the hill watching that blasted slave auction they had there. Said you pulled a pistol on Booth and stood him down."

"That is true. He provoked me."

"I also heard you paid him off, washed your hands of him and his practices."

Stottish seemed to know everything. I couldn't tell from his demeanor if that meant he was angry with me or pleased. I said nothing.

"I've been talking to the man upstairs," Stottish said.

"God?"

"No, you idiot. Lincoln."

I blinked, but couldn't help smiling.

Stottish's tone softened too. "All that talk about Father Abraham, pah!" He looked about and spotted Chastity peering through the crack of a nearby door, listening. " The last few evenings I've been talking to him about business—the slave business."

"I saw your factory in Pittsburg."

"It's not working."

"What do you mean?"

"I have the most modern of facilities, the best food and lodging. But they still don't work. Production is terrible!"

I was surprised to hear this. "They seemed efficient when I was there. They seemed to be working hard."

"They are efficient. And they do work hard, after a fashion. They only lack one thing—their *hearts* aren't in it. My plant in Youngstown, where you can hardly find a soul who speaks English, produces twice the steel. I've just received the figures for the last six months. The immigrants are widening their lead in production. Those Youngstown workers don't make much money, but by God they *work!*"

"They have one thing the slaves lack, if I may say so, sir—they have hope."

Stottish nodded silently and reached out a hand to my sleeve. He brushed past me, his face set like stone and slammed the door at the end of the hall as he went out.

Chastity came to me then, looking thoughtfully after her father.

"Where's he going?" I asked.

"He's going to speak to John Wilkes-Booth. Things have not gone well between them since Lydia broke off the engagement." She took a quick look up and down the hall and seeing no one, she leaned in to let me kiss her.

"I'm supposed to be upstairs," I said.

"I am also."

"Do you think anyone would notice if we were delayed in the linen closet for a few moments?"

"I would notice," she said, pulling me in after her.

* * *

Upstairs, I found the other young Bucktail private who was on guard that afternoon. "Better check in with the boss," he told me. "You'll want to meet his guest."

I stepped into the room and saw a smaller, brown-haired man and a young boy in the two Antimacassar chairs by the window. Grant, in full uniform, and his teenage son, I supposed.

"Captain Edwards, General Grant," said Lincoln, his wry smile anticipating my surprise.

Without thinking, I saluted. "Pleasure to meet you, sir."

"This uniform is merely ceremonial, Captain. I'm retired. Take your ease." With the stub of a cigar, he indicated a nearby chair. I noticed his tan cotton gloves, frayed at the fingers.

"Edwards was at Gettysburg. A casualty of the first day's fighting," said Lincoln.

"Weren't you in on those train raids in Tennessee?" asked Grant.

"Yes, sir." I said, surprised he had heard of them, but also noting he had changed the subject away from the great battle we had lost—without him.

"I liked that raid," said Grant. "Showed gumption!"

"Thank you, sir," I said, and with a nod to his uniform I added, "If you're marching on the capital sir, I'd like to fight again."

"I *am* assembling troops. More than half a million veterans will join me. But not to fight. At least, that's the plan so far."

I looked at Lincoln, who said, "They are marching to the capital to deliver a message. Like Moses said to Pharaoh: *Let those people go!*"

"No artillery?" I asked.

"No rifles, no bayonets. Just men in blue, standing up for what they think is right," said Grant.

"And if they greet you with guns and canister?"

"Then we might come back with the same."

"Do you really think all those soldiers will go?"

"Most of them are already on their way. Easter Sunday we all assemble to march into Richmond."

"I'd like to go," I said.

"Not wise," said Grant. "Mr. Lincoln needs you and your company of guards."

"But tell all those Union men down in the valley!" said Lincoln.

"I'll pass the word after my shift is over in the afternoon."

"Ah, we were wondering if you might be available tomorrow evening?"

"Sir?"

"Yes. I have been trying to talk Mr. Grant into accompanying my party to the theatre. Edwin Booth is doing *Macbeth*—my favorite of all Shakespearean dramas."

And the most bloody and depressing, I thought, but didn't say so. "I'm not sure Booth will let me in his theatre, sir. We've had something of a falling out."

"If you could just assist us in the transportation department," he said, a statement that seemed puzzling until there was a knock on the door. The hotel porter stood there with a large brown paper package in his hands.

"Who could that be from?" asked Lincoln.

That he was expecting no packages alarmed me, and I arose and met the porter at the door. The postmark said simply "Kaufmann's" and beneath that, "Pittsburg." With the door closed to Lincoln's room, the young Bucktail guard helped me unwrap it. Inside, I was puzzled to find two bright Easter bonnets and what looked like a large number of white kid-leather gloves.

"What's in there?" Lincoln called out from the other room.

I came in the room and tilted down the box so Lincoln and Grant could see. "It's women's clothing, sir. Hats and such."

A broad grin lit up Lincoln's face, and he slapped his knee. "Molly!" he said to Grant. "She's feeling better! She's got her old shopping bug back! I can't wait to see her."

Chapter Forty-one

The next day was Good Friday, though what should be called good about the day our Lord was crucified always puzzled me. I took more care in dressing than usual, not sure if I would have a chance to return to the flats. It was a balmy, early spring morning or appeared so when I looked out the door, so I left my heavy overcoat behind.

When I arrived at town, I spotted Lincoln greeting well-wishers from the window of his second-floor hotel room. Each day the crowds grew. His appearances now rivaled the daily parade of the doves. I noticed more Africans in the streets than in days past—in spite of the depredations of Booth and his cronies. I went to the second floor and entered Lincoln's room, where he was being held up slightly by the other Bucktail guards so he could more easily wave to his admirers.

I came to him and looked out at the crowd. Most were smiling and shouting words of encouragement. A few waved flags. But I scanned the crowd for those who were not glad, for those dark and scowling faces that might do him harm. It didn't take long to spot one. A small, handsome, dark haired man with his lips compressed in fury—John Wilkes-Booth. He had his hand in his jacket, like those images of Napoleon.

"That's enough," I said, to the guards, "take him away from the window."

"I'm in charge here," said Lincoln.

"Not of your safety," I replied. "That is in my charge and care on my watch."

Lincoln grumbled a little as they wheeled him away while I leaned out to latch the windows shut. The sky above turned a sickly yellow, casting a pallid glow on those still standing and gazing up, including Booth who still stared with malice at me. For a moment, I remembered just a bit of a dream I had had last night. It was a snake, slithering through a strangely colored ooze, not unlike the dreadful lemon pallor of the muddy street below.

"What is it, Captain? You don't look well," said Lincoln as I turned back to him.

"I'm afraid I didn't sleep well last night, sir. Pardon me if I was not polite in voicing my concern for your safety."

"I slept exceedingly well!" said Lincoln. "I had my dream again. That always means something wonderful, something momentous is about to happen."

"What sort of dream is that, sir?" one of the other guards asked.

"It is hard to describe. I seem to be on a vessel in a fast-moving stream. I am carried along at a torrid pace, and it is very exciting! I had the same dream before Bull Run, Antietam and Gettysburg!"

"Good to see you in such high spirits, sir," I said. But inwardly, I still felt a sense of foreboding. After all, Bull Run and Gettysburg were defeats, and the death toll at Antietam was the greatest in the history of our country. I tried to smile, but I couldn't shake the feeling of heaviness in my heart.

* * *

We moved the president late in the day. He shared a carriage with Solomon Stottish, and we walked along the route to the theatre in procession—two guards in front and two in back, with Sharp's carbines at the ready. Chastity Stottish sat with her father, dressed for the theatre and not as a nurse. It was not without some jealousy that I saw that those lining our route gave her almost as many fond looks as the former president and his wife. Grant, I learned from the other guards, claiming illness, had declined to come.

We marched into a stiff breeze, and I wished for my heavy overcoat that I had left down in the flats. After the sun had set, the temperature of the air dropped sharply. Heavy clouds, already spitting snow, conspired to hide the moon and stars. I resolved to fetch my coat as soon as Lincoln was safely delivered—no use freezing to death on the march back to the hotel after the show.

I had been a guest of honor at Booth's theatre many times before, but now I felt like a spurned old lover at his sweetheart's wedding for the opening of *Macbeth*. Mortenson, Stiles, and the others accompanied him in, and I saw them carry his chair backwards up the stairs to Booth's private box. Lincoln waved to the crowd of patrons as he was carried away, and I heard a low chant of "Lincoln, Lincoln, Lincoln."

Booth eyed me frostily while his minions ushered me out the door. I heard the bell clang for the patrons to take their seats. There was something odd about Booth's appearance that struck me as I walked out the heavy doors. He was wearing his thick outer coat. Yet it was stifling in the anteroom of his theatre, and there was sweat on his forehead.

I went down the hill to get my coat and heavier boots so I would be warmer when I returned to get the president after the play. Already, the snow was piling up, soaking my footwear and chilling my bones. "When does spring come to this god-forsaken place?" I asked Tinker, who was warming himself by the fire in the boiler wearing just his union suit and wrapped in a Union army blanket, a pipe in one hand.

"June."

"In Boston, by Easter, it is spring."

"Not here. Have a little cider, Captain. Warm yourself. You're shaking."

"I wish I could have stayed at the theatre up there. It was quite warm with that whole crowd—"

And then it struck me. The reason Booth had a coat on in the hot theatre.

"I've got to get back up there. Something's wrong."

"Captain?"

"Got to go, Tinker. I'm worried about the president."

* * *

Peanut, the errand boy, got me in. He had just crossed the street from Josiah's and approached the side door to the theatre with a fresh bucket of roasted peanuts when I called out to him, "Peanut, wait!"

The steward of the side door kept the door open, and we both stepped inside. "He's allowed in, sir, but you are not," Booth's doorman said to me.

"That's fine, I just wanted to give him his change purse," I said, smiling down at the confused boy. That gave me the instant I needed to pull Tinker's revolver out of my pocket and give the steward a sharp rap on the side of the head. He crumpled to the floor.

Peanut's eyes went wide with fright. "It's okay, Peanut. I'm here to protect Mr. Lincoln. I fear he's in danger. Please watch this man…"

I ran past him out to the lobby, hearing the actors' voices from the stage, including the sharp cries of Edwin Booth. I crept behind the doormen who were fixing their attention on a crowd near the front doors, to make sure there were no gatecrashers at intermission. Now that I was moving more quietly toward the stairs, I could hear what was going on—it was the scene where the king is killed by the usurper, Macbeth. A cold hand gripped my heart, and I hurried up the stairs where I had seen Lincoln go.

In the upper hall were several doors. I quickly opened the first one and for my pains got an angry look from Stottish sitting right beside the door. Lydia and Chastity were beside him, with Chastity holding his hand. She saw the terror on my face as the action on the stage reached a crescendo. I looked past Stottish and saw Lincoln in his chair and just to his right, the formidable presence of Tom Mortenson. No sign of Booth, thank God. I slipped back out of the box, and that's when he struck.

There was a piercing scream, not from the stage, but from the president's box just yards away. I sprinted to that door and found it slightly ajar. I stepped inside just in time to see Mortenson fall forward into the aisle in front of me, his hands at his neck, drenched wet with his own blood. Mary Lincoln stood screaming beside him. And just behind her, John Wilkes-Booth, holding a derringer with both hands and smiling as he pulled the trigger. My motion was to dive forward and protect the President, but I was too late. A horrific spray of gore erupted from the base of Lincoln's head, and he cried out "Ahhh!" just as I reached his side.

My heart sank, but I had no time to reflect. Acting more from instinct than thought, I struggled past his wife and reached out to tackle Booth, but to my astonishment he leapt forward over the rail, just his fingers hanging on to allow himself enough purchase to drop safely below. With my clenched fist I hammered at his fingers. One hand came free, and he fell crookedly toward the floor, crying out as he went.

The entire crowd erupted in cries of outrage and fear. I staggered forward to the rail, my thoughts intent on capturing the man I knew had just killed the president. Down below me, Booth hobbled forward to the stage and with his derringer raised above his head, yelled out words in Latin that sounded like some oath about death to tyrants, though most of his words were drowned out by the pandemonium that reigned in the assembly. I raised the pistol to shoot, but before I could get a clear shot, the kerosene lights came up to full bright and in that instant, Booth was gone. Standing dumbfounded in the middle of the stage was his brother, Edwin, holding out his hands that were covered with the fake blood from the killing of the king.

There were more screams from the balcony, from women and even from men. But the voice of Mary Todd Lincoln cried out above them all, "He has killed him! He has killed my husband!"

Chapter Forty-two

John Wilkes-Booth

Booth darted out the side entrance, vaulting over the prone body of one of his stewards and racing up to Holmden Street. He felt as if he had sprained his foot in his fall from the balcony, but now was no time to stop and dress injuries. Once on Holmden, he slipped into a side alley just down the hill from Josiah's Saloon and ran through thick snow up the alley to the place where he had hidden the horse. A nicely crafted sign bore the legend *David Jarrett, Master Carpenter*. He fumbled for the key in his pocket, dropped it in the snow, but his shaking fingers finally found it. "Damnit," he cursed, looking over his shoulder to see if anyone pursued him. He inwardly cursed the weather gods who had made it snow this late in the year so that the rabble could follow his footsteps to this shop.

He found the key, popped the mortise lock and stepped inside the dark shop. He heard a snort from Star, the prize horse he had won at the raffle yesterday. *Forrest will be pleased to hear his horse was instrumental in my escape!* Booth thought as he pulled some dried apples from his pocket and fed them to the young, black stallion. While Star munched on the apples, Booth made quick work of the saddle and bridle, and he donned his long white duster.

From outside, he heard the approach of the angry crowd. *Damn again!* He had intended to exit that way, but now they were massing at the front door. He lit a lantern that sat on a nearby workbench to see if there was another exit to the shop; but to his dismay, he found none. Outside, there were shouts of "The murderer! We've found him!"

Murderer! By Jove, he thought. *The murderer is the man I killed back in the theatre. I'm just the instrument of God's justice.*

But be that as it may, he needed to escape. So he led the horse to the back of the shop where light shone through the slats of the siding boards. He began kicking them loose and found they gave way easily. Soon, he had a space clear that was about three-feet wide, but with one problem—

the sideways nailers stood in the way of getting the horse out. And he had another problem—the mob seemed close to breaking through the stout, double plank front door.

"Jarrett's here!" Someone shouted. " He's got a key. Stand back!" Booth heard from behind him as he looked about for some tool to break the remaining boards in his way. He found none. What could he do to delay the mob?

"Give him some room! Give him some room!" he heard them shouting. He turned back toward them and threw the lantern hard against a workbench out front. The kerosene ignited the thick wood shavings on the floor, and the flames leapt into the air.

"Fire! Sound the Alarm!" someone shouted, spotting the blaze.

In the meantime, some of the crowd had circled around back, and one of them shouted, "He's making his escape! He's breaking out back here."

There was a tumult in the crowd with the sound of voices circling the building, and a panic seized Booth. He began kicking hard at the last of the boards that held him and the horse in. Finally, one gave way and then the next, and then he circled his arms around the strong neck of Star and kicked at the last one.

It didn't break. Instead, a man's face appeared at the opening in the boards. Booth pulled out his derringer and fired a shot. The crowd backed off. But now they were streaming in from the other entrance, trying to get around the flames to capture him. He grabbed the saddle horn and kicked one last time, and he heard a sharp cracking sound and thought: *Oh God, I've broken my ankle.*

A searing pain confirmed that he had done something bad to it, but all he could do was push off the other foot and swing himself up into the saddle. He ducked his head, and the terrified horse leapt through the opening into the snow at the back of the building. He rode past men who were screaming oaths and waving fists at him, and he even heard the discharge of a pistol close at hand. But to the crowd, there was now a greater problem than catching a fleeing assassin. His path was lit by the raging fire he had started in the row of tinder-dry buildings behind him. The flames reached up to the sky before Booth even made it to the end of Holmden Street. He dug in his heels and with his heart soaring, galloped out of town.

Chapter Forty-three

Ezekiel Edwards

When Booth exited to the left of the stage I knew he was going to the same door where I had come in. I could vault the railing, but already the aisles below were filled with panicked, screaming people. I fought my way past those who now surrounded Lincoln. Chastity rushed to his side, her expression wild with grief.

"I'm going after Booth!" I shouted, and our eyes met.

She mouthed one word, "Careful." And then, I was gone.

I flew down the stairs as fast as I could, but the doors were jammed with fleeing patrons. People were being crushed and injured trying to get out the doors, and the only way to keep from injuring or killing those in front of me was to wait my turn to get out. My stomach churned with frustration as minutes passed until I finally made it out onto the porch. I could see that a mob of men had already headed off after him through the heavy snow, and more were joining the chase. If he were on foot, they would catch him. But what if he wasn't? There were always a few horses available in Pithole; and if Booth had a mount he might easily escape. I ran to the livery stable.

"Henry, I need a horse!" I yelled to him as I rounded the corner.

"Captain Edwards, there's a fire!"

I looked back over my shoulder and saw that he was right—a fire had broken out in one of the buildings. I heard shouting and the breaking of glass, and then I wondered. Had Booth planned a diversion? Of course he had. That was a common tactic during the war.

I entered the stable and saw that Henry was unlatching the gates to each stable bay and readying the horses to leave in case the fire reached this far. They stamped and neighed in fear, already having spotted the flames lighting the sky.

"There's only one horse saddled. He's a big stallion," Henry yelled over his shoulder as he continued to release the gates and free the beasts. "I don't have time to saddle your mare."

Damn! I thought. *I can't ride some big, mean stallion.*

"Come on," Henry said to me, "I'll give you a boost up."

I hesitated. Just then, through the open door I saw John Wilkes-Booth gallop past, his head down and his free hand mashing his hat down like a pony express rider on a tear. And right behind him, a man with a team of fast trotters was giving chase and shouting, "It's the murderer! Give chase!"

Henry yelled again for me to mount. My heart was in my throat as I turned back. My breath caught at the sight of a huge beast with wild eyes that were lit by the reflection of the approaching fire. I had put a foot in the stirrup just as Tinker dashed in the front door. My actions at the well had spurred him to follow me to town, and he had arrived just now. He saw me hesitating with one foot up in the stirrups and shouted, "Come on, Ezekiel. Take him!"

I had no choice. I swung my leg up and over and felt Tinker pushing me up from behind. Already, most of the horses were bolting from their stalls, whinnying and bucking their way out the doors. My horse made to follow them, but Tinker still held the reins, his feet dragging stripes through the hay strewn on the thick plank floor.

"Which way did he go?" Tinker shouted over the tumult. Beside him, I saw Bobby Lee jumping and barking at the horses to herd them out of the stables.

"North! A man in a carriage is giving chase!"

Tinker nodded and then gave the stallion a great slap on the rump. I ducked my head as the horse broke free and dashed out the door. From behind me, I thought I heard Henry shout, "We'll follow!"

But it could have been just wishful thinking.

The stallion tried to follow the freed horses that were galloping to the relative safety of the flats, but I yanked hard on his reigns and shouted, "No! This Way!" I was practically standing in the stirrups to try and force my will on him as I pulled his head to the left with all my might.

Like a ship coming about in heavy seas, the stallion slowly came around to the path back up the hill that I wanted to follow. He bolted past McTeague's saloon and darted in and out around the men who raced the opposite way to fight the fire. I saw men carrying buckets wearing only their union suits and boots, some with clothes and no boots. One man was bare-chested, trying to shoulder his arms into his jacket as he ran. The stallion dodged and wove past them, the roar of the approaching fire making him gallop faster than any prodding of mine could ever do.

I looked down and saw Bobby Lee racing along beside us, barking at anyone in our path, trailing a length of hemp rope.

At the end of the street, two pencil-thin marks headed to the right, with faint hoofprints in the snow in that direction, as well. I slowed the horse, trying to see the tracks in the dim light and again had to force my will on the stallion to take that path. Bobby Lee barked at him to turn also, and the horse lowered its head once more and took off. I had never ridden a horse like this one before, and it was as exhilarating as it was frightening to try to hold on as he raced forward up the hill and out of town. The lights and noise of Pithole were soon left behind, and I drew myself down close to his neck as he galloped on.

It wasn't long before I spotted a carriage stopped in the road ahead. There was a fork in the road, and the driver stood on the footboard, peering ahead and looking disgusted. "He took the tram road," he yelled to me as I pulled back on the reins, the stallion rearing up.

The carriage driver pointed a black-gloved hand to the left, where a snowy road led into the forest. There was a huge drift of snow churned to mush by the passing oil caravans but no track, save one, into the forest on the old logging road.

"You must follow and apprehend him. Are you armed?"

"Yes," I said, feeling the weight of the Navy revolver in my coat pocket.

"I was not at the theatre, but the crowd chasing him said he shot the president." To my surprise, I realized that the man spoke with a Southern accent—yet he was chasing Booth.

"I *was* there. The president will surely die from his wound." I didn't want to add the grisly detail that I was splattered with the gore of his wound, but it was true.

"Do us all a favor, sir. Kill John Wilkes-Booth."

"Surely," I said, and tried to turn the stallion about to give chase. But the stallion had other ideas. He pawed and pranced and refused to leap the piled snow in our way. Even Bobby Lee's barking didn't move him.

"Use your crop, man!" the Southerner said.

I looked down and did indeed find a riding crop in a slot in the saddle. I pulled it out and whacked the horse on his haunches, and he responded. He took one step and leaped the pile, flying so high in the air that my head brushed the overhanging pine branches, and he almost threw me. "More men are coming. Show them the way!" I shouted, hoping he could hear me.

The stallion picked up his pace again and raced down the tram road. Racing with us was Bobby Lee, still dragging his lead. Snow continued to fall, but the sky grew lighter, as if the moon might come out. We circled past some loggers' cabins that looked dark and deserted. The road followed a swale through some marshy land, but the path remained frozen. There was but a single line of hoofprints through the snow. We came out onto a flat where I could see a rider up ahead. Booth! He must not have expected anyone to follow him and had slowed to conserve his mount for the long journey. I saw his head turn, and then he leaned forward and spurred his horse to a gallop and disappeared from sight.

The snow and dark closed in on us, but the trail along the road remained clear. We galloped on, giving chase. I strained to hear the sound of his horse ahead, but heard only the wind in the trees. Suddenly, Bobby Lee gave a yelp and dove off to the side. Had he seen a deer?

No. For now I saw that the line of hoofprints had ended. Booth had ridden his mount off the road and into the woods. I pulled hard to turn my horse to follow. He refused. I pulled out the crop and hit him hard again as I yanked the reins back with my free hand. That's when he bucked me off.

I flew through the air like a doll tossed aside by an angry child. I landed hard in a snowdrift in the thick underbrush, feeling like I had fallen off a ladder. There was pain everywhere. I stood up, checking my limbs for breakage, but found none. But I had another problem—no horse and no Bobby Lee. The horse was running back toward town, bucking and snorting, kicking up its heels. "Damn you!" I shouted after it.

I could run after the stallion and try to retrieve it. Try to get it to take this path through the woods. Or, I could try to follow on foot. In the distance, I heard another bark from Bobby Lee. From the hoofprints in the snow, I could see that Booth had slowed the horse to a walk while navigating the thick woods. Perhaps I could catch him on foot, if Bobby Lee corralled him for me. Neither option seemed good—I was angry with myself for being such a poor horseman. I'd had opportunities to learn during the war, and now I was paying the price.

I dusted myself off to keep the snow from soaking my clothing and gave chase. I saw a line of hoofprints, a line of dog footprints, and a thin line in the snow where Bobby Lee's rope had dragged—a trail even a city slicker like me could find. The trail led through the woods, dodging in and out of trees and rocks. We were on a high plateau, with mountain laurel and hardwoods. The snow picked up, and the wind increased; the trail in the snow began to blur. Then, it seemed the hoofprints vanished, and all I could see was the path of the dog running, with the rope dragging. Bobby Lee must have taken a short-cut through a laurel thicket.

I broke my way through low branches, ducking under some laurels to keep the trail. A branch struck me hard in the face, and it sparked the beginning of fear in my gut. A voice inside said: *You don't know what you're doing. You're no outdoorsman.* I ignored it. I was a Bucktail Raider. I had been on many night missions in the woods of Tennessee, the Carolinas, Western Virginia.

But none alone, the voice reminded me.

Deep in the laurel, the dog had circled, looking for his prey. And then I came on some brown, bare patches in the snow where he had kicked out some deer. There was a welter of prints in confused circles, bushes with broken branches. Coming out of the laurel, I found the trail again. But I had lost time. I could hear no dog yapping; no fleeing horseman. I yelled his name, "Bobby Lee! Bobby Lee!"

Still, I could see the faint trail, so I followed on. *It's the president's murderer! You can't just let him go!*

I found a line of hoofprints again, spaced farther apart—he was speeding up. I saw the line of the rope dragged over logs, giving chase. And then, another laurel thicket. And another snow squall. And now, it was so dark I could barely make out my own footprints.

I stopped. How far from the road had I run? What direction was it? I labored my way back to the first laurel thicket—I would head back to the road and get help. If I could find the road. All the old prints were getting drifted over with snow.

I looked at the trees and the circle of mountain laurel. I chose a path out of the laurel bushes that looked correct. The only sure guide I had was that the wind out of the west was blowing snow against the west side of trees and making it stick. I kept this to my right. I must be heading south toward the tram road.

But after about a hundred yards I came to a stream. I was going the wrong way. I stopped and listened to the wind swaying in the treetops, whistling derisively at me. My heart pounded in my chest. It was the panic of being lost in an immense forest. I could easily die out here tonight. My feet were soaked and chilled. *Take some laudanum,* the inner voice said. I pulled out the bottle. Held it up to see how much remained—perhaps half a bottle, enough to induce a deep sleep. *Drink ye all of it.*

Some sort of aversion came over me. I felt as if I were holding a spider by a thread—and it was crawling upward to bite me with deadly poison.

I pulled the cork and put the bottle to my lips, feeling the seductive warmth. But then, I took it away from my mouth, held it at arm's length and poured the contents out into the snow. *You'll regret that...*

I turned around and headed away from the stream, back to the laurel thicket. I realized now that if I ventured away from this spot I might continue walking off in the wrong direction and just get further and further away from the tram road. But if I stopped here, I might at least be able to find the tram road at first light—if I could survive the night.

Mixed in with the laurel were some small pines. I would spend the night here. Under one of the pines I found some bare spots, broke off the lower branches and laid them on the ground to keep my body from the damp earth. Too bad I didn't have a knife, some matches, a flint, or anything else a sane person would have with them in the wilderness. I took my coat off and wrapped it around myself like a blanket, then pulled my hat down over my eyes and ears and waited. Booth was gone. I had failed. I would be the laughingstock of the country, the man who had let Lincoln's killer get away because he had fallen off his horse and gotten lost in the woods. Maybe it would be better if I didn't return from the woods, just went to sleep here in the cold and never woke up. Yes, that might be best.

Chapter Forty-four

I awoke from my sleep, shivering. There was an odd light in the thicket of mountain laurel—a lantern!

"Here! I'm over here!" I yelled.

The light came closer. But even without it I could have seen Tinker and Henry for the snow squalls had ended, and the moon had come out.

"Look, Henry," said Tinker, "there's a scrawny old porky-pine under this tree here."

He held the light up and it illuminated both me and the thicket of laurels that surrounded us. "Took you long enough. I was nigh unto death," I answered, standing up and shivering as I slipped my coat back on.

"You've only been here about half an hour. Even my old lady could have survived out here that long."

"Bobby Lee is still chasing Booth. If we follow quickly with the lantern we can catch them."

Tinker exchanged glances with Henry and shook his head. "We can see Bobby Lee's trail. But we'll never catch him on foot. There's a cabin back at the tram road where we tied the horses. If it doesn't snow too much tonight, we can follow the trail in the morning."

"The snow is letting up. I can tell that from the sky," said Henry, concurring. "We'd have a much better chance in the morning of finding that trail. I've hunted these woods before. It's much easier tracking in daylight. Much less chance of becoming casualties ourselves."

"You've convinced me," I said. Actually, my cold and nearly frozen feet had convinced me, but I didn't want to let that keep us from catching Booth.

The horses snorted and whinnied at our approach to the tram road—all three of them. The damned stallion stood beside the other two, looking contrite. "Troublemaker," I said to him. He looked away. He knew what I meant.

"With three fresh mounts we can follow the trail in the morning. I think the cold and dark will have slowed Booth," said Tinker when we had reached the cabin and lit a fire.

"He can't have gotten far at night," said Henry. "It's all cliffs and ravines up ahead. You'd need a mountain goat, not a horse, to ride over that hill."

"Will we be able to track him?" I asked.

Tinker looked out through a chink in the logs to where the moon shone through breaks in the clouds. "If the weather holds, we might be able to track him in the morning. Boot prints and horse trails are pretty easy to see."

Bundled in my coat, I drifted off to sleep, and I dreamed…

> *I was in an empty house. White walls streaked with gray surrounded me. I saw a set of stairs, and so I climbed them, wandering from room to room. Searching. I knew I had lost something, but I couldn't remember what—and it was cold…so cold. My feet ached with each step.*

> *Then, I heard a dog's bark from behind a closed door. Bobby Lee! But when I opened the door, it led to a porch, and the porch stood in the midst of a forest. Then, I heard another bark, a bit further on. He had cornered something—perhaps treed an animal. I started walking through the woods toward the sound. The forest was thick and green, yet my feet were icy cold. It didn't make sense, but I kept on walking anyway. Not long thereafter, I came to a thicket of mountain laurel growing in a circle. I could hear Bobby Lee's low-pitched growl. It sounded much closer now.*

> *I ducked under laurel branches and pushed my way into a thicket. The growling became louder. Bobby Lee had something cornered in the brush ahead. Something dark and furry—a bear? Through the thick, leafy brush I couldn't see it clearly.*

> *But it seemed as if it watched me—the monster from the house. I saw its hands—human, but not human. Bobby Lee crouched behind me, growling and snarling, yet backing away. And then, the branches parted. It was coming after me. I tried to run on my frozen feet, crying out in my sleep…*

…and then, I woke up.

As I came fully awake, a line from Emerson came to mind: *Why should I travel? I take my monster with me wherever I go.*

* * *

The sun was not even above the horizon when we headed out again. My feet had finally warmed, but with the snow yet deep on these hills, they might soon be frozen again.

"Henry should head back into town and get reinforcements," I said as we mounted up. Tinker took the unruly stallion.

"But he knows these woods better than us," Tinker said. "You go on back. We'll follow Booth," he said, indicating Henry and himself.

But I couldn't give up the chase of Booth to them or allow them to go toward the danger. "I'll follow Booth with Henry. You go get help."

Tinker looked at me seriously. I knew what he was thinking—that he was a better horseman and outdoorsman than me.

"I want him, Tinker. He shot Lincoln on my watch, and I want him."

"You can't make up for the past, Ezekiel."

"Just go."

With a sigh, he pulled the Sharp's carbine from his saddlebag, ratcheted a shell into the chamber and handed it to me. The implication was clear, "This one's for Booth." He gave me a nod of acquiescence, leaned forward and spurred the horse away.

Henry and I quickly found the trail of the night before. We found the laurel thicket and the welter of tracks leading in circles out of it. Leaning low over the neck of my horse, I followed slowly along the trail of dog footprints and hoofprints. It would have been much harder, but for one thing; the clear line through the snow where Bobby Lee's rope had dragged behind him. It was like an arrow saying *this way*. Wherever it was Booth had gone, Bobby Lee had followed.

Eventually, we came to a spot where more brown patches of earth showed that they had kicked out sleeping deer. Henry nimbly dismounted and peered intently at the tracks left behind.

"Looks like he's still headed toward the ravine," Henry said. "We won't be able to ride much longer."

I shrugged and led the way slowly, thankful I was not riding that headstrong stallion. It would likely toss me off the edge of a cliff for sport. Half of me wanted to ride slowly and not lose the trail. Another part of me wanted to gallop ahead and catch Booth before he got away. Up ahead, the light through the woods seemed different. We were approaching the edge of the plateau. I held up a hand, and we halted.

"What's ahead?" I asked Henry.

"A steep ravine they call Bear-Wallow Hollow."

"Why would Booth come this way?"

"Pleasantville is just over the next ridge."

"And?"

"The railway to Corry has a station there. It heads east to New York City."

His escape route, for sure. "We'll have to walk now. We'll tie the horses here. Tinker and the others should be able to follow us—but we must hurry. Are you armed?"

"I've got this," Henry said, beaming. He pulled out what must have been an ancient family treasure, an ornate old flintlock pistol. I tried not to let my dismay show on my face. He needed courage, not doubt for what might lie ahead.

"Okay, let's head down," I said, shouldering my rifle and heading forward.

We climbed over the steep cliff side. The hoofprints showed Booth was leading his horse down the steep defile at a walk—still being trailed by the dog. But there was no rope line any more. Booth had captured Bobby Lee.

"He's got the dog," I yelled over my shoulder to Henry.

"I see."

The climb down was difficult and dangerous, the thick melting snow like climbing through porridge. My legs soon began to ache from the exertion. *Where was my laudanum?* I thought, and then as I patted my pockets I remembered. I had gotten rid of it last night. *Damn!*

We climbed over a large boulder and then slipped down the other side. Gravel and small rocks rained down, and we slid together down to the next ledge. The sound of rocks falling echoed down into the ravine below. And then I heard a clear bark.

"Sounds like he's down by the stream," Henry said, pointing to the right. "That way."

Below us, a log skid angled steeply to the left where the trail of footprints and hoof marks still led. "Let's keep on their trail—might just be some dog at a logger's cabin over there."

Henry nodded reluctantly. That way down looked easier.

We descended for perhaps another quarter mile. The log skid was joined by a tram road. There was a new smell now—wood smoke. We were getting closer.

Now, another bark. Henry pointed ahead.

"Bobby Lee!" I called out, and he answered back with an excited bark. Looking up ahead, I saw him tangled in a laurel bush, the rope snagged on low branches. He began barking and whimpering, lowering his haunches as we approached.

Something in my gut signaled danger, and I put a hand out to the side to restrain Henry. The setting of the road, the trees and the thick brush to one side looked like a scene from my nightmare last night. "Wait," I said. "I'll go."

I trotted forward in a crouch and laid down my rifle when I reached the happy dog. I pulled out a knife to cut Bobby Lee free, and as I lifted it to him, the sound of gunfire echoed through the hills. A trap! Booth was using the dog as bait!

I dove forward just as the rope was sliced free, and Bobby Lee leaped away. Another roar came from Booth's rifle as I rolled deeper under the laurel bush, and right beside me a rock shattered from a direct hit. I was partially covered by the laurel bush and wedged into the rocky hillside. Good cover, but my rifle lay just out of reach.

Another rifle shot, and I heard a yelp. Bobby Lee went tumbling, end over end. Henry saw it too, and it galvanized him to action. He came running out of the brush with his ancient derringer held forward, a war cry issuing from his lips. But he was no match for Booth and his rifle. I saw a dark circle appear on his forehead, and he pitched forward in the snow, landing right beside Bobby Lee, his hand reaching out for the injured animal. Bobby Lee's tail lifted and then fell—and they both lay still as the gunshots echoed back and forth off the rocky canyon walls.

A great anger came over me. I scrambled to my feet and swung the rifle to my shoulder. A bullet whistled past me, but I didn't flinch as I aimed the nub of the rifle barrel at Booth, who was standing in the stirrups of his great horse across the stream. I pulled the trigger. The rifle recoiled as the shot fired, and I heard a scream from his horse which reared up as I chambered another round. I pulled the trigger again, ignoring the pain in my shoulder from the gun's discharge. This time I missed, and the bullet thunked soundly into a hickory tree beside the fleeing horse and rider.

I ran forward to the swift moving stream and saw Booth galloping away. I shot again, missed again. He was out of range. But I could see that jets of blood issued from the horse's side as it ran, staining the snow pink and brown. I raised my fist in the air, whether in anger or triumph, I didn't know.

Then, with sadness, I turned back to Henry and the dog. I approached the animal where it lay in the snow, patting the soft fur of his head and neck. He was still warm, but already stiffening with death. I dragged him over to the hillside and with the butt of my rifle covered him as best I could with loose dirt and gravel from the exposed bank.

Henry lay still with his arm outstretched, the gun lying loosely in his grip. His mouth was still open in a war cry, a custom of his people during battle. I did not weep for him, for a life cut off in its youth. He had given his all. I thought of what Lincoln had written in that letter I had found: *the last full measure of devotion*, and I thought of those other young men, running forward with me that last day at Gettysburg—pressing forward, charging ahead for something they believed in. And it seemed to me that they had not died in vain; they had died with honor.

I picked Henry up off the ground and put him over my shoulder—my good shoulder. The words of the scripture came to mind: *You will not suffer your holy one to see corruption.* I would carry him back to town. He would be buried with respect. I would make sure of that.

Chapter Forty-five

It was no small feat to carry the body of Henry to the top of the hill. But before I had made the crest I heard other riders. Tinker and three men came into view, leading their horses to the edge of the ravine. I knew none of them, but they all had the look of veterans—hard riders with unyielding stares. None of them seemed surprised to see me carrying the Seneca boy, dead over my shoulder, to the crest of the hill. Two came down to help, one wearing a weatherbeaten Black Hat, like Mortenson. Another wore a soiled Kepi, with a dangling Bucktail.

"You look a sight, Captain," Tinker said, reaching a hand to pull me to the top.

"Booth laid an ambush for us. He used the dog as bait," I said and saw a cloud pass over Tinker's features. He knew what it meant that Bobby Lee was not with me. "We had a shootout. He killed Henry and the dog, then took off."

Tinker looked at me.

"I shot his horse with the carbine. Don't think I hit Booth, though, unless I got his leg, as well…"

"How long ago?" asked the Black Hat.

"Fifteen minutes at the most. The horse is badly injured, trailing blood. He's headed toward Pleasantville, but most likely won't be able to ride that far."

"There's a railhead there," said Tinker.

"Hurry," I said, pointing down the hill while still trying to catch my breath. "If you go to the left of that big rock you can walk the horses down, then you can ford the stream on horseback like Booth did."

"He planned this route," the Black Hat said, his dark eyes narrowing.

"He's dangerous," I said. They looked at me and at Henry lying motionless in the snow. "He won't surrender. Watch for ambushes."

"I'll leave Nicholas here to help you get Henry back to town," Tinker said, with a tilt of his hat to the Bucktail soldier."

"No!" I said. The men turned to me and stared at the sound of my voice, which held a note of hysteria. "For God's sake, track down Booth and kill him. I can manage Henry. Go!"

They hurried down the slope, rocks clattering before them as they descended. I saw Tinker look down at the barely covered form of Bobby Lee as he mounted up and spurred his horse right through the stream. He leaned down and spotted the bloody trail, visible even from up here on the crest. The riders spurred their mounts and galloped off.

I hoisted Henry up over the back of his horse, which snorted in alarm. I cinched him to the saddle with his belt, wrapping it around his thin, youthful waist. I thought of Henry and Bobby Lee this morning—of the dog leaping in joy at being free and Henry running with a smile on his face to greet him—just before they were cut down.

I made it out to the tram road and led the horses back toward town. I passed a young, straw-haired teamster, his freckled face wearing a pleasant expression until he saw my grisly companion and stared with alarm at my bloodstained face and hands. He looked down and yanked his reins to pull the team forward to pass more quickly.

As I approached the town, I was greeted with the same response by those I passed on my way to the stables. But as I came in to town, I noticed something was different. The streets were clogged with men, but few were transacting business. They stood stunned, spitting tobacco, heads inclined, talking to one another. It was as if the whole town were the anteroom of a funeral parlor. Only fitting, I thought, for a whole town, indeed a whole country, in mourning.

More than was normal wore their blue woolen coats, with the faded brass buttons proclaiming U.S. So much for the good old US of A, I thought, as I pulled up to the stables and found the manager.

"I'll pay for his funeral, sir," I said.

"He saved all the horses last night during the fire," said the manager. "He was a good lad."

"He died trying to bring Booth to justice."

But the man did not hear me. He was overcome with grief. I crossed the street to McTeague's saloon, putting my hand to the familiar oak door, but was stopped by a youth in a blue uniform who said, "You can't go in there, mister."

"Let him in. It's Captain Edwards," came the voice of Elisha Stiles.

I entered and found that, in addition to the Bucktail guards, there were others present. Local politicians, some I recognized, some not.

"They have him on a table over there," the guard whispered.

"I was sure he must be dead," I said, overcome with shock

remembering his injuries from the gunshot.

"He was shot in the neck, at the base of his skull. He can speak a little, but he can't move."

Lincoln was so tall he took up two tables. Beside him stood his wife, holding his hand in both of hers, his sad eyes fixed on hers, whispering something, smiling. I must have looked like she did, her face stained with blood and streaked with tears.

I stood transfixed; tears came to my eyes again at the sight. I felt a strong arm under my shoulder, a quiet voice in my ear saying, "Come this way, Captain. Let's get you cleaned up." It was Josiah McTeague.

In the kitchen, over an iron stove boiling kettles of water, stood Susanna. Seated in a chair, drowsing but looking much better, was Daniel.

"Why Cap'n, you made it back," Daniel said, coming awake.

'I lost Bobby Lee...and Henry," I began. I was too distraught to question when they had returned.

In his soft drawl, Daniel said, "Cap'n, if you lost 'em we can fetch 'em later. I can help you."

"They're dead," I said and noticed Josiah leaning in to listen at the door. "Booth ambushed us."

I saw Susanna reach out to Daniel. It was he who had found Bobby Lee and had named him.

"I did manage to shoot Booth's horse as he fled. Tinker and the others may be able to catch him at Pleasantville, if he doesn't catch a train."

"You done your best, Cap'n. S'all a man can do is do his best."

*My best...*I thought. *My best was not good enough.* I looked away. Self pity was not going to help the situation.

"How is Mr. Lincoln? Can he live?"

"He'd be dead now if it weren't for Miss Chastity. She compressed the wound by holding cloths on it. The doctor said he would have bled to death."

"Dr. Miller says he's stable now," Josiah said. "But he doesn't know for how long. Perhaps hours, a day, maybe two. It's hard to say. There's a very slight chance he might yet live. Reverend Steadman is leading prayer right now in the very theatre where he was shot."

"It's in God's hands now," Daniel said, getting a nod from Josiah.

"I should go there and join them," I said and turned to leave.

"Ezekiel Edwards," Susanna said in a sharp voice.

I looked back.

She held out a steaming towel and commanded, "Wash up first."

Chapter Forty-six

John Wilkes-Booth

There was soup on the table when Booth entered the kitchen from the back door at the Widow Charlotte Davis' house. It smelled heavenly, especially since he had eaten nothing since yesterday.

"John! You're hurt!" she cried as he limped in and headed for a wooden chair. She gasped as she looked down at his blood-soaked leg. "What happened? Were you shot?"

"No," Booth said, collapsing into the chair. "My horse was. This is not my blood—but I think I might have cracked my ankle."

"Oh, my," she fussed and then turned to her maid and said, "Betsy, run next door and ask Dr. Mudd to come here directly. Tell him we have an emergency."

"No, Charlotte. Nobody else must know I am here," said Booth.

"Not to worry, John. Samuel is my loyal friend and very discrete. You mustn't leave again until you've received medical attention or I'll be quite distraught," she said. "I was up half the night worrying about you."

"I told you in my wire that I might sleep in the cabin, Charlotte. It all turned out fine, other than losing poor Star."

"But your horse? The horse you won?"

"He was a valiant animal. Forrest will be so proud of him. He suffered greatly from his wound, but he led me right to the edge of the town before expiring. He saved my life!"

"You're being pursued?"

"I may be. We must be cautious." He smiled as Charlotte placed a bowl of steaming vegetable soup before him—he was famished. But he ate hurriedly. He must not tarry long. Let the doctor do what was necessary, and then be on his way. "Were you able to gain the articles I needed at the apothecary?"

"Yes, John," she said, moving behind him and placing her warm hands on his neck, rubbing it. "I have Richard's old things laid out upstairs." She paused, and he felt her hands reach under his collar, and then she leaned down and pressed her cheek against his. "They are in the bedroom. I can help dress you," she said and then giggled.

Booth smiled, caught her arm and let her kiss him. He wished he did have the time to stay and enjoy her pleasures as he had before, but he had many miles to go and she was a temptation he could not afford. Not now—and his ankle hurt like a son-of-a-bitch.

* * *

They rode in her carriage to the train station, acting as if there were nothing out of the ordinary. People would not expect a fleeing man to be riding in broad daylight with the pretty young widow. Her husband had been much older, and it was in the disguise of an elderly veteran that he made the trip. Even the old man's cane came in handy as he moved about the platform. A limping old soldier with a sore foot was all too common a sight these days.

As he stood in line to purchase a ticket, he spotted the newspapers. The Corry paper proclaimed: **LINCOLN SHOT!** That brought a smile to his heart, if not his face. But the *Pithole Daily Record—Special Edition*, published just an hour or two ago said: **LINCOLN CLINGS TO LIFE!** Below the bold headline, he read that Lincoln had been shot in the head, and that the bullet had damaged his spinal column leaving him paralyzed, not dead. The doctor thought he might yet live.

Booth stamped his good foot in disgust. The bastard lived! He had failed! All that danger and risk, and for what?

"That's how I felt too!" a portly man standing behind him said, "I'd like to get my hands on that Booth fellow! I'd wring his scrawny neck!"

"I agree with you. It's a terrible shame," Booth replied. *A terrible shame I missed*, he thought.

"As an injured old soldier, sir, I know you must feel this keenly, my friend," the man said, leaning closer. He smelled of onions and tobacco. "But don't lose heart in our cause. God will have vengeance. I think Lincoln will yet rally the Union from his death bed—just you wait and see!"

Lord no, Booth thought as the line snaked forward toward the ticket-master. I have not only failed, but I might have effected the very result I most feared—the North rising again. Booth lifted the newspaper to deflect the man's attention. "I must read all about this, sir," he said, raising it up to hide his face. For all he knew, his photograph might be printed somewhere therein.

Booth could hear the man sniveling on about his beloved Union and how the North would rise up now that Lincoln had been attacked. He ignored him and turned the paper over to find the railroad timetable on the back. He needed to find a way back to Pithole as soon as possible.

Chapter Forty-seven

Chastity Stottish

Chastity Stottish woke with a start. She tensed as a cold chill worked its way down her body. Someone was in her room! She pulled the covers up to her chin, suppressing a frightened whimper, afraid to move lest she alert the intruder that she was awake. Whoever it was, she could smell him. Her father? No, he wouldn't come here. Yet, it was an old-man smell—wood smoke, sweat, wet wool. But there was also another smell—expensive cologne. A smell she had noticed at the theatre…Booth!

Her heart pounded and cold sweat formed on her brow. She could feel him there, crouching behind her somewhere in the dark. She lay there blind and helpless, wishing she hadn't pulled the thick draperies shut before falling asleep. Very slowly, she snaked one foot out of bed, hoping to find the floor and make a run for it before he knew she was awake. The bedsprings squeaked, and she held her breath for what seemed like a long time. No sound. Then, she reached further out, her leg coming out of the covers, feeling cold air on her bare skin. Then, she heard the sharp click of a gun being cocked, followed by a scratching noise. The room was suddenly bathed in the soft glow of her bedside candle.

"My, what long legs you have, grandmother," Booth said.

His leering grin looked as evil as Lucifer's in the flickering light, and she drew back in horror. She made a quick decision and leaped from the bed trying to escape, but he caught hold of her nightgown and dragged her back roughly. Laughing—as she wept in terror.

He was behind her now, his bristly face rubbing against her ear. His cologne was a nauseating stench and she felt sick. The gun poked her in the ribs—the same gun he had used last night, most likely. He reached his hand down, and she felt his cool palm on the inside of her thigh moving upwards. She jerked away from him and felt the gun jab into the back of her neck. "Stop right there, Miss Stottish—unless you want to end up like your hero, Lincoln."

"Take your hands off me," Chastity demanded, her heart in her throat. "I'd rather be dead than to let you touch me."

"That can be arranged," he said. "But there are some things worse than death, you know."

His hand, that had been on her thigh, was now gone. But then she felt it again, this time with the knife he had used the night before. She looked down. It still had Mortenson's dried blood on it. He placed it flat on her belly and began drawing it upward toward her breast. As her breath came even more quickly, she could feel the sharp edge beginning to cut through the thin fabric of her gown.

"Some women fear being disfigured more than death," he said. "I want you to take me through the kitchen door downstairs and in to Lincoln."

"Then you might as well just kill me now," she said. "I'll not."

"I could make you look like your mother."

He brought the knife up to her face. Chastity felt her stomach turn over.

"I've heard that your mother went insane after her face was ruined. What will *you* do?"

The knife tip came closer to her face. Despite her best efforts to control herself tears began flowing, and she could no longer stifle her sobs. She cringed when she heard Booth's laughter, as crazy as a hyena's, and she realized that her show of emotion seemed to add fuel to the fires of his cruelty.

"I think I'll start with these pretty dimples—by cutting them out," he said dramatically.

She felt the knife poke into her skin, and she gasped in pain. He was actually cutting her and enjoying it. She felt a trickle of blood start at the corner of her mouth and run down her neck. She licked her lips and tasted copper. Then, her mind went back to the image of Mortenson, dead in a pool of his own blood in the theater last night, cut from ear to ear with this very knife. It was too much. She cried out, "No! Stop! I'll take you to him."

And I'll scream bloody murder the second we get near the door.

Chapter Forty-eight

Ezekiel Edwards

I felt more at peace with myself after talking with Reverend Steadman and attending the vigil for Lincoln. I stood on the porch of the theatre and gazed out across the town, steam still rising from where the fire had burned its way right up to this street. The same snow showers that had given me fits last night had saved the town—miraculously, some said. And by some miracle, Lincoln was still clinging to life. Booth would be caught and punished for his crimes. All would be well. If only this headache from giving up laudanum would go away, I'd be fine.

Across the street, I saw Tinker and the two others ride up and tie their horses to the rail in front of McTeague's. They quickly dismounted, and I hurried forward to find out what had happened. But as I went to cross the street, a band of Negroes came and stood in front of the saloon. They were here to pay homage to Lincoln, and they did so by starting to sing. They were the railroad slaves I had heard singing before, and if I had not been in a hurry to catch Tinker, I would have stopped to listen. As I circled around them, they sang, "*Oh, come, angel band; Come, and around me stand . . .*"

Going this way took me closer to the kitchen entrance. Close enough to see someone come down the stairs and turn toward the back door: Chastity. And then I saw a man holding a hand to her shoulder, guiding her. At first, it looked like an old man in a deep-blue Union coat. But in the light of the setting sun, I could see his exposed wrist and the three letters clearly tattooed there—J.W.B. I did not see his face, for he was behind her. He did not see mine for that reason, also. In an instant, they were gone from sight, but not before Chastity's frightened eyes had met mine, and she had mouthed the word *help*.

They entered the kitchen from the back—I would never reach them in time if I went that way. Besides, I knew what his ultimate goal was. I vaulted forward over the steps and shoved aside the Bucktail youth guarding the door. In an instant, I was into the saloon, heads turning in shock as I came flying in through the door. In the same instant, there was a piercing scream from the kitchen, and Booth burst out from the kitchen door, a bloody knife raised like a bayonet in front of him. The bright gaslights of the barroom lit the scene like the final act of a tragic play. I saw Tinker and the Black Hat pulling their pistols out and turning toward Booth as he sprinted forward. But I was quicker. I took one step and launched myself through the air to stop him.

There was a huge cacophony of sound, and I felt my hand on Booth's as it traveled downward toward Lincoln's unconscious form. Mary Lincoln screamed and pushed one hand forward to try to deflect the blow. My fingers tightened on Booth's wrist, which was still traveling downward. And then the bullets intended to stop Booth struck me instead, knocking me down and away from him. The last thing I remembered was Lincoln's deep-throated moan as Booth's blade plunged to the hilt in his chest. Then, Booth also was shot, and he fell on top of me.

I had failed.

Chapter Forty-nine

In my dream I was back at Gettysburg lying in a pile of fallen Rebels with a terrible pain in my shoulder. Negroes with lanterns sang songs of the Underground Railroad—crossing the River Jordan to freedom—and they were crying out for Father Abraham. Then the scene shifted, and I was at the banks of the Allegheny down by Oleopolis where I had first started to hike to Pithole.

And I dreamed I saw Father Abraham across the swift flowing river. He stepped from a boat onto the shore, and he turned to me, waved and smiled. He had on his tall hat and his dark suit and I thought, he is dead, that's why he's dressed like that, but it didn't seem to bother him. He had crossed over the river. He turned to walk away, and then I saw a white flash coming toward him, and he bowed his lanky frame and let the dog lick his face, and he was laughing, and the dog ran jumping and leaping beside him as they moved up the gentle slope on the far side of the river out of sight...

...and then I woke up.

I was upstairs in the same room I had shared with Susanna—, which seemed like years ago. Chastity sat beside me, a damp cloth in her hand.

"Ezekiel, you're awake!"

I tried to talk, but it felt like I had a handful of copper pennies in my mouth. My tongue felt swollen, dry. A familiar feeling—one I felt if I had taken too much laudanum. "Water," I whispered.

She crossed the room to get a pitcher—and that's when I heard the singing through the open window. One singer's voice rose above the crowd, "*'Zekiel saw de wheel!*" he cried out, and the chorus answered, "*Way up in de middle of de air!*" I tried to look out the window to see if I could find that one singer who had helped me, and as I watched, a butterfly wafted in on the warm spring breeze, fluttered its wings and settled on the bed beside me.

"Who's singing?" I asked in a gravelly voice, when I had taken a sip of water.

"The colored people have come. They're hoping for a glimpse of Lincoln before Steadman takes him home today."

I sighed and shook my head. I had indeed failed.

"You did the best you could, Ezekiel. It was my fault, too. I should have fought Booth up here…I never thought he could get past all those guards."

"Tinker was there. He shot him."

"He shot you, too. In the upper arm," she said, nodding toward my bandaged shoulder. Dr. Miller operated and pulled this out of your shoulder, also." She held up a dish. A sharp piece of sheet metal lay on it. It looked like something a barber might use to shave a man. "Your shoulder should be much better now."

I lifted my arm slightly. It felt bruised, as if someone had punched me in the upper arm, but there was surprisingly less pain in my shoulder. "I feel better already. I'd like to sit up and look out the window."

Chastity bit her lip with uncertainty, a girlish gesture that belied her age. "I don't know."

"I do," I said, struggling to a sitting position while gritting my teeth and pressing my lips together in pain.

"How do you feel now?" she asked.

"Like I drank too much whiskey last night," I said, the blood pounding in my temples.

"Not likely. You've slept for three days."

"Where's the snow?"

"It's been warm and sunny the last three days. Look! The birds are returning."

I looked out the window, but I didn't see birds. I saw a multitude of Africans surrounding the building. They struck up another song, *Dark Days of Bondage.*

"It looks like there are hundreds of Negroes here," I said. She was sitting beside me, and her hand was gently rubbing my back and shoulders.

"Not hundreds, but thousands. Lincoln's death was the cause of it. They left their masters and came any way they could, train, carriage, mule."

"So, Steadman is taking Lincoln back to Springfield for burial?"

"Yes," she said. Her voice sounded different. She leaned close against me, and her hand slipped inside my collar. Her fingers felt cool on my skin, and I shivered.

"I'm not making you cold, am I?"

She was up to her old tricks again—caressing, not nursing. No wonder they didn't let young girls become nurses. But I was not going to complain. "Continue," I said simply, and she snorted with laughter.

I lay back, and she snuggled in close beside me. She pulled the blanket up to cover us both and rested her head on my neck—on my "good" side. In spite of her caresses, I felt a great drowsiness settle over me, no doubt from still having a large amount of sedative in my system. We both drifted off to sleep, embracing.

Epilogue

When I awoke, it was to music again. This time it was not a spiritual, but a martial tune. A band was playing *John Brown's Body*—or was it *The Battle Hymn of the Republic?* They both used the same tune.

At first, I thought the Negroes had filled the streets again, for in the gathering twilight I saw a dark mass of people congregating. One man carried a sign which read: AND THE NORTH SHALL RISE AGAIN! Then, I leaned closer to the window and saw that they were Bluecoats—thousands of them. There were Black Hats and Bucktails and the bright sashes of Zouaves—men from all sorts of units. What were they doing here? And then a roar went up. I had heard shouts like that before, in the early days, when Little Mac led the troops. But Little Mac was gone now. I strained to see who now inspired the men.

"Who is that over there?" I asked.

A voice behind me said, "Why, Captain. That's General Grant."

With a little pinch of pain, I turned my head and said, "Tinker Evans, did you come to admire your handiwork?" I noticed he was dressed like the men below.

"If I'd a been tryin' to hit you, I coulda done much better than that little scratch," he said, grinning. "Just a nick, really. To encourage you to finally get some surgery on that bum shoulder of yourn."

"Much obliged," I answered. "If I die from gangrene I'll leave you something in my will."

"How 'bout your share in the well?"

"Lot of good that would do you."

"I wouldn't be so sure. We hit the grease at eighty feet yesterday."

"You drilled on the Sabbath?"

"And the Lord blessed us. It's flowin' 'bout fifty barrels a day, so far."

"Then maybe I'll decide to live, so I can spend my newfound wealth."

Out the window there was another roar from the crowd, and the band struck up its tune again. This time I could hear the verse: *Mine eyes have seen the glory of the coming of the Lord*, and then the tromp of boots.

"They're leaving?"

"You *have* been snoozin' for too long. We seceded two days ago. They're headin' south to present an ultimatum to President Lee. Slavery ends, or the war starts—his choice."

"Have many answered the call?" I asked.

"About half a million men are there already, camped in a ring around Richmond. He put on his cap, which I noticed had a fresh Bucktail attached, the source of our Company's name. "I'm going too."

"What about our well?"

"Daniel's tending it, and Enos returned—which reminds me—if you're up, someone else wants to see you."

With that, he ducked out the door. Chastity smiled at me, but I didn't know why. I heard footsteps on the stairs, the door opened, and Susanna came in. Then another Susanna appeared behind her. My jaw dropped.

"Captain Edwards, I'd like you to meet my sister," she said. "Jerusha, this is Captain Edwards."

They could have been twins they looked so much alike. Her sister curtsied to me—and stepped aside to let someone else in the room—my daughter, Abigail. She dropped a tattered looking doll to the floor, held out her hands and rushed to me.

I reached out and embraced her, ignoring the pain. All I had been through the last few weeks seemed to pale in comparison to the joy I felt now. I wiped tears from my eyes with my sleeve and noticed that the women in the room did the same.

"We read in the papers about you, Captain Edwards," Jerusha said. "Your ex-wife thought you might recover better if you had a visit from *your daughter.*"

"Thank you," I said, noting the emphasis on "your daughter." I looked past Jerusha to Susanna as I held Abigail close to me. "You had a hand in this," I said, but she only smiled.

Abigail stayed for a short while as the sky grew dark outside and lanterns were lit. Then, Jerusha took her off to bed in a nearby hotel. Chastity was about to close the window when I heard the mournful sound of *Taps* being played out the window. I leaned forward to see a flag-covered coffin being loaded into a wagon for transport to the railroad. Abraham Lincoln was going home.

"Do you regret coming here?" Chastity asked. She must have seen the sadness in my face as I pulled the window down and closed it.

"No, not in the least. In fact, I've achieved almost all my goals in coming here to Pithole, save one."

Chastity leaned close to me. I could feel her warm breath and see her deep brown eyes close to mine in the candlelight. "What have you not yet accomplished?" she asked.

"Just one thing," I said, putting my arm around her and drawing her in for a kiss. "Perhaps we can discuss that later."

"Ezekiel Edwards!" she cried, pulling away and staring at my face, trying to look serious, but failing miserably. "You tell me right this minute what it is you haven't yet accomplished."

"Well, all right," I conceded. "But only if you give me a little kiss."

"Ezekiel…" She was giving me her *stern* look now, her head lowered, with chin tucked down.

"All right, all right. But I'm *not* getting down on one knee."

THE END